Get **more** out of libraries

Please return or renew this item by the last date shown.

You can renew online at www.hants.gov.uk/library

Or by phoning 0845 603 5631

27/10/15

21/11/20

Hampshire
County Council

WITCH HAMMER

WITCH HAMMER

M. J. Trow

CRÈME de la CRIME

This first world edition published 2012
in Great Britain and the USA by
Crème de la Crime, an imprint of
SEVERN HOUSE PUBLISHERS LTD of
9–15 High Street, Sutton, Surrey, England, SM1 1DF.
Trade paperback edition first published
in Great Britain and the USA 2013 by
Crème de la Crime, an imprint of
SEVERN HOUSE PUBLISHERS LTD.

British Library Cataloguing in Publication Data

Trow, M. J.
  Witch hammer.
  1. Marlowe, Christopher, 1564-1593–Fiction. 2. Great
  Britain–History–Elizabeth, 1558-1603–Fiction.
  3. Detective and mystery stories.
  I. Title
  823.9'2-dc23

ISBN-13: 978-1-78029-029-4 (cased)
ISBN-13: 978-1-78029-530-5 (trade paper)

All Severn House titles are printed on acid-free paper.

Severn House Publishers support The Forest Stewardship Council [FSC],
the leading international forest certification organisation. All our titles that
are printed on Greenpeace-approved FSC-certified paper carry the FSC logo.

MIX
Paper from
responsible sources
FSC
www.fsc.org   FSC® C018575

Typeset by Palimpsest Book Production Ltd.,
Falkirk, Stirlingshire, Scotland.
Printed and bound in Great Britain by
MPG Books Ltd., Bodmin, Cornwall.

ONE

As his horse splashed along the lane, Kit Marlowe, late Scholar of Corpus Christi College, Cambridge, late intelligencer, late . . . he was in the mood to call all his life so far late; all his twenty-one summers. He was riding to London; he was sure he was this time. It was where all men, old or young, went to secure their fortunes for the streets were paved with gold. He could hear the city calling, a siren call he knew, but not one he could ignore any longer. He had a play in his knapsack, the words so clear still in his mind that he could almost feel the last lines on the last page pressing backwards into his skin, through canvas, leather, silk and wool. 'This shall I do, that gods and men may pity this, my death, and rue our ends, senseless of life or breath.' He could feel the weals rising up on his back as if the still-hot ink frazzled into his hide. He shook himself slightly to dispel the feeling of the black dog over his shoulder and the rain sprang off his curls like sparks. The horse trotted two paces at the unaccustomed movement from the man on his back and then returned to the plashing amble it had been in for many miles.

There was water everywhere. It scarcely seemed like rain but more as if the air had turned to water. Some summer. Occasionally a vicious little wind sprang up and gusted it into stinging lashes, but otherwise all was much the same; wet, wetter, wettest. The horse gave a snicker and shook its head as a rivulet of rain grew big enough on its harness to run off the oiled leather and down into its eye. Huge drops flew up and hit Marlowe in the face, smelling of wet horse, bran and a warm stable hours ago.

'I've had enough of this, haven't you?' Marlowe asked the horse. It wasn't like him as a rule to talk to animals, just in case this was the day one of them chose to reply, but neither was it his custom to go for so many hours without uttering a word to a living soul. This going out on the road was all very fine and well, but it was a lonely game at the best of times and in this vile weather there had not even been a casual passer-by with whom to exchange a word. He had seen harvest men across the fields earlier in the day, looking at the corn bowing in the rain and shaking their heads in disbelief, but they were too lost in their own troubles to notice him.

Marlowe's mother always told him he had a lovely face and because she was his mother he naturally did not believe her, but in one respect she was right. Although his heart was at best a shade of grey, what showed on the outside was only the good and he had never had to travel far without being offered food and drink, shelter and often more by people he met along the way. But all souls but his were tucked up warm and dry in this downpour which seemed to be sent from Heaven by a wrathful God. Marlowe was not a God-fearing man himself, but he had seen what others believed and was not keen to be out and about if the Flood was coming. He needed to be near other people; experience had taught him that with his luck, one of those people would have a boat. At the moment, any shelter would do him. The horse would have to fend for himself.

He remembered tales his grandfather had told, about sheltering under his horse in wet weather out in the fields of Kent. It had never sounded a very efficient way to keep dry and downright dangerous when you gave sober thought to what went on under a horse, even leaving the hoofs out of the calculation. He also reminded himself that, as far as he knew, his grandfather had never knowingly chosen to spend time outside, even in clement weather, so he had to assume that the anecdote fell into the category of something the old man had once heard. Dover was like that, full of travellers, with tales taller than the houses. Since one of his grandfather's other anecdotes featured a talking pig very prominently, he decided not to try sheltering under his horse. He needed a cottage, for preference one with a barn for the poor creature to dry off in, but anything would do, any old port in a storm. A wagon, a lean-to, however mean and full of sheep. His grandfather had had tales about sheep too, but when they began the children were usually shooed out of the room.

The horse snickered again and blew down its nose, shaking its head and spraying Marlowe once more with greasy water droplets. Over the roar of the rain, man and mount heard a horse snort in reply. It sounded near, as far as the scholar could tell, and Marlowe stood in the stirrups and looked over the hedge. Indistinct in the downpour, there were three wagons, hitched in the lee of the bank, their horses still in the shafts and standing, heads down, as the water poured over their backs. Marlowe patted the horse and in doing so soaked the palm of his leather gauntlet, so far dry around the reins. Muttering, he slid from the animal's back and led him through a gap in the hedge, tethering him next to the lead horse and slipping under the wagon it had been pulling. It was hardly the driest place he had ever been in, but at least the ceaseless drumming of rain on his head had stopped and his ears seemed to ring with silence.

He wriggled out of his knapsack, and delved into it for a handkerchief to dry around his neck and the hair around his face, which he pushed back behind his ears. He dried his hands and spread the cloth optimistically out across the top of the bag and leaned against a box which was under the cart, pressed against the axle. The rain was coming from the other direction so by and large his little nest was dry and he settled back, arms down by his sides to let the front of his doublet dry out a little and thought he might try to have a few minutes' sleep, hopefully to wake to sunny skies and drier weather for the rest of his journey. He closed his eyes and prepared to drift off.

'When shall we two meet again?' a voice said, just by his ear, making him jump in his half sleep.

'Hmm, yes, yes, that's not too bad,' another voice spoke, further away. 'Not very threatening though, perhaps?'

Marlowe eased himself to a more alert position. He knew those voices; he just needed a second or two to work out where from.

The younger was the nearer. 'When shall we two meet again?' he said. 'In . . . the town or in the lane?'

'Dreadful,' said the other. 'Dreadful. The audience will walk out.' He sighed. 'Just like they have been doing lately, Thomas, I have to admit.'

Marlowe smothered a laugh. He knew now where he had heard those voices before. Ned Sledd, actor, manager and entrepreneur extraordinaire and Thomas, the pretty boy who played all the women's parts, while his voice held and his beard had not come through. These carts must be their travelling company, their glamour rather hidden by the thundering rain. Lord Strange's Men on the road, bringing their special magic to the dull lives of country folk. Marlowe crept forward, so he could see over the box he had been leaning against. He could just see the very top of Thomas's blond head, but Ned Sledd was facing him, appearing to look him in the eye, although he clearly had no idea that he was there.

'They all love witches, though, Ned,' Thomas said. 'They like a good scare. Especially the ladies.'

'Oh, yes,' Sledd said, his voice heavy with sarcasm. 'We mustn't forget a little something for the ladies. I seem to remember you said that when you helped me with the last play.' He glared at the boy, not speaking.

Thomas gathered his pride about him like a tattered cloak. 'A maid I had been seeing told me . . .'

'Just seeing, Thomas, I hope,' Sledd cut in. He reached forward and Thomas gave a small shriek. 'We have to think of the balls, Thomas, the voice and the balls.'

'I'll have to stop doing the girls' parts eventually,' Thomas said, his voice rising in hope. 'Staying away from girls won't change that. It's an old wives' tale, that is.'

'Well, let's not tempt fate.' Sledd looked up at the underside of the cart, but in his imagination into the eyes of the Muse. 'When shall we two meet again?' he intoned. 'In the town or in the lane. Make sure that you are not late. That way we will tempt not fate . . .' He looked hopefully at Thomas. 'That's better, don't you think? Coming on?'

Marlowe could stand the suspense no longer. Without showing himself and dropping his voice to an eldritch whisper, he said, 'When shall we three meet again? In thunder, lightning, or in rain? When the hurly-burly's done, when the battle's lost and won, that will be by set of sun.'

Looking through the gap over the box, he saw Sledd's face change, through horror to realization.

'Kit!' the man yelled. 'Where did you spring from? Thomas!' he aimed a kick in the boy's general direction. 'It's Kit!'

'Yes,' said Thomas, in the lacklustre tone of someone who sees his playwriting days are over. 'Kit. But what about . . .'

But Ned Sledd was shoving the box aside and enveloping Kit Marlowe, playwright and saviour of Lord Strange's Men, in a bear hug.

'Ned?' The voice sounded puzzled and not a little worried. 'Ned? Where are you?'

'Under here, Edward. Under the wagon. Come in, quick, out of the rain.'

'Rain? How long have you been under there? The rain stopped hours ago.'

Sledd looked up from the manuscript he was reading, squinting in the half light. 'Stopped?' He peered out at the sky, an innocent blue without even a fluffy white cloud to spoil its perfection. 'I didn't even notice. Kit?' He turned his head to where the playwright had been, but there was no one there. 'Kit was here. Have you seen him?'

'He's over by the main wagon. Ferdinando is here. They're talking . . .'

Sledd was out from under the wagon in one fluid movement, adjusting his laces which he had loosened for comfort. He shoved the papers he had been reading into the actor's hands and pulled madly at the trailing cords. 'For the Lord's Sake, Alleyn, do none of you listen to what I say?' Edward Alleyn never tired of telling everybody that he was the greatest actor ever to stand in the wooden O of London's new theatres. There would never be another like him. Listen to Ned Sledd? Hell would have to freeze over first.

'Often,' the actor said, all hurt and innocence. 'There's a lot to listen to, Ned; you don't mind if I say that, I'm sure.'

'Droll, Edward, droll. Don't let me forget to cast you as the fool in the next production. Take care of those sheets, by the way. It's a new version of *Dido*.'

'New version of . . .'

'I accidentally burned it last time. So take care of it. A mighty line. A mighty line.' He sighed for the beauty of all he had just read, quoting softly as though rehearsing for the part, 'What can my tears or cries prevail me now? Dido is dead.' With a final tug on a recalcitrant lace, Sledd was off at a trot. 'And don't call Lord Strange Ferdinando, please. It's Lord Strange, to you, sonny. Sire, things of that nature. You *do* realize his father's great uncle was His Majesty King Henry VII and his mother the daughter of the niece of His Other Majesty, King Henry VIII?'

'As you wish,' Alleyn said, who had realized nothing of the sort. He wandered off, reading as he splashed through the steaming puddles in his path. '*Dido*, eh?' he muttered. 'Fool, indeed!' He read more and his left arm started to wave about of its own volition, as he tried the rolling lines out in his head. This was good stuff. It made sense and it rhymed; was he reading it right? *Five* beats to the bar? Excited and not a little alarmed by the shock of the new, the actor wandered off down the lane, the towers of Troy burning in his mind.

Sledd slowed from his half-hysterical crouching run as he approached the small group over by the biggest wagon and raised his voice in greeting as he did so. 'Lord Strange!' he declaimed, bowing as he walked. Ferdinando Stanley was not a large man but he had the presence of all the Derbys who had ruled the bitter North for so long. His dark hair cascaded over his shoulders and his curls made twisted patterns against the white of the square cut collar he habitu-ally wore.

'By our Lady, Sledd,' his patron said. 'Have you hurt your-self, man? Whatever is the matter with your back?'

Sledd paused. Here was a quandary and a half. 'A passing malady, My Lord,' he said. 'I was too long crouching under the wagon, sheltering from the rain. I will be well presently.'

'Sit down, man,' Strange said. 'You make me feel quite unwell looking at you listing like that.' The man looked around him. 'Is there a chair for Master Sledd?'

None of the actors moved. Sledd was their manager and their meal ticket, but most of them held him in friendly contempt. He had never been a good actor and now that Strange's gold had come on the scene, men who knew how to wring the meaning out of a line were joining the company and making him look worse than ever. Even Thomas, who relied on his pretty beardless face and fluting voice for parts, even Thomas could give him a run for his money.

'Well?' Ferdinando Stanley, Lord Strange, related to so many kings, was not used to being ignored.

'Sorry, My Lord.' One of the bit-part actors pushed forward a chest.

'That's better. Now, be off with you, lads, and rehearse, or whatever it is you actors do.' They stood around, looking uncertain. They had the odd practice if anyone remembered, but otherwise they just went on stage with a hazy notion of the story to be told and with any luck the play staggered to its conclusion without anyone being brained by a flying vegetable. But Lord Strange was, after all, the man with the fat purse, so they took themselves off in as purposeful a way as they could.

Strange turned back to Sledd and Marlowe. Sledd was sitting at attention on his crate, Marlowe was at ease on the throne that Sledd managed to bring in to every production, usually as his seat as the King, Duke or other authority figure he played every time. He felt mildly annoyed that Marlowe had commandeered it, but on the other hand was anxious that the newly reborn *Dido, Queen of Carthage*, should not slip through his hands again, so kept quiet.

Strange spread his hands to the men. 'Ned,' he said, 'Master Marlowe here has been telling me of his new play. It sounds exciting. May I read it?'

'Of course, My Lord,' Sledd said, smiling.

'Where is it, Ned?' Marlowe spoke for the first time.

'Hmm?' Sledd looked at him with a rather frantic expression on his face. 'Where's what?'

'*Dido, Queen of Carthage*. You were reading it under the wagon.'

'I was indeed.' Sledd played for time. 'And a very good read it is too. Better than the first draft, if I may say so.'

'Thank you very much, Ned,' said Marlowe, leaning forward. 'Where is it?'

Sledd looked around, as if it might possibly appear in a

puff of smoke, just as the Devil was meant to do in *The Devil and Mistress Maguire* – he was finding it difficult to get the right amount of gunpowder calculated though and so it didn't often work. His mind wandered off at a tangent, as it so often did these days.

'Sledd!' Strange had a way of speaking which made all of Sledd's nerves stand on end, with the hint of the Derbyshire dialect coming through as it always did when he was angry. 'The play!'

'Yes. The play's the thing,' said Sledd, slumping. 'I had it under the wagon . . .' Suddenly, he brightened. 'Young Alleyn has it! I gave it to Edward Alleyn.' The relief brightened his face like the sun coming over a hill.

'And Alleyn is . . .?' Strange looked around.

'Thomas!' Sledd yelled. 'Get Alleyn. Here. Now.'

All the actors muttered amongst themselves, eavesdropping as they were on the far side of the wagon. Just like Alleyn to get singled out. Always toadying up to the management for the best parts and barely out of his hanging sleeves. They huddled together and muttered some more.

Thomas looked around him helplessly. Alleyn was nowhere to be seen and now he would have to go and winkle him out. He would have found an inn, a cottage, somewhere where a pretty girl would be giving him food, drink and as much more as he wanted. Thomas sighed and slouched off in the direction of the lane. He hated it when he had to interrupt Alleyn at play.

'He'll be back with it shortly,' Sledd said to the two men before him. 'Have you been planning a production, My Lord? Master Marlowe writes a mighty line.'

'We need to plan something, Ned.' Ferdinando Stanley might be a bit of a rebel, as the aristocracy went, but he watched his money like any Northerner and didn't like to see it pouring down a drain. 'The pennies aren't coming in, Ned, are they? We need to do something to keep the groundlings in the theatre till the end, so we get their money, don't you think? We can't just rely on the food they throw – most of it is definitely past its best by the time it hits the stage.'

'Theatre, sire? We haven't played in a theatre these past three months. Not since the plague closed them all.'

'Plague?' Marlowe asked. 'What plague?'

Strange shrugged. 'You know how it is, Kit. Someone sneezes, a few people die, everyone shouts plague and before you know it, London is empty and all the theatres closed.'

'But . . . plague?' Marlowe asked again. He was no coward, he would face any man with any weapon he might choose, but the plague was a different kettle of fish. There was no sword on earth proof against the plague. He had known people bowed down with the weight of talismans and prophylactic charms who had nevertheless died in days. 'Plague in London? I was on my way there.'

'Nothing to stop you going,' Sledd said. 'The gates are all open as far as I know, but you won't find anyone still there. Well, no one who is anyone, if patronage is what you're after.' He flashed an ingratiating smile in Strange's direction.

'I'll have to reconsider my plans,' Marlowe said.

'No need,' Strange said, expansively. 'Join Lord Strange's Men, Kit. You can act, I suppose?'

'I can't say that I have ever tried,' Marlowe said, to an accompanying snort from Sledd. 'I can sing, if that's any help.'

'It's a start,' Strange said. 'It's a start. Can you learn lines?'

'I can write them.'

'Yes, as you say. Now, where is that boy with Alleyn? You have little control over this troupe, Sledd. We must talk.' He turned to Marlowe. 'Kit, go for a walk or something, will you? I must talk to Master Sledd here. Privately.'

Marlowe stood up and bowed. 'Sire. Ned. I'll join Thomas in his search for *Dido*.'

'Alleyn,' Sledd said, absent-mindedly. 'The name's Alleyn, Kit. He gets very funny if you forget his name.'

Nicholas Faunt had sat in Francis Walsingham's anteroom for well over an hour. He had served the spymaster now for more years than he cared to remember, but he never got used to the little irritations that Walsingham threw his way. Waiting came with the territory; standing in the pouring rain or the melting snow by a great man's door. It was the only way to get on.

Nicholas Faunt had a timepiece – better, he believed, than the Queen's – and it had cost him a year's pay. He was just

reaching into his doublet to find it when the door crashed back
and the man he was waiting for stood there, a quill in his hand
and a furrow on his brow. The cares of State had etched themselves into the face of Master Secretary Walsingham and his
carefully trimmed beard and moustache were iron grey in the
white crispness of his ruff. His eyes, however, still burned for
England and they missed nothing.

'Nicholas, dear boy.' He looked vaguely up and down the
corridor. 'Why wasn't I told you were here? Come in, come
in. How've you been?'

'Well, Sir Francis, thank you.' Faunt was on his feet already,
bowing low.

'Enough of that,' Walsingham chided him. 'We've known
each other too long for such niceties.' He ushered him into
the chamber. 'Er . . . do you smoke?' Walsingham waved to
a pipe rack on the far wall. 'I can never remember.'

'Can't abide the stuff,' Faunt told him, smiling.

'Quite right, quite right. Abominable habit, although they
say it's good for you. Wine, then? I do remember you are
partial to a good Rhennish.'

'Thank you, sir. Indeed.'

Walsingham clicked his fingers and a flunkey appeared from
nowhere, wearing the livery of the Queen. He was carrying a
tray with two goblets and he laid them down on the low oak
table by the leaded window. 'This isn't good Rhennish, I'm
afraid,' Walsingham said. 'It's a rather indifferent Bordeaux,
but in these straitened times . . .'

'I'm sure it will be excellent, Sir Francis.' Faunt took the
goblet. Walsingham took one too and noted that Faunt was
waiting for him to take the first sip. He did and jerked his
head in the direction of the door. The flunkey bowed and left.

'Now.' Walsingham ushered Faunt to a chair and looked out
of the window at the busy Whitehall day. 'To business.' He
took in the scarlet-clad guards drilling in the courtyard below,
the clerks in their raven black hurrying in pairs with parchment
and quills, cooks and scullions and draymen all going about
their business in this little world where Walsingham, not
Gloriana, ruled. He turned sharply to Faunt, the bonhomie
gone, the smile vanished. 'Marlowe.'

Faunt put the goblet down. He'd been expecting this for a while, for weeks in fact. And he had hoped, by now, to have prepared a better answer. 'Gone,' he said.

Walsingham's eyes narrowed and his lips pursed. He sat down opposite his man and sipped from the goblet again. 'You have an explanation, of course.' It was a statement, not a question.

'I last saw Marlowe at Corpus Christi College two weeks ago. He had become . . . disenchanted.'

'With Corpus Christi?'

'With life, as far as I could tell.'

Walsingham sighed. 'That Delft business.' He nodded, staring into his cup.

'He is very young,' Faunt reminded his master.

'You mean we sent a boy to do a man's job?' Walsingham's eyes were fixed on Faunt again, searing into his soul.

Faunt stared back. 'I mean it was an impossible job,' he said in a level tone. It was never a good idea to let Walsingham know he had you rattled, although that state of mind was almost automatic when in the room with the man. For many, it was a state of mind which never left them, day or night.

There was a silence. Faunt had challenged Sir Francis Walsingham, bearded the Queen's spymaster in his own den.

'To save the life of the Statholder of the United Provinces; to keep alive a man who was the target of just about everyone in Imperial Spain? Of course it was.'

'I mean, Sir Francis –' Faunt was warming to his subject – 'in this great game of ours we all have our failures. We take them on the chin, move on. Fresh fields, pastures new. Marlowe perhaps feels more deeply.'

Walsingham nodded. He'd been a young man once and a Cambridge scholar too, like Marlowe. As for feeling more deeply, that wasn't a luxury he could allow himself. 'So where was he going?' he asked.

'As I understand it, he was on his way here, to London. Had a hankering to write for the theatre.'

'The theatres are closed,' Walsingham reminded him. 'You must be aware, Nicholas, that there is plague in the city.'

'There is always plague somewhere, Sir Francis,' Faunt

replied. 'These days I tend to take these constant crises with a good pinch and a half of salt.'

Walsingham nodded, his enigmatic half smile flickering over his face. 'Indeed, Nicholas. I do think that the Master of the Revels overreacts occasionally.'

'Marlowe would not have known about the plague, so I assume he is still on his way,' Faunt said, 'but I've had men watching at the city gates. No sign as yet.'

Walsingham chewed the ends of his moustache, deep in thought. 'He'd come from the north. Aldgate. Bishopsgate.'

Faunt hid his annoyance. 'I have covered all of the gates, sir,' he said. 'In my experience, Dominus Marlowe often does the unexpected. He's just as likely to come from the south. What are the points of the compass to the man they call Machiavel? And don't forget, he has family in Kent. Even Christopher Marlowe needs to see his mother, once in a while.'

A smile crossed Walsingham's lips and this time stayed a trifle longer. 'You like him, don't you?' he said.

'Yes,' Faunt admitted. 'As a matter of fact, I do.'

'So do I,' said Walsingham, nodding. 'And we can't afford to lose men like him. Spread your net wider, Master Faunt. Send your people out to the villages. Today is . . . what . . . Thursday? By Monday, I shall expect word on the whereabouts of Machiavel. Are we at one on this?'

'We are, Sir Francis.'

'I'm glad, Nicholas. Losing one man would be bad enough, two would be a disaster. Again, do I make myself plain?'

Faunt bowed, swigged the rest of his wine and bowed himself out of the room. He had learned long ago that when Sir Francis Walsingham said jump, only a fool lingered to ask how high.

TWO

Kit Marlowe had hidden his anxiety well in front of Sledd and Strange, but the thought of rewriting his *Dido* all over again was almost too much to bear. He had managed to recreate much of the original, lost by Sledd in riots in Cambridge no more than a year before, but some lines were gone for ever, leaving just a ghostly imprint on his soul, but too faint to be grasped and put down on paper. Michael Johns, the fellow of Corpus Christi who had read both versions, and whose opinion Marlowe valued above all others but his own, had told him frankly that the second version had flashes of genius that the first had largely lacked, but Marlowe was not fooled by that. Johns was an honest man, but possibly kinder than honest; he would walk on hot coals rather than hurt another man's feelings. He would crawl on hot coals, should that other be Kit Marlowe. So the playwright cleared his throat before peering round the corner of the wagon where the actors sat, to make sure his voice wouldn't give him away.

'Which way did Thomas go?'

'Thomas?' boomed a voice. It held the tragedy of the world in that one word, which seemed to have taken on extra syllables.

'Yes.' Marlowe tried not to let his surprise show. It had seemed a rather overblown question, given the subject matter. 'Thomas. You know him – the lad who plays . . . well, who plays the girls and women.'

'Aaah.' The voice rumbled and boomed like weeping thunder over a distant mountain range. 'Thomas.' This time the syllable fell like the final beat of the drum that signals the end of the world. 'He went after that fellow, Alleyn. The tragedian. Hah!' and the voice broke into a peal of humourless laughter, clearly based on the sound of earth on a coffin lid. As heard from the inside.

Marlowe kept his question short and pithy, to try to avoid more interjections from Job. 'Which way did he go?'

One of the young actors leapt up and grabbed Marlowe by the elbow, turning him to face the lane. 'That way,' he said, pointing. 'Through that gap and to the right.' He dropped his voice. 'Now clear off and find him. But don't use the A word, or you'll only start him off again.'

Marlowe raised an eyebrow and mouthed, 'A word?'

'Alleyn,' the actor mouthed back and moved a few paces further from the group. 'Old Joseph was the tragedy expert in the troupe until Alleyn joined us. The poor old chap is past his best, I'm afraid. Can't remember his lines and his legs have started to go. Can't do the really great tragedy roles with dodgy legs, as I'm sure you agree.'

Marlowe nodded, making a private note to look closely at the actors' legs next time he was watching a play. Clearly, he had been missing all kinds of subtleties he didn't know were there.

'Alleyn is an annoying little tit, but he can do a good speech, you have to give him that, at least. He has them in floods of tears every night and that's just the men. The women throw all manner of things we try to stop young Thomas getting too good a look at; it's his balls, you know.'

'So I understand,' Marlowe said. 'But, I must be away. Alleyn has my play with him and I . . .'

'Good?'

'Not at all – it's a disaster. I've already rewritten it once, thanks to Ned Sledd.'

The actor turned him round and looked him up and down. 'I remember you,' he said. 'Cambridge, wasn't it? That riot . . . that was a night to remember.'

'Yes. But my manuscript . . .'

'I remember. Someone lit a torch with it. Shame – good it was, as I recall. Dido and the . . . something.'

'*Dido, Queen of Carthage.*'

'No, that wasn't it. Anyway, if you don't hurry there's no telling where Alleyn and the lad will have got to. I wouldn't trust either of them an inch.'

'Thank you,' Marlowe said.

'You're welcome,' the actor said, with a very theatrical bow. 'Come back soon and write me something good to say. I'm tired of Ned's old rubbish, to be frank.'

'I hope I'll be back soon with *Dido, Queen of Carthage*,' Marlowe said.

'No,' the actor muttered as he turned his back. 'That's not it.'

Marlowe turned his back on the ragbag crew and walked past the wagon where Strange was still giving Sledd a piece of his mind. Overheads apparently needed to be cut and some of the troupe were being let go. Ham was mentioned. Marlowe wanted to be a playwright. He didn't want to have anything to do with actors; what would be the point of that? He quickened his pace out on to the lane and looked hopefully back and forth, in case Thomas was hurrying towards him, a manuscript in his hand. Marlowe realized he wouldn't mind if it were to be mud-stained, in the wrong order or even mildly singed at the edges. Just so long as it was back. He had been a fool to let Sledd have it for even a minute. But look though he might, there was no sign of Thomas and he turned to the right and trudged off down the lane. For a moment he toyed with fetching his horse, but hoped that wouldn't be necessary. How far could the man have gone in the short while since he had first been missed?

As he walked, his thoughts seemed to get into step with his feet and the desolate boom of the old tragedian's voice seemed to become the voice in his head. This was no job for an intelligent young man, it seemed to say. Get yourself back off to Cambridge, where you belong. Finish your degree. Get a good job in the College, marry a nice girl while the College rules let you, settle down, stop this stupid nonsense about going to London. And above all, put all thoughts of Francis Walsingham out of your head. These kinds of things aren't for the likes of you, a humble lad from Canterbury. A pot boy at the Star whose dad makes other people's boots. Stick with what you know.

Hold on just a minute, another voice chimed in. He recognized it as that of John Dee, magus to the Queen and in one grey and dusty package at once the wisest and the most frightening person he had ever met. And, just now, the saddest, still mourning his beautiful wife. Don't listen to this idiot, Dee's voice said. Find your play, if it is to be found. If you can't find it, write another. Write one with my Helene in it, but don't let that spotty boy play her. He'll not be playing women much longer anyway, the magus said. He'll be playing with them soon and then where will his pretty treble be? Follow your stars, Kit Marlowe, and don't let anyone stop you. You are fire and air.

Aaah, the tragedian was limbering up in his other ear, don't let that . . .

'Ow! Master Marlowe! Look where you're going!'

Marlowe and his voices were suddenly struck in the chest by an immovable object and before he could refocus his eyes he was flat on his back. Thomas was looking anxiously down at him.

'Are you all right, Master Marlowe?' the lad asked. 'You were . . . well, you were talking to yourself, in all kinds of different voices. Until I came round the corner, I was expecting a crowd. Indeed I was.' He reached down and helped Marlowe up.

'Sorry, Thomas. I was just thinking aloud. As one does, you know.'

'As you do, perhaps,' Thomas said. 'I would soon be in trouble if I started doing that kind of thing. People where we go are only too pleased if they can put us away on some trumped-up charge. Talking in tongues, they'd call that. Have us in chains as soon as look at us. Witchcraft, some would say.'

'Thomas.' Marlowe was making conversation without thinking of what he was saying, so busy was he looking round behind the boy, for the manuscript he was surely hiding behind his back. 'Thomas, these are modern times. I'm sure no one would put you in chains for talking to yourself.'

'Hmmph!' Thomas turned his eyes to heaven. 'Master Marlowe, you live in Cambridge, where everyone is enlightened. Me, I live on the road and by my wits. When my voice goes, I'm finished here. I can't act at all; I just look good in a dress and can carry off a straw wig. Modern times mean

nothing to we folk who live in them. It's only men like you
who can manage modern times.'

'Men like me?'

'Who live through modern times in a place which takes no
notice of them as they pass. The rest of us they chew and spit
out as they please.'

'But I want to join you, Thomas. I want to be one of the
players.'

'If you say so, Master Marlowe,' Thomas said, with the air
of one who seldom wins an argument. 'Bad news about the
play, I'm afraid.'

Marlowe stopped trying to see behind the boy. 'Burned?'
he said, in a defeated tone.

'Worse. I can't find Alleyn anywhere. I've tried all the
cottages for a mile around and the village inn and no one has
seen him. He will be hiding up, for sure, but if he has had
five minutes start on some farmer's wife somewhere, we'll
never winkle him out. You can write it again, surely?'

'No.' Marlowe was adamant. 'No, I cannot. I have already
written it twice.'

'Well, can't you remember some of it at least?'

'Of course I can,' Marlowe said, outraged. 'Most of it, in
fact. But not the best bits. You always forget the best bits.'

'I can remember some of it,' Thomas said, diffidently.

'You can?' Marlowe grabbed him by the front of his jerkin
and shook him till his teeth rattled.

'Yes. You have to be a quick study when you play in Lord
Strange's Men and with Ned Sledd's troupe before them. Ned
is too penny pinching to get copies made, so we have to pass
just the one copy around. I can scan and learn a page at one
sitting. I have a lot of *Dido, Queen of Carthage* in my head.
Martin has a lot as well. Different bits, of course, seeing as I
was going to be Dido and Martin was to be Aeneas. But we
might be able to remember quite long pages if we can sit
somewhere quiet.'

Marlowe had stopped shaking the boy now and was
bouncing him up and down, ruffling his hair and otherwise
scaring him out of his wits. 'Let's get back to the camp,
then. Is there paper and ink?' Thomas tried to nod but wasn't

sure if the playwright noticed the gesture. 'Which one's Martin?'

'Dark. Tall.'

'Does he talk like this?' Marlowe asked in the tragedian's dark brown voice.

'Lord love you, no,' Thomas said. 'That's old Joseph. You must be grateful we're not relying on him. He often gets the play completely wrong and as for the costume . . . well.'

Marlowe sensed a story in the wings and despite being in a hurry knew it was best out in the open, so asked politely, 'Costume?'

'Let's just say things go all right as long as he remembers to wear one,' Thomas said. His head was spinning but at least Marlowe had stopped bouncing him now. 'Shall we go and look for Alleyn again? He can't be far.'

'No, no,' Marlowe said, starting to drag him back to the camp. 'We've got a play to remember.'

As they entered the field again through the gap in the hedge, Strange had stopped haranguing Sledd, for the simple reason that the actor-manager had stormed away across the field and was even now standing in the furthest corner, yelling at a rather bemused cow. Strange was sitting where Marlowe had left him, trying to look as though people ignored him all the time. He brightened up when he saw Marlowe and Thomas.

'Master Marlowe! What luck in finding your play?' Thomas he ignored.

'No luck, My Lord,' Marlowe said, 'but Thomas and Martin can remember quite a lot of it, and so we are off now to find somewhere quiet where we can write it down.'

Ferdinando Stanley looked at Thomas as if he had just arrived from falling from the sky. 'Remember it? That is a useful skill.'

'We all learn to be quick studies,' Thomas said. 'We don't have extra copies in Lord Strange's Men.'

'Really.' Strange reached into a bag beside him and brought out a small book. He opened it and ran his finger down a page and his eyes popped. '*How much* to copies of *The Devil and Mistress Maguire?*' he read and looked up with a quizzical expression.

'That can't be right,' Thomas said, without thinking. 'We've only ever had one copy of *Mistress Maguire* and I don't think we even have that these days.'

'Hmm.' Ferdinando Strange looked back at the page and ran his finger down it, nodding his head from time to time.

'Oh.' Thomas suddenly realized what he had done. He knew that Sledd had problems making both ends meet in the middle sometimes and a few copies which were never made had probably made the difference between food and starvation on more than one occasion.

'Oh, indeed, lad,' Strange said, ominously. 'I think that these books will take another look.'

'I need to copy out my play,' Marlowe said. 'May we . . .?'

'Leave the boy here,' Strange said, in a peremptory tone. 'He seems to know how this troupe works better than most. Not just a pretty face, eh?'

Thomas smiled a mirthless smile at this witticism. He thought it best at least to pretend that he had never heard it before, given the present company. He turned to Marlowe. 'I'm sorry, Master Marlowe,' he said. 'There is parchment and ink in the main wagon, and I think the quills are sharp.'

'Here, Master Marlowe,' Strange said, delving into his doublet. 'Take one of these. Newly brought from Borrowdale.' He offered the playwright a piece of wood, smoothly planed, thinner than a finger and tight-corded with string.

Marlowe had been brought up to accept gifts politely and so he did this now. 'Thank you, Lord Strange,' he said, trying to keep any emphasis from the last word. 'A very kind gift.'

'From your reaction, Master Marlowe,' Strange replied, 'I can only assume that you have never seen a pencil before.'

None the wiser, Marlowe agreed. He had never seen a pencil before and now he had he still was wondering why the man had given it to him.

Smiling, Strange took it from his hand and motioned him to come round to his side. Holding the small accounts book in one hand, with the other he drew the end of the cylinder along the page, underlining the spurious copies of *Mistress Maguire*. A black line followed the path of the pencil and Marlowe finally understood.

'It is a pen,' he said.

'In a way,' Strange said. 'I don't fully understand it myself.
It's called graphite and it is an easy way to write things down
when on the road. Ink and quills and the rest can be so messy,
my secretary finds.'

Marlowe knew full well the ruin that an upturned bottle of
ink could wreak on a shirt in a knapsack and reached out his
hand for the pencil. Strange handed it back and smiled up at
the man.

'Much quicker too, I think you will find. It takes a bit of
getting used to, but once you have the knack, it is much easier.
My secretary says it will never replace the quill, but for these
purposes it seems to be just what you need, Master Marlowe.
When the point is dull, sharpen it with your penknife as you
would a quill.'

'Thank you, My Lord,' Marlowe said. 'A very generous gift.'

'Loan.' Strange was back in his account books and didn't
look up.

'Of course.' Marlowe bowed. 'A loan. Thank you all the
same.'

'Martin's over there,' Thomas said. 'He can help you until
I have finished here. There's paper in the wagon.'

Marlowe walked back over to where the actors were still
arguing. He stood back from them for a while, then looked
at Sledd, still telling the cow all about his life. Behind the
main wagon he could hear sounds of the women, as usual
getting the work done without fuss or bother, making the
world wag as it should and taking no credit. Suddenly, he
didn't want to write a play about a queen, of Carthage or
anywhere else for that matter. He wanted to write about what
happens to people when their world is turned upside down,
through war, famine or death. Or love. He needed to think,
to get the plot straight in his mind. He veered away from the
noise of the camp and wandered off back into the lane, crossing
into the opposite field. He moved along the hedgerow and
tucked himself under the bole of a willow, old and hollow
and very private. No one would see him there, with his legs
tucked in and his brown cloak over his shoulder. He leaned
his head back against the spongy wood inside the hollow and

looked into the far distance, eyes unfocused as his mind wandered wherever it fancied.

But Kit Marlowe was not just a playwright. Or just a scholar. He was also, though he fought against it, an intelligencer, a spy. And so his eyes never stayed unfocused for long. They wandered along the horizon, half seeing the trees, the wandering sheep, the blue sky, the few scudding clouds as they wisped past across the top of the hill opposite. Then they stopped and his head snapped up. His young eyes had seen what most would have missed; the man on the horse among the trees, a silhouette against the sky. But although there was no detail to be discerned, he knew in his bones that the man was looking down the hill at the camp below. And he knew from the set of his shoulders and the immobility of his stare that the man would follow them for as long as he need follow, until he had done whatever he was there to do.

THREE

The sun was already high by the time Kit Marlowe rolled out of his wagon. The women were tending a large pot of stew over the campfire and the smoke was drifting lazily across the Hertfordshire fields, snaking to the east and the cluster of villages known as the Pelhams. The pretty girl with the red hair smiled at Marlowe and he smiled back. The older ones crouched around the fire with silly grins on their faces. Now that Alleyn had gone, this newcomer was the handsomest in the company and, anyway, Alleyn was anybody's. His smiles were usually followed by groping hands and a tumble in the hay. This one was altogether more mysterious and – unusual in theatrical circles – he was playing hard to get.

There were raised voices coming from a stand of birches where Lord Strange, Ned Sledd and Martin were standing. His Lordship was struggling to look suave while coughing and spluttering over a pipe and Sledd and Martin were actors enough to pretend it wasn't happening.

'All right,' Marlowe heard Strange rasp. 'Convince me.'

'Oxford,' Sledd began, delighted as always to have an audience. 'City of dreaming spires.'

'Isn't that where they burned Bishop Latimer and Bishop Ridley?' Everybody turned to the direction of the voice. Nat Sawyer didn't really have the temperament for a comic. He'd have been better as a tragedian except that he couldn't act nor, as Martin would be quick to point out, did he have the legs for it. Give him a pig's bladder on a stick, a saucy-shaped vegetable and a funny hat and he lit up a theatre. But on a day-to-day basis, misery was his middle name. He did have one skill though; he crept up unbidden on conversations and was a natural for hiding behind trees.

'What's that got to do with the price of fish, Nat?' Sledd rounded on him. He'd set his heart on Oxford and irrelevancies from the camp comedian he could do without.

'Go on, Ned,' Strange commanded. 'We're all agog.'

'Think of the gate, My Lord.' Sledd knew that the way to Strange's heart was through his wallet. 'Merchants, scholars, craftsmen, artisans – the place is crawling with them. Kit!' Sledd raised his voice and beckoned the playwright over. 'Tell His Lordship about Cambridge.' He turned back to Strange. 'Kit and I met in Cambridge last year.'

Marlowe raised a sardonic eyebrow. 'Do you really want me to tell Lord Strange about last year?' he said. 'About the . . .'

He watched the light dawn behind Sledd's eyes as he realized that possibly it would be a huge tactical error to tell his sponsor about the riot at the Stourbridge Fair. He seemed to sniff again the smoke of burning wagons, he saw Thomas go down, straw wig awry, under a pile of tussling townsfolk intent on finding out what he had hidden under his skirts. He felt the rough hands of the Constables on his collar as they made sure he left town. In his ears rang the words 'And stay out!'

'No need to go into that kind of detail, Kit, there's a good boy. Just tell Lord Strange about the pickings to be had in Oxford.'

Marlowe smiled. 'Cambridge is a different animal, Ned,' he said. 'Altogether superior to the Other Place.'

'Er . . . yes, yes, of course,' Sledd agreed. 'But scholars will go to the opening of an envelope, won't they?'

'To avoid lectures, certainly. But . . .'

Sledd was in no mood to hear 'buts'. Strange, however, was.

'Go on, Master Marlowe,' he said.

'Half your scholars are sizars,' the scholar told him. 'Poll men who can't afford to eat, never mind the gate money to a travelling play. The gentlemen scholars can afford it but half of them are Puritan and would rather cut their own throats than watch a play. It all depends what you're putting on.'

'Sappho and Phao,' Sledd answered proudly.

Marlowe shook his head. 'Don't know it,' he said.

'Neither does anybody else,' said Strange. 'John Lyly's, isn't it, Ned?' He looked the man in the eyes.

'It might be.' Sledd shrugged.

'There's no might be about it, Edward Sledd,' Strange

snapped, his dark eyes flashing. 'You lifted it from Master Lyly without his express permission or so much as a groat changing hands.'

'Well, that's show business.' Sledd dismissed it.

'Master Marlowe . . .' Strange turned to him. 'You're a playwright – a university wit?'

'I try,' said Marlowe modestly.

'What can you do for us? Something small scale now we've apparently lost Alleyn.'

Martin looked hurt, but there were enough egos already in that stand of trees. He didn't want to let his out as well.

'We need some love interest.' Strange was warming to his theme. 'Young Thomas's got a couple more seasons in him before he's put out to grass.' He looked Martin up and down. 'Handsome lead, Martin?' he asked.

The actor beamed, delighted that his time had come.

'No.' Strange was already thinking better of it. 'Ned, you'd better do that. Unless . . . Kit?'

Marlowe put up his hands and stepped back a pace, shaking his head. 'I'm no actor, My Lord,' he said, smiling. 'I'm a scribbler, leave it at that.'

'As you please. Give old Joseph a little part and keep it simple.'

'Bless,' chorused Sledd and Nat.

'Now, then –' Strange was beginning to walk about in creative mood as the sun through the trees warmed his back – 'a bit of light entertainment. Drunken porter, Nat?'

The comic looked bitterly at him. 'Why, marry, I'd as soon be a warmed-over crumpet on a drab's plate at Lammas tide as a pickled herring in the barrel of a lord.' Sawyer turned his head and spat volubly.

'Is that a yes?' Strange asked, looking helplessly from man to man. They all shrugged and Sawyer ignored him completely.

Marlowe came to his aid eventually. 'I think what Nat is trying to say, My Lord, is that the drunken porter character is a little old hat.'

Strange looked a little crestfallen. 'I've always rather enjoyed that bit, but it may be that you're right. Well, I'll leave it to you. Can you rustle something up by . . . let's say . . . next Friday?'

Marlowe nodded. It would not be easy, but it could be done. 'If everyone lends a hand,' he said. 'Copies and so on.'

'That won't be a problem,' Sledd said, rubbing his hands together at the deal which seemed to be thoroughly done. 'Plenty of scholars in Oxford, half of them, according to Marlowe, desperate for a groat.'

'That is doubtless true,' Strange said. 'Except that we're not going to Oxford. We're going to Stratford.'

The two women squatted in the coppiced trees and watched as the men walked away, Sledd and Strange still in animated discussion, Marlowe and Martin, heads together already planning the play, Sawyer on his own, as always.

'I like the look of the small one,' one said to the other. 'He has evil in his soul.'

'When evil is already there, where is the fun?' the other asked. 'The work is done already when the soul is already black.'

'True, true, sister, but fun is not the object. Garnering another soul for the Dark One is what we are about, isn't it?' She spat, but unlike Sawyer's random expectoration, she took a butterfly out of the air without even seeming to take aim. 'They are packing up to leave so we must be quick, if we are to have him.'

'There will be others,' the other pointed out.

'But he is so ripe for the taking,' the other one whined. 'I want him.'

The other, older, wiser, forced both eyes to focus on her companion. Her glare was brief, as the left-hand one flew back into the corner, where it usually dwelt. 'Margaret,' she said, curtly, 'we can't always get what we want, can we?'

The other looked puzzled. 'I thought that all this –' she swept an arm down across them both, taking in their rags, damp and mildewed – 'was all so that we could have other things we want. I would rather live in a nice warm cottage, if I told the truth, rather than in a ditch, but the Dark One doesn't want us living in houses, so I am always told. So I live in a ditch. Now, just because I want the little one's soul, because I want to take him into the Night and play with him just a little, you say I can't.' Her last words rose to a high pitched scream, which set the hairs standing on the backs of all necks in the camp.

Nat Sawyer shuddered and turned to old Joseph. 'A goose just walked over my grave.'

'Eh?' Joseph's hearing was going, but even he had heard that scream.

The old woman turned to the young one and pointed a crabbed finger at her, right between the eyes. 'Well,' she croaked, 'you can't have him. If I'm any judge, his soul hasn't been his to give these many years. We must go now, at any rate. We have places to be and the road is hard and long.'

'There is the broomstick, sister, the cat, the winged horse.'

The old woman shook her head. These youngsters had much to learn, about what was and what was not. Hemlock was all very fine and dandy, but it didn't eat up the miles like plain shoe leather. She gathered up her bag, full of herbs and name-less things. 'Let's just walk, sister, this time. I have much to teach you on the road.'

'Where?' Thomas winced as the wagon jolted on the hard-rutted roads of summer.

'Stratford,' Nat told him, munching an apple as if it was poison. 'Stands on the Avon. Gateway to Hell.'

'You been there?' Thomas asked.

'Yes,' said Nat, 'but it was a long time ago.'

Thomas looked ahead at the first wagon where Ned Sledd sat on the board with Marlowe, declaiming as he went. He looked behind at the third wagon, groaning with flats and drapes and fluttering costumes. 'I thought we were going to Oxford.'

'His Lordship's got other ideas.'

Thomas saw His Lordship in the far distance, his dappled grey caracoling as he criss-crossed the road. 'Ah.' The lad who played the ladies held up a hand from the reins. 'I know what they call that. It's called "Noblesse Oblige". Only bit of French I know.'

'Good for you,' Nat muttered.

They drove in silence for a while.

'So where are we going, then – exactly, I mean?' Thomas asked.

'Some country house or other. Place called Clopton, on the edge of Stratford. Some old mate of His Lordship. He owes him a favour, apparently. God, I hate private house shows.'

'Oh, I dunno,' Thomas said brightly. 'You get a bed of sorts. A roof over your head. Decent food, probably. And who knows?' He nudged Sawyer in the ribs. 'Bit of slap and tickle with the serving wenches, eh?'

'Oh, yes,' the comic grunted. 'Wonderful. And then it's: "Tell me something funny, Nat." "Say something funny." "Do that funny falling over thing, Nat." Why do they always want me to be funny? There's nothing funny about being a comedian, take it from me.'

Marlowe saw it first, riding on the first wagon with Sledd. All afternoon, Lord Strange had led the rattling, groaning wagons, starting his horse in this direction, then that. But now, far in the distance, His Lordship had stopped. He sat motionless in the saddle for a while at a point where the road crossed the marshes and the tall reeds stood still and silent to his left. Sledd had stopped declaiming now and was concentrating on driving the horses, clucking and clicking softly to them every now and again as they plodded on.

Suddenly, Strange's grey shied and whinnied, swerving to the right and throwing her rider. His Lordship hit the dusty ground with a thud and he lay there, ominously still.

'God's teeth!' Sledd's head came up at the commotion. 'Kit, your legs are younger than mine. Run and see if he's all right.'

Marlowe was already out of his seat and running for the reeds. It was no distance but it seemed miles to where Strange lay, his body shimmering in the heat rising from the road. The horse had wandered away, shaking its head as though tormented by an unseen spur and lashing out with its hind hoofs. Marlowe reached Strange and lifted his head. The man was deathly pale, but he was conscious and blinking in the sun.

'My Lord.' Marlowe held his face firmly in one hand and supported his neck with the other. 'Are you hurt?'

Strange winced. 'No,' he said, easing the dagger from the small of his back, 'dented pride is all.' He let Marlowe help him up. Then he caught the playwright's sleeve. 'Did you see her, Kit?' he asked. He had a wild look in his eyes, swivelling his head from side to side.

'Who, My Lord?' Marlowe asked, seeing nothing but the silent reeds and the road.

'She was there . . .' He pointed to his right. 'In the rushes. A faerie's child. Tall, gaunt. She . . .'

'My Lord?' Marlowe frowned at the man, who was clearly terrified.

'She had no eyes, Kit. She had no eyes.'

FOUR

Edward Alleyn knew the Smock Alleys like the back of his hand. And he knew a hundred ways to reach them without bothering the Gentlemen of the Watch. The problem was that the Smock Alleys after dark were no place for a respectable player like him to be seen; unless it was dead – which was always a possibility in the Smock Alleys. So instead he decided to risk the Aldgate before making his way west.

'Who goes?' he heard the guttural bark and the rattle of pikes as lanterns swung to and fro in the gathering gloom, sending their beams bouncing off cobbles and buttresses. To his left loomed the ancient stones of the Ald Gate, half ruined now where generations of Londoners had helped themselves to refurbish their own homes in these fast-building times. If only stones could talk most of the houses for a mile around would say 'take me back to Ald Gate.'

'Edward Alleyn,' he answered, 'Keeper of the King's Bears.' True, he had won the title in a dice game, but the Gentlemen of the Watch didn't know that and it sounded grand enough.

'Advance, Master Alleyn,' the gruff voice came again.

Alleyn marched into the lantern light and looked at the grizzled face lit eerily by the lantern held low. The helmet rim reflected it back down again, giving the man's face planes and hollows which in the daylight were merely the curves of a normal face. A second lantern was shoved into the actor's nose and, although he loved to be the centre of attention as a rule, he pulled back, blinking, turning his head to avoid the singeing flame. He had to consider his looks, above all else and a singed actor was not likely to be as successful with the ladies.

'What's your passport?' the grizzled guard wanted to know.

Alleyn flipped the man a groat and the guard caught it with

a flourish born of years on the take. He bit the coin and pocketed it in one fluid movement. 'Yes,' he said, for the ears of anyone passing by. 'These papers seem in order. Pass, Master Alleyn. Welcome to London.'

Alleyn grunted in acknowledgement. All in all, the journey had not gone well. He'd been harangued by a religious maniac on the road, warning him not to go south because the Pestilence was in the English Jerusalem and it was God's judgement on the place, damned to eternity as it was. He himself had seen the Dance of Death on the wall of Paul's churchyard and he knew the end was near. To cap it all, Alleyn's horse had pulled up lame as he trotted through Highgate and from there he'd endured the Hell the Puritan spoke of on the jolting back of a farmer's cart. He was thirsty, he was hungry, he was tired. But he had in his knapsack a play that he knew would earn him a pretty penny from Philip Henslowe or even that malevolent bastard Burbage if the mood took him. He might even nip it round to the Earl of Worcester, whose purse, men said, was the heaviest in the kingdom. It might not make him enough to retire for good but at least he could get out of Strange's company and, for a man staring nineteen in the face, that seemed a good option.

He was just sauntering down Shoreditch with the old city wall to his left when he became uncomfortably aware that he was not alone. There was the distinct thud of somebody else's boots behind him and, when he stopped, they stopped, too, just one pace later. His ears became so attuned to the abiding echo of the following footsteps that they seemed to ring in his head the more he listened for them. Like all good strolling players and Keepers of the King's Bears, Alleyn carried a dagger in the small of his back. It was literally and metaphorically a two-edged weapon. On the one hand, its silver-damascened hilt would attract any footpad north or south of the river; on the other, it could kill him.

He quickened his pace. Around the corner, he knew, where the stalls of the squatters lay scattered under the dark jut of the wall, were alleyways of utter blackness where he could lose anybody – Money Bag Alley and Harebrain Court. Once

there, he defied any cutpurse to find him. But he wasn't ready
for the pincers, *two* footpads working as one and even as his
right hand snaked back for his dagger hilt, he felt the tip of
a sword jab into the collar of his doublet and force his head
upright. In a second, his knife was gone from its sheath and
he stood alone between two points of steel glinting wickedly
in the firelight.

He glanced to right and left, his chin still in the air, the
sword blade tickling his tonsils. In the soft glow of the fires
he saw a little girl looking at him, then her squatter mother,
all rags and dirt, swept her away. Gulls fell to footpads every
day in Shoreditch. No one saw it. No one heard a thing. The
man behind him, who had his dagger, reached forward and
thrust a hand into his wallet. The other prodded with the blade
to make sure he stood still. He heard the hiss of parchment
as *Dido, Queen of Carthage* left his person and with it, a
happy and contented future.

'Hm-mm,' he heard the footpad mutter in the half light.
He sounded satisfied. What were the odds that the thieving
bastard could read? Suddenly, the sword point dropped from
his throat and Alleyn found himself bundled around a bastion
into a black corner. He heard one sword being sheathed but
not the other and knew the nearby footpad was still carrying
his knife. The shadow was not just as black as night, it was
suddenly silent as well, except for the sibilant whisper of one
of the cutpurses to the other. Then, a grunt of assent and a
low laugh.

'Welcome to London, Master Marlowe,' a voice said, in his
ear.

'Who . . .?' Alleyn said, startled and confused.

Both footpads chuckled then. It was no good these
amateurs trying to sneak in to the city under false names if
they dressed like peacocks and carried papers with their real
identities written in their back packs. Would they never
learn?

Alleyn risked turning his head and saw, in the dim light
filtering round from the squatters' fires, the embroidered 'E'
on their shoulders and the leather jacks and tall boots.

'We know a gentleman who's been looking for you,' one

of them said and Edward Alleyn, player and Keeper of the King's Bears was bundled into the night.

Alleyn had never been to the Clink before. It was one of those Hell-holes into which the Privy Council and the Lord Mayor threw their human rubbish. Even before dawn had crept into his cell, he knew he was in the filthiest prison in London. His eyes had become accustomed, in the predawn light, to the walls around him, slick with green slime and cold to the touch. Outside in the air it was high summer and the sun would be beating down on the tenter grounds and the bear pits, the markets and merchants' houses. The footless martlets would be swooping around the eaves of the houses, growing fat on the flies that swarmed from the filth, human and animal, that filled the gutters.

In the Clink it was chill and dead like a vast ice-house on some great lord's estate. He was manacled to the wall, the clammy iron chafing his wrist. He was aware of dried blood under his chin where the Queen's guard had pricked him the night before and his voice was still hoarse from yelling at them that his name was not Christopher Marlowe. With luck, he wasn't scarred and his voice would recover its honeyed tones in time. He would need careful nursing from a plump and pliant wife; someone else's wife, that is. They were better nurses than one's own, or so he had always believed.

Alleyn had already realized that time stood still here. Every now and again he heard a cry beyond his cell, a scream or a curse, it was hard to tell. He'd heard about the Clink, of course, that there were large courts where hags who once passed as women were to be had for the taking and a grilled window, where, for a suitable fee to the turnkey, you could buy your beer, your wine, your coney, your chicken. Lawyers of course cost more, but no one in the Clink could afford a lawyer and they never came near the place.

He couldn't tell, then, how much time had passed before he heard the rattle of locks and the squeal as his cell door opened on protesting hinges. The turnkey thudded in first, a man with shoulders like linen presses who had banged Alleyn's bracelet into place an eternity before. But it was the man behind him who grabbed the player's attention. He was tall and elegant with a plumed cap and a Colleyweston cloak. Alleyn noticed he carried no sword but wore a baldric, so perhaps he had left his weapon at the door. The man looked down at him.

'Stand up!' The turnkey kicked Alleyn viciously in his outstretched leg.

'It's all right,' the dandy said. 'I can squat. Leave us, Master Gaoler.'

The turnkey hesitated. He'd guided gentlemen through the Clink before, pointing out the immense attractions of the place and the dubious celebrities who lived there. Some of them would pay good money to jab a stick into the vitals of Mad Will Udall just to see him react. Others were more interested in just what was under the skirts of Mistress Earthworm, who had breasts but the pocky of a boy. One or two Puritans came to bring bread and hot soup, but most of them were repelled by the oaths and curses and left in a hurry. But no one, ever, asked to be left alone in a place like this.

'*Now*, Master Gaoler.' The tone was insistent and the dandy looked as though he could take care of himself, so the turnkey shrugged and left.

The dandy squatted in front of Alleyn. 'I am Nicholas Faunt,' he said. 'Who are you?'

'Who I am not,' Alleyn told him, 'is Christopher Marlowe, whoever he is.'

'I know you're not,' Faunt said.

'You do?' This was the first sound of sanity Alleyn had heard in several hours. Or was it days?

'Of course. A case of mistaken identity, I'm afraid. The lads who brought you here are a little long on overzealousness and a little short on brains. But then –' he produced a sheaf of paper from beneath his cloak – 'you were carrying Kit Marlowe's play.'

'You know it?' Alleyn blinked, preparing all sorts of subterfuges in his head.

'I know his hand,' Faunt said. 'And, in case that sounds over-clever, his name is on the page at the beginning and end

of every scene. Perhaps he had reason to mistrust people; I
wonder why.' He fixed Alleyn with a gimlet stare. 'How did
you come by it?'

'I found it,' Alleyn said.

'Liar.' Faunt smiled. 'Try again.'

'All right.' Alleyn changed tack. 'I bought it.'

'Liar.' Faunt was still smiling and although Alleyn didn't
know it, it was a good sign Faunt was still smiling. He should
have been more grateful than he was.

'Very well.' The player decided to brazen it out. 'I stole it.'

'Ah.' Faunt's smile had vanished and Alleyn didn't know
what to make of that. 'From Marlowe?'

Alleyn nodded. 'The same. Tell me, Master Faunt, is this
play so important?'

Faunt stood up. 'Not in the slightest, any more than you
are. Where is Marlowe?'

Alleyn began to breathe easier. If the play was nothing,
then there would be no charges for its theft. If Marlowe was
Faunt's target, he, Edward Alleyn, player and Master of the
King's Bears, was in the clear. 'When I last saw him, he
was in a travelling players' camp. Somewhere outside Ware.'

'Which troupe?' Faunt asked.

'Lord Strange's Men,' Alleyn said.

'Where are they bound?'

'Oxford, as far as I know. With the plague here . . .'

'You shouldn't believe everything you hear, Master Alleyn.
If there is plague here, I am the Queen of Scots. It's just a
ruse to get you strolling charlatans out of town and give us
all a rest.'

'Who are you?' Alleyn frowned up at the man. 'Why this
interest in Marlowe?'

'That's my business,' Faunt said. 'Turnkey!' He straightened
up and banged once on the door. 'Ho!'

The door screeched open again and the oaf stood there,
blocking the space.

'This is Master Edward Alleyn,' Faunt told him. 'He claims
to be a travelling player which, as you know, Master Gaoler,
is in itself a felony.'

The man nodded and smirked as Alleyn scrabbled to his

feet in indignation. The chain held him fast and all he could manage was a humiliating crouch.

'He was also in possession of stolen goods.'

'Holy Mother of God . . .' Alleyn mumbled, but his usually stentorian voice trailed away. He didn't want to add blasphemy to the charges against him.

'For enacting lewd and libidinous entertainment in the street, Master Player, you'll get six months, quite possibly right here. For impersonating a Cambridge scholar, another six.' He paused, apparently deep in thought, keeping count on his gloved fingers. 'For the theft of the play, we're looking at two years, the lash and possibly, depending on the magistrate, the loss of your right hand.'

Alleyn slumped to the ground, a broken man.

'As for the unfortunate outburst a moment ago, taking the Holy Virgin's name in vain . . . If the magistrate is of the Puritan persuasion, you'll have an iron spike driven through your tongue. Good day to you, Master Alleyn.'

And he was gone, leaving the Keeper of the King's Bears in a blackness of despair.

In the dark passage outside, well away from the cell door, Faunt pressed a couple of coins into the turnkey's hand. 'I have seen Master Alleyn on the stage,' he said, 'and he turns in a good performance, when he remembers to act and not just display himself for the ladies. Keep the arrogant bastard on bread and water for three days,' he said, 'then give him his traps and let him go. And, Master Gaoler . . .'

'Sir?'

'Don't tell him a God damned thing.'

'Where are we, Nat?' Thomas wasn't a born navigator. When you spend all your time applying lead make-up and lacing yourself into farthingales, points of the compass aren't the first things on your mind.

'Warwickshire.' Nat was munching on another apple. 'Haunted Warwickshire. Piping Pebworth, Dancing Marston, Haunted Hillbrough, Hungry Grafton, Dodging Exhall, Papist Wixford, Beggarly Broom and Drunken Bideford.'

'What are you talking about?' Tom asked.

'Villages hereabouts. I knew 'em as a lad. My old dad was a forester in Arden – before he took his foot off with an axe. Trust me, this shire's haunted.'

'Why do you say that?' Thomas looked at him. The horses snorted and tossed their heads.

'They sense it,' the comic grunted. 'I was last here . . . what . . . nine years ago, when the Queen came to Kenilworth. Stood in Echo Fields.'

'Echo Fields?' Thomas repeated.

'You've got it,' Nat said and tossed his apple core away to the side of the road.

Thomas looked confused and ran the conversation back in his head. Ah, that must be a joke. Not one of Nat's best, but no one could be hilarious all the time. He gave a short laugh and said, 'Where is Echo Fields?'

'Outside the walls at Kenilworth,' Nat told him, wrestling a piece of apple skin from between his teeth. 'The Earl of Leicester, God rot him, flooded the land for his barges and his pretty fireworks, all to impress Her Majesty of course. I was in Sir Christopher Hatton's household then.'

'But why is it called Echo Fields?' Thomas persisted.

'They say –' Nat huddled nearer to the driver – 'that houses were drowned, a whole village beneath the waters of the lake. There was a church and if you stand in Echo Fields you can sometimes hear its bell, tolling, as if for a funeral. The funeral of the Kenilworth drowned.'

Thomas nodded, his eyes wide. He was trying to focus on the road ahead, but all he saw were bobbing heads and dead men rolling in the weeds, their arms and legs trailing in the wet green slime, their faces eyeless, mouths gaping.

'And that's not all,' Nat Sawyer added after a perfectly judged pause. For all Thomas was a boy actor, he made a damned fine audience. Gullible was clearly his middle name. 'If you stand at a certain point and whisper your name towards the castle, it'll come back to you on the wind.'

'Get away,' Thomas mouthed.

'But sometimes . . .' Nat looked sideways at the lad. 'Nah.' He shook his head and smiled a crooked smile. 'Best not,' he said.

'What? What?' Thomas said, shaking him by the arm.

'Halloah!' Ned Sledd's shout halted the little column. They saw him stand in his lead wagon and call back. 'Flags, boys. Music. Stratford's over the next rise and you know how important an entrance is.'

FIVE

Lord Strange had ridden on ahead, taking Marlowe with him for company after the fright by the lakeside. They had gone to Clopton Hall but Sledd's commission was to ride into the town and spread the good word. A play was toward in three nights' time at the Hall and all were welcome, admission one groat, half for the lame and incurables. Children – if they behaved – were to be allowed in free.

'William Clopton,' grunted the old man at the bridge head. '*Papist* William Clopton?'

'*Sir* William Clopton.' Ned Sledd had a moment ago doffed his cap to the Warden of the Bridge, but now regretted his civility and put it back on with his most theatrical flourish. 'My Lord is, as we speak, paying his devoirs to Sir William.'

The old man only had one eye and it shot like a watery blue arrow into the actor-manager's face. 'Who did you say your lord was, again?'

Sledd looked him up and down. The man would never see sixty again and he was squat with the urban guile of the country bumpkin who has been allowed to edge his gown with squirrel and put a tin chain around his shoulders. He'd seen his type in every town south of the Wall.

'Lord Strange,' Sledd repeated loudly, so that all the traffic on the bridge could hear him. 'Son and heir to Lord Derby.'

The old man spat so that his grey bristles were coated with it and he wiped his face with the back of his hand. 'This is Stratford Upon Avon, sir,' he growled, 'and we have no truck with strange lords.'

Sledd took in the situation. Beyond the grey stones of Clopton Bridge, with its green-dripping arches and the roaring brown of the river, stood a handsome town on a hill. Smoke rose from the tanneries and the distant sounds of commerce came and went on the breeze. Behind him, behind Lord Strange's wagons, a hostile queue was forming, geese honking

in their impatience, sheep bleating in their keenness to reach
the place of slaughter. Market day. And market day meant
street theatre, acrobats, tumblers, tabors and pipes. The rattle
of coins in the cup. On the other hand, the bridge-keeper had
four stout-looking constables with him, large and surly. Nat,
Martin and Thomas and a few of the others could look after
themselves, but he had the women to think of. And anyway,
starting out a town tour still bleeding from a clash with the
constabulary was hardly going to draw big crowds.

Even so, honour was at stake here. 'Who are you, sir?'
Sledd asked. It was the voice he always put on to play Nero;
deep and patrician with just a slight underlay of incipient
homicidal mania. It usually worked.

'George Whateley,' the old man said, standing as tall as he
could and squaring his shoulders. 'Wool draper and Warden
of Clopton Bridge.'

Sledd rubbed his nose – always a sign as the others knew
that he was furious. He had run out of options already and
his hand was straying to the dagger in the small of his back.
Perhaps slicing off a little squirrel fur might do the trick.

'Whateley?' a voice called over his shoulder. 'George
Whateley the wool draper?'

All eyes turned as Nat Sawyer slid down from his wagon
and trotted on to the bridge. It wasn't exactly Horatius, but
the clown had, as usual, the attention of the crowd.

'Who might you be, sir?' Whateley wanted to know.

'Nathaniel,' Nat said, widening his eyes and spreading his
arms even wider. 'No,' he said, laughing and grovelling, all
at the same time. 'No, of course you wouldn't remember. I
was at the Mop Fair last year, buying trifles for our troupe.'

Sledd's mouth hung slack. In all the years he had known
Nat Sawyer he'd never known him buy anything at all. Steal,
yes. But buy? Never.

'I asked around –' Nat was in full swing now – 'in the
Rothermarket. I asked 'em, I asked, "Who's got the best wool-
lens in town?" To a man, they all said, "George Whateley."'

The Warden of the Bridge clutched Nat's sleeve, drawing
him closer. 'Not Barnhurst?'

Sawyer shook his head.

'Badger?'

'Who?'

'You know,' Whateley grunted out of the corner of his mouth, 'wool draper. Sheep Street.'

Sawyer looked from left to right, aware of the mounting hostility of the farmers on the road behind Sledd's wagons. 'A beginner,' he said softly. 'No, I had it on good authority. Whateley . . .' He let the name roll around his tongue. 'The one and only. Look.' He held out his sleeve. 'Yours.'

'Is it?' Whateley tried to focus with his one good eye. 'Well,' he muttered, 'it certainly *looks* like one of mine.'

'Depend on it,' said Sawyer, beaming. 'So –' and he clapped a too-familiar arm around the Warden of the Bridge – 'where would you like us to set up, George? The stage, I mean? Er . . . the Rothermarket? Sheep Street?'

Suddenly, George Whateley frowned and pulled away. 'You, sir, are the lackey of a Papist lord and are unwelcome in this town. For all I care you can set up your stage at the bottom of the river, for you'll not pass this point.'

The staves of the constables, long and heavy, came to the level.

'Now –' and the little Warden, knowing he had burly men to protect him, drew himself up to his full but very inconsiderable height – 'now, clear those wagons and let honest folk pass.'

'Oh, well done, Nat,' Sledd hissed in the man's ear as he slunk past. 'Next time I'm looking for an actor, remind me not to call on you.'

The Cloptons had lived at the Hall since before anyone could remember. The old house had been refurbished in Sir Hugh's time and now that Sir William was aware of the scythesman at his elbow, it was time to find a match for his daughter, Joyce. To that end, Lord Strange's company and to that end, Lord Strange. Strange was married with a couple of children under his belt, but he was a good friend and knew many eligible bachelors, some of them young and not all of them stupid. Joyce was a lovely girl, but given to study and not likely to settle for a simpleton, no matter what his wealth and status.

'Your health, Ferdinando!' The old man raised a goblet in the mellow evening light of the solar, his wolfhounds dozing in the empty grate, his goshawk mewing softly on its perch and rattling its chain every now and again. The room was pleasantly cool after the heat and dust of the day and his guests were sprawling at their ease in his most comfortable chairs. Marlowe and Strange fitted easily into the shabby splendour of Clopton's solar and Sledd, with the strange, chameleon quality of the actor, was fitting in more every minute. High above them, where the gentle light couldn't reach, cobwebs like hammocks, thick with the shed skin and long-exhaled breath of Cloptons without number, swayed slightly in the draft that crept through the windows, under the door and down the chimney. The whole room was pregnant with Cloptons dead and, if Ferdinando Strange did his duty, as yet unborn.

'And yours, William,' Lord Strange replied and everyone raised their cups.

'So, Master Sledd.' Clopton was still tucking in to the sweetmeats that lay in bowls on the vast oak table. 'I gather you had some trouble at the bridge today.'

'Trouble, sir?' Sledd smiled. 'No, no. All in a day's work for we strolling players. We've seen it all, from cold looks to the cart's tail. I have the scars to prove it.'

But Clopton was frowning. 'Gentlemen,' he sighed. 'I'm afraid there's more to it than that. If it weren't so grim, you could write a comedy about it, eh, Master Marlowe?'

The scholar-playwright smiled into his goblet and said quietly, 'I don't do comedy, Sir William, but the grimness intrigues me.'

'William.' Strange put down his goblet. 'You and I have known each other . . . what . . . fifteen years?'

Clopton nodded his old grey head. 'You were a boy,' he remembered, 'chasing the deer on your father's estates.' He smiled sadly. 'Happier times.' And he sipped from the goblet again.

'Is there something rotten in the state of Stratford?' Strange asked, leaning back and stretching his legs out on an accommodating wolfhound. He noticed the old man's watery eyes flicker to Marlowe and Sledd. 'Come, come, William. We're all friends here. These men work for me.'

'Whateley,' Clopton said after a moment, suddenly standing up and wandering to the window. Through the leaded panes he watched the sun gilding the spire of Holy Trinity, the church he no longer dared to attend, where the Puritans had smashed the face of God Himself.

The others looked at Sledd.

'A clod,' said the actor-manager. 'Man acts far above his station. What is he? A shopkeeper?'

Clopton chuckled and turned back into the room. 'Never underestimate the power of the guilds, Master Sledd,' he warned. 'But no, Whateley is not the problem. He is merely the mouthpiece of the man who is – Edward Greville.'

'I know the Grevilles,' Strange said. 'Charlatans and rogues to a man.'

Clopton nodded. 'He owns Stratford,' he said. 'All of it. Cross him and you'll pay. Some . . .' he faltered. 'Some have paid with their lives. John Shaxsper daren't leave his home – he's a virtual prisoner in Henley Street. Ben Badger, he's another. They say he'll never walk again after the accident.'

'Accident?' Marlowe echoed.

Clopton looked hard at him. 'Some barrels fell off a cart in the Rothermarket and Ben Badger just happened to be under them.'

'You suspect . . .?' Strange began.

'I suspect that one of Greville's thugs laid him low with a cudgel first. Badger wouldn't sell his wool shop. He has now, grateful for the pittance Greville gave him for it.'

'Can't the man be stopped?' Strange asked. 'By law, I mean?'

'He *is* the law, Ferdinando. Lord of the Manor. He appoints the mayor, the guildsmen, even the bloody Warden of the Bridge. And there's more . . .' The old man's voice tailed away.

'More?' Strange asked.

William Clopton stood up as straight as his years would let him and pulled his gown into position over his paunch. 'It's late, gentlemen,' he said. 'And I do not have the staying power

I once had. Please, help yourself to more food . . . wine. Whatever you need and Boscastle will attend you.'

'Magic!' beamed Sledd, unused to such largesse so easily come by.

Clopton took Strange's hands in his own. 'It is good to have you here, Ferdinando,' he said, his eyes wet with tears. 'So very good.'

Strange rose and hugged the man, trying with the close contact to give him the strength to carry on for just a while longer.

'And you,' Clopton said with a sniff, turning to the others, who stood up respectfully, 'lords of the stage. I look forward to your offering.'

'Goodnight, sir.' Marlowe said and they watched the old man shuffle away, his wolfhounds slinking silently behind him.

'A troubled spirit,' said Marlowe when he had gone. They all sat back down.

'Indeed,' murmured Strange. 'There was a time when the Cloptons ruled Stratford – half of Warwickshire, in fact.' He shook his head. 'Sore decline indeed.'

'What did he mean?' Sledd walked to the trestle and poured another claret, lifting the jug in the others' direction in silent question. '"And there's more"?'

Strange shook his head to the offer of more drink and shrugged. 'More examples of Greville's baseness, I suppose.'

'No,' said Marlowe, after a moment's pause. 'No, it's not that simple.'

'Well.' Sledd quaffed the cup and left it on the trestle next to the jug. 'I must be off. Some of us have props to attend to. If I leave it all to Nat Sawyer, we'll be fencing with pig's bladders on sticks in the Masque. His mind does tend to be rather narrow when it comes to acting. Goodnight, My Lord. Kit.' He bowed to the one and nodded to the other and was gone.

Marlowe and Strange sat opposite each other with the great, grey carved stonework of the fireplace between them. 'Sir William is of the old religion, isn't he?' the playwright said.

Strange stared at him, all the emotions of a generation hurtling through his brain. 'Is he?' He decided to smile as he brazened it out. 'What makes you say that?'

Marlowe could not begin to explain that, until what seemed like yesterday, this was what he did for a living. He was not proud of it; in fact he hated it. But Francis Walsingham was the Queen's spymaster. He had a nose for treason, for Papist intrigue. There were Jesuits abroad in the land, fanatical, black-robed priests pledged to snuff out the life of the English Jezebel. And Walsingham couldn't have that. For every murderous priest on the road, there was a family to house him. A family like the Cloptons, with hidden rooms and secrets and the low, deadly chant of the Catholic Mass. When he had worked for Walsingham, Marlowe's job had been to join such households himself, to expose their rabid idolatry, to save the Queen. That was what he told himself in the long, sad watches of the night – he was playing Judas to save the Queen. And it didn't help one little bit. Because what he had suspected from the start had proved to be true; the evil plotters had turned out to be just people, trying to do what they thought best in an uncertain world. He had looked for the cloven hoof and the black heart and had found only human flesh that could bleed as readily as any other man's. He forced a smile.

'A lucky guess,' he said. 'But I *am* right, aren't I?'

Strange looked at the man, with his dark, watchful eyes, the sensitive lips and the flowing hair. He had only known him for a few days and here he was, baring his soul in a situation in which men went to the flames. 'Yes,' he said, quietly. 'Yes, Master Marlowe, you are right.' Then, suddenly, Lord Strange remembered where he was and who he was. He sat up straight in his chair and then leaned forward, one hand in the small of his back. 'But if you breathe a word of this, Marlowe, by God . . .'

The playwright held up his hand. 'Sir,' he said. 'Sir William's secret – and yours – is safe with me.'

Ferdinando Strange acknowledged the man's sincerity with a brief inclination of his head. Then, as the sun sank to a magenta death in the west, the two sat, alone together with their thoughts.

SIX

'Red sky at night, shepherd's delight,' the maid said, craning up on her toes to see out of the high window above the slop table in the kitchen of mighty Clopton Hall.

'Red sky at night, hayrick's alight, more likely,' grated the old crone in the inglenook corner. 'There'll be rain before bedtime, I can guarantee it.'

'No, Mistress Merriweather,' the girl sang out. 'It's a beautiful evening.'

'Puthery,' the old woman remarked, shutting her toothless jaws with a snap.

The cook spun round, a short paring knife, worn to a half moon by sharpening, in her hand. 'I have said it before and I'll say it again, Mistress Merriweather,' she said, sternly. 'I will have none of that language in my kitchen.'

The woman in the chimney corner looked affronted. 'It's just a word to describe the weather,' she said, in a wheedling tone. This was a comfortable place to be when the weather was closing in, when winter was nearer than you might think and the cook was generous. There was no bed on offer, but the settle in the corner was wide and accommodating and no one bothered her at night. Not worth annoying the woman; and anyway, it really was a word to describe the weather, that thick, soft feeling to the air, shot through with little shocks which foretold thunder and lightning to come.

The cook looked dubious, but after a busy evening conjuring up little sweetmeats for His Lordship and his guests and great pies and puddings for the players she was in that happy place inhabited by those who knew that a job had been well done. She wagged the knife at the woman. 'Very possibly, Mistress Merriweather, but mind your tongue.' She turned back to cleaning off her pastry board and so couldn't read the old woman's lips as she mouthed a foul oath at her broad back.

The maid was twirling now, her feet picking out complicated steps on the greasy flagstones. She was intoning, 'Shepherd's delight, shepherd's delight,' to herself, half song, half chant.

The cook clapped a floury hand to her forehead. 'Dorothy, can you please stop spinning around like that? Mercy, girl, you'll have me as giddy as a gander. I'm getting a mazy head.'

The girl carried on spinning round, but stopped singing. Instead, she moved her lips silently, but otherwise took no notice of the cook, who stood at her table, head bowed, hands braced on the butter and flour-daubed board. The old woman heaved herself up from her seat in the inglenook and tottered across to her and put a grimy claw on her shoulder.

'Get off to your bed, Mistress,' she crooned. Her voice, usually harsh as a corncrake was softer and persuasive. 'I'll finish cleaning your board off for you.'

The cook raised her head and winced with the pain. 'I think I will, Mistress Merriweather. You know how to clean my pastry board? Scrub it down and rub it with rosemary to keep it sweet. Otherwise the butter goes rancid and taints the paste.' She went a strange shade of green at the thought and, clapping her hand to her mouth, ran to the door. The girl and the crone could hear from the noises that something had definitely disagreed with the cook. After a few moments, they heard her dragging footsteps as she made her way to her truckle bed tucked under the back stairs. The kitchen was quiet for a moment, with only the settling embers of the cooking fire to be heard. The kitchen was usually loud with shouting pot boys and serving men, but their work was done for the night and they were all out at the wagons, mingling with Lord Strange's Men – and women – with dreams of the stage and running away to a better life filling their heads.

The crone looked at the girl, who had started her solitary dance again. She had lived a long time, mostly on her wits, and had learned a lot in that long life. She had once had a name of her own, but her talent for predicting rain, snow and other conditions which could affect her fellow men and beasts had earned her a new one; Merriweather. She cocked her head on one side.

'Stop that, now. You've done your work, now go outside and have some fun.'

The girl stopped spinning and looked at the old woman from under her brows. She was not a pretty girl at first glance, with a glowering look and hair which hung in elflocks round her face, but the crone could see that with a better expression and a ribbon, she could be quite a heartbreaker. There was a moment when the two glances met with an almost audible crackle, but the old woman had been around a long time and no chit of a girl could beat her. Yet. Then, the tension broke and the girl gave one last twirl.

'You're sure?' she said, but she was already heading for the door, clapping her hands as if to rid them of any remaining flour.

'Certain sure,' the old woman said, with a toothless smile. 'Off you go. Find yourself a nice young man to dance with. It's not healthy to dance with yourself.'

With a glance over her shoulder, the girl was gone in a swirl of skirts and shawls and Mistress Merriweather was alone. A snatch of pipe and drum had come through the door with the girl's exit and the forecaster gave a slow, arthritic turn of her own, one hand shaking on her hip and the other held curved above her head. She stopped and looked around with a sheepish smile to make sure no one had seen her, pulled her clothes into what passed, on her body, for tidiness, and then went back to her seat in the inglenook and her thoughts.

Outside, under the spread of a glorious chestnut tree, Lord Strange's Men were taking their ease. Nat Sawyer was entertaining a couple of the village girls behind the tree, to an accompaniment of smothered giggles. There were tricks he could do with various parts of his body which the rest of the troupe preferred not to know about. A couple of the women had the details but could never bring themselves to talk about it. Thomas, still an innocent in many ways despite his best efforts, thought it might be something to do with being double jointed. Martin was making the most of Alleyn's absence and had been last seen slipping away into the coppiced wood to the west of the estate with one of the more attractive household servants. Joseph was asleep in the arms of his favourite companion, alcohol, and Ned Sledd was playing his favourite role of actor-manager, standing legs akimbo like the old king and for much the same reason; it was a stance calculated to make lesser men quake and peers to step aside. A gaggle of impressionable youths surrounded him. He bowed, cleared his throat and stepped forward a pace.

'Gentles, all,' he began.

Thomas, sitting to one side mending the hem of his dress, groaned. Nothing good ever came of it when Sledd began that way.

'Gentles, all,' Sledd repeated, with a venomous glare at Thomas. 'I give you a few lines from a play which I penned as a lad, *Rafe Roister Doister*.' He bowed low to hide his grin; he loved these country places that had never heard of Nicholas Udall and all his works.

'I thought Nicholas Udall wrote that,' came a voice from the crowd.

Sledd straightened up, leaned back from the hips and boomed back, 'Pen name, good sire. My pen name merely.'

'I thought Nicholas Udall was dead,' the voice continued. 'And I thought he was done for buggery.'

Sledd shaded his eyes and looked into the crowd but could see no one in particular that he knew. Some trouble maker; there was one in every audience. He straightened again and struck his favourite stance, one leg held stiffly in front of him, one arm flung out, one hand on his heart. He dropped his chin on his chest and growled, 'From *Rafe Roister Doister*. A snatch only, for your delight.' He took a deep breath in through his nostrils and exhaled like a winded horse. 'Where is the house I go to, before or behind? I know not where, or when, or how I shall it find?' He took another whistling breath and changed arms.

Recognizing that his leader was about to forget the next line and not wishing to witness the sorry scene, Thomas rolled quietly off his stool and crept on hands and knees around the tree. Nat Sawyer and his audience looked at him with startled eyes and Thomas grew up several years in one second. He quickly turned away but with an unforgettable image burned forever into his brain.

Covered in confusion, he blundered off across the sheep-cropped grass, towards the coppiced wood, deciding on his destination as he went by veering away from the cries of obvious delight coming from behind a big elder clump. Looking over his shoulder, he missed his footing and went flying over an ivy-covered stump and lay there, face hidden in his arms, waiting until he felt steadier.

'Are you hurt?' A voice from above his head startled him, and he looked up slowly. At first, he could just see a pair of feet, bare and rather dirty, leading to slender ankles which in their turn disappeared under the frowsty hem of a skirt. Looking onwards and upwards, the next thing he saw was an apron, kirtled up into the waistband of the dress and above that a pair of swelling breasts under a hastily knotted shawl. Above that, a smiling face, not pretty, not clean, but friendly.

Thomas scrambled to his feet and dusted himself off. Something of his acting persona had rubbed off on him over the years, and he liked to look nice in company. Sometimes he had to hold himself in check to keep the girl within in her place. 'No,' he said, consciously trying to lower the timbre of his voice. 'No, it was just a trip.'

Now he was on his feet, he could look the girl in the eye, but only just. She was tall and well made, with a body that looked almost as hard and boyish as his own. He found himself wishing he could make his breasts look as good as hers in a gown. She was still smiling, with her head on one side, making an elflock fall over one eye. She brushed it aside and tucked it behind one ear. 'Are you with the actors?'

'Mmm.' Thomas decided that until he could get his voice a little lower, he would stay in the safety of mumbles. Perhaps she would think he was just too masculine to speak. It seemed to work for George, the stupidest of all the actors, who always played third spear-bearer and who had shoulders like linen presses and the intellect of one of the bed sheets within. He had a wife and six children back in London, so a grunt must have done the business at least that many times.

She stepped forward half a step and put her hand on his chest, rubbing just one finger tip up and down the laces of his jerkin. 'That must be exciting,' she said, huskily. 'I'm a maid in the kitchen of the big house.' She tossed her head in the direction of Clopton Hall. 'It's very . . . dull.' Somehow, without Thomas being aware of how it had happened, her finger had pulled the laces loose and his jerkin flapped open. In another deft movement, she had pulled the shirt loose and her hand was now scratching at his chest. Somehow, his breathing seemed to be giving him trouble and he had to really concentrate on not passing out.

She smiled at him and her face seemed very near. He could smell the sweet pastry smell of her, like honey and warm butter. Her teeth gleamed in the half light and her eyes flashed. He tried to pull his head back. He had told everyone that it was just an old wives' tale, all that about his balls and his voice and all, but when push came to shove, he didn't dare risk it. But it seemed that her reach was longer than his and her mouth found his and he had no choice but to kiss her.

And such a kiss. He felt as though his brain was falling out through his mouth, to mingle with hers in a tangle of tongues and teeth. And then he felt the hand in his breeches and knew he should stop all this, before his voice was gone for ever. And then he felt her leg wrap around his and something warm envelop what he had tried not to think of too much lately, for fear. And he thought of Nat Sawyer, and he thought of Martin, and he thought of his career, such as it was. And the ground came up to meet them and he stopped thinking altogether.

Back under the chestnut tree the audience was beginning to melt away. Ned Sledd had begun to descend into random lines from any play he could remember, Joseph was awake now and joining in like some kind of demented echo, making it hard for the actor-manager to keep his concentration on his performance. Nat Sawyer's party trick had reached its natural climax and the girls had wandered away, giggling.

Suddenly, from the coppice there came a yell to freeze the blood. Sledd's head snapped up and he counted his flock with a quick flick of the eyes, then grinned. He looked at the women, sitting to one side, chatting together now it was too dark to sew and saw they were smiling.

'Martin's in good form, by the sound of it,' he said and they all laughed.

Through the dense foliage of the tree, fat drops of rain began to drum faintly on the hands of the leaves, like distant applause.

In the coppiced wood, behind the elder clump, Martin sheltered his temporary love under his cloak, a gentleman player to the last.

And deeper in the wood, Dorothy sheltered under the panting figure of Thomas and turned her face up to the rain. And laughed.

The rain which had come with the night was lashing down and with it had come a wind which was roaring through the oaks that ringed Clopton Hall. Every casement in the building rattled and in the Great Hall Sir William's dogs whined in their sleep before the huge unlit logs in the grate, dreaming of the horns and the hunt.

Kit Marlowe was still awake when he heard the tap on his bedroom door. The bed was high and soft with feather down and the candle flickered its lurid shapes on the tapestries, velvet and brocade. Men like Marlowe often slept alone but his dagger was always within reach and he slid it noiselessly from its sheath now before sliding off the four poster and snuffing out the candle. He waited behind the heavy oak door and felt rather than saw the thing creak open. Candle shafts darted in the darkness and he heard a voice.

'Master Marlowe? Master Marlowe – are you awake?'

She almost floated into the room, her face lit by the candle, her eyes bright. He couldn't see her heart, of course, but he guessed it would be pounding, like his. Joyce Clopton, his host's daughter, had long dark hair, hanging in a long and tapering plait now down her back, rather than the elaborate pearl-speckled coil wound around a cap as she had worn it at dinner. Her feet were bare and she clutched a long velvet cloak around her, her left hand holding it closed at her breast.

'Tolerably,' he murmured and she spun at the voice behind her, gasping as she saw the outstretched steel. He caught her wrist with his left hand and steadied it and the candle. 'My Lady,' he said, 'it is late and I am not sure that Sir William . . .'

She pulled away sharply and placed the candlestick on the table. 'This is not exactly a social call, Master Marlowe. And you need have no fear. Neither of us shall be compromised.'

'Even so,' he said. 'For decorum's sake. I am a guest in your father's house.'

'Quite so,' she said. 'Quite so.'

For a moment they looked at each other, the squire's daughter and the playwright. Then she cleared her throat. The man was in an open shirt, to be sure, but he still wore his leather pantaloons. And his dagger was tucked back into the belt at the back. There was no doubt about it, he was very attractive, especially when compared to some of the spavined aristocrats her father had trotted out for her delight over the last months. But she was not here on pleasure bent, so she put his looks to one side.

'What are you, Master Marlowe?' she asked, arching her neck and looking up at him.

'Somewhat surprised,' Marlowe said.

'No.' The ice broke in her voice for the first time. 'No, I mean, *what* are you? Father says you are a playwright.'

'That is so.' Marlowe nodded and relit his candle with the tinder flash. She watched his eyes sparkle in the half light and smoulder in the half dark.

She moved away from the table and sat down on a gilded chair in the corner. 'And what else are you?' she asked.

'I am . . . I was a scholar,' he told her. 'From Cambridge. Corpus Christi College.'

She frowned. 'I thought the men of Corpus went into the Church.'

He found himself chuckling, for all sorts of reasons, but mostly in surprise. 'You are well informed, My Lady; Cambridge from here is the far side of the moon.'

'When I was a girl,' she said softly, 'I used to look for the man in the moon. When the moon was full in the faerie time.' She smiled, a smile warm with memories of long ago. 'I never found him.' She flashed him a glance, suddenly serious, direct, urgent. 'Perhaps I have now.'

'My Lady?' he crossed the room and placed his candle beside hers. He perched on the side of the bed and waited.

'At dinner,' she said, 'you spoke of . . . oh, so many things. Of Tamburlaine, the Scythian shepherd. Of the great magician, Dr Faustus. Have you written plays about these men?'

'No,' he said, laughing. 'One day, perhaps. But . . . I have to get to London first. *That's* where my destiny lies, if I have one.'

She nodded. 'You are ambitious, Master Marlowe,' she said.

'One of my many failings.'

'And you need money – to get your plays accepted, I mean. They say the Master of the Revels does not come cheap. Nor, I'll wager, does the Lord Chamberlain.'

Marlowe nodded. 'Palms will have to be greased, that is true.'

'Here, then.' She threw him a leather purse which appeared from nowhere under her robe. He caught it expertly. It was heavy and it jingled. He weighed it in his hand.

'My Lady.' He smiled. 'I cannot accept such kindness. I have a patron, of sorts, in Lord Strange . . .'

'It is not kindness, Master Marlowe,' she said. 'It is a down payment for a little task I'd have you undertake. There's more – much more – when the job is done.'

He carefully laid the purse down and leaned back. 'What job?' he asked.

'That,' she said, pointing to his waist with a curving finger, 'that dagger behind your back. How good are you with that?'

'I get by,' he said.

'Tell me, Master Playwright, Master Scholar . . . have you killed a man?'

He sat upright slowly. 'No one told me you worked for the Star Chamber,' he said. He saw Joyce Clopton gnaw her lip. She was in too far to pull out now and time was of the essence.

'What do you think of my father, sir?' she asked him.

'A good man,' Marlowe said, 'a generous host. And a good father, I am sure.'

'The best.' She smiled fondly. 'My mother – God rest her soul . . .' She crossed herself, instantly regretting it and putting her hands behind her back as a child would do when caught out. 'My mother bore four children and I alone survived. Father says I am his all. And I've never wished that I was a man more than I do tonight.'

Marlowe shrugged. 'You've lost me.'

'My father is a good man, but he is too kind, too soft. There is one in the town who intends to ruin him.'

'Sir Edward Greville.' Marlowe nodded.

'You know him?' Joyce said, wide eyed.

'I know of him,' Marlowe corrected her.

'A fouler bastard never drew breath,' Joyce growled. 'He will hound my poor father to his grave, unless . . .'

'Unless?' Marlowe knew exactly where this was going.

She looked at him from under heavy eyelids. 'Unless you kill him.'

The wind rattled the casement and the curtain rippled like something living as the candles shivered and shook. Marlowe got up from the bed, taking the purse with him and crossed to the girl. He lifted her gently to her feet and holding out her right hand, placed the gold into it. 'I am a poet,' he whispered. 'A playwright, a scholar. I am not a murderer.' And he turned away.

For a moment, there was silence, then the rustle of her gown and when he turned back, Joyce Clopton stood naked before him, the robe at her feet, her shoulders and breasts gleaming in the candlelight. He kept his eyes on hers, although he was aware of the shape of her, her waist and the swell of her belly leading down to the dark v between her legs.

'If not money,' she said, 'whatever is your wish . . .'

The silence between them now was an eternity. Then Kit Marlowe, gentleman as well as scholar, bent and picked up the gown, carefully draping it around her shoulders, covering her nakedness. Joyce Clopton did not know what to do. Men the length and breadth of the country would have given their right arm for what Marlowe had just turned down. And in a burst of frustration and shame, she sobbed violently, her body convulsing with the humiliation and failure.

He held her close, smelling the fragrance of her hair and wiped away the tears that ran down her cheeks with his still ink-stained thumb. 'I will not take your gold,' he told her. 'Nor will I take you. But tomorrow –' he held her at arm's length and held up her chin – 'tomorrow I will take me a walk into this Stratford of yours and pay my respects to Sir Edward Greville.'

'You . . .' Her tear-filled eyes widened with hope, but he placed a hand softly over her mouth.

'This,' he said, sweeping out the dagger from the small of his back. 'This I will leave here.' And he threw it on to the bed. 'Now, My Lady,' he said. 'It is late.' He turned his back so she could scramble back into her gown and cloak. Turning back, he snatched up her candle and handed it back to her. 'It's a wild night,' he added, as the window shook again, 'but when it's over and the clouds have gone and the moon's awake, look again for that man. Perhaps you will be able to find him now.'

He turned back to his bed and blew his candle out. Behind him, the darkness swelled and with a creak of the door and a gust of air, she was gone.

SEVEN

'What do you make of this weather, Kit?' Ferdinando Strange wanted to know as he swung from his horse outside the Swan.

'Fair and foul, four seasons in one day,' Marlowe said. 'Typical summer, surely?'

'There's nothing typical about this summer, Kit, believe me. Well . . .' He waited until Marlowe had dismounted and threw a coin to the pot boy, a job Marlowe had had not so many years before. 'What's the plan?'

'My Lord?' Marlowe arched an eyebrow.

Strange looked at him, hands on hips. 'I tell you I'm paying my respects to the Lord of the Manor and you say "what a coincidence – so am I". Now, I don't believe in coincidences, Master Marlowe. We've ridden all the way from Clopton discussing the might of Spain, the cost of enclosure and the various merits of Masters Tallis and Byrd; *anything* in fact but the matter in hand – Sir Edward Greville.'

'You are the son of an earl, My Lord,' Marlowe said. 'I merely follow.'

Strange snorted. 'I've not known you long, Kit Marlowe,' he said, 'but I don't believe you've ever followed anyone in your life. Are you armed?'

'No, My Lord.'

'No?' Strange stopped dead in the doorway. 'Was that wise?'

'I made someone a promise,' Marlowe said.

'Hmm.' Strange nodded. He liked the sound of this less and less. The Swan was a vast, ramshackle barn of a place, dark with heavy beams and reeking of Warwickshire ale. But it was cool out of the morning sun and the travellers found a table. Mine host knew a gentleman when he saw one and was soon hovering in person, service guaranteed.

'Good morning, My Lords. What can I get you?'

'Sir Edward Greville.' Strange looked the man up and down.
'Now.'

'Er . . . very good, sir,' the host grovelled. 'Who shall I
say . . .?'

Strange flashed the man a withering glance then wrenched
the ring from his finger. 'Give him this.'

The innkeeper stared at it. He had never held so much
gold in his hand before and his eyes shone.

'I did say "now",' Strange reminded him and the landlord
vanished.

It was less than two minutes before a figure appeared at the
top of the stairs that led to the wooden gallery. Both men
recognized the livery the man wore – the arms of Greville
Strange knew by sight and the lion rampant of the Earl of
Lincoln. The man himself was short and round and he clutched
a leather satchel to himself. He also carried Strange's ring.

Two other men followed him down the stairs, each of them
in leather jacks with daggers at their hips and Greville's arms
gilt on their shoulders.

'My Lord.' The man bowed as he reached the flagstoned
floor.

'Who the Hell are you?' Strange barked at him.

'I am Henry Blake, My Lord, Bencher of Lincoln's Inn.'

'I *knew* it!' Strange slapped his thigh. 'I *knew* Greville would
send his heavies. One –' he pointed at Blake – 'to lie his way
out of trouble; the others –' and he tossed an imperious glance
to the men with him – 'to provide the muscle if legalities fail.
Where is Greville?'

The lawyer smirked. 'I'm afraid Sir Edward is unavailable
at the moment, My Lord.'

'Don't tell me he's at Milcote. I was reliably informed he
spends his Tuesdays here at the Swan.'

'Not today, My Lord.' Blake was the epitome of reason.
'Neither is he at his country home. He has been called away
to London, on urgent business.'

Strange pursed his lips. 'Very well,' he said, 'to my urgent
business. Shall we discuss it here, lawyer, or do you need a
more secret chamber to conduct your crooked business?'

'Sir Edward has nothing to hide, My Lord.'

Strange guffawed. 'Except his coercion in forcing good men off their land and buying up property at cut-throat prices.' He looked at the men flanking Blake. 'Is that where these two come in?'

They both took a step forward and Marlowe rose to face them. Strange raised a hand. 'Give your master notice, lackey,' he said. 'I intend, on behalf of Sir William Clopton, knight of this shire, to oppose him in his current ventures. Whatever scraps of paper you're hiding in that satchel, you might as well tear them up. They know me in the Court of Chancery. And he shall know me too.'

He stood up, scraping back his stool and he strode for the door. Marlowe crossed to the lawyer and lowered his head towards his. 'Lord Strange is an honourable man,' he said, 'one who deals with the law and in the light of day. I'm sure that's the fair way to stop your master, lickspittle, but there are other ways. Ways of the dark.'

'Oh, yes?' one of the thugs grinned, standing half a head taller than Marlowe.

Marlowe closed to him and smiled back. 'Oh, yes,' he said.

Greville's hired men stood their ground for a few moments more, then, clicking like automata, turned on their heels and walked away, back up the stairs, the lawyer leading the way.

Strange turned to Marlowe with a wry smile. 'That went well.' The question lingered at the end of the sentence like a wisp of smoke when a candle is snuffed out.

'We're still alive, so I suppose it did,' Marlowe said. 'Never mind. Sir Edward Greville knows we are here and on his trail, so this morning has not been wasted.' There was a muffled cough behind them and the men turned.

'Yes?' they said in unison.

The man who stood before them was unusual looking, to say the least. His head seemed too big for both his hair and his body and although his features were, individually, all quite normal they nevertheless seemed to belong to several different faces. His forehead seemed enormous, wider and taller than any they had seen and the mouth was petulant, burrowed into a neat goatee beard. His eyes were hooded and just a threat too close together, with a slight hint of a divergent squint.

They flicked now, from one man to the other, under a querulous frown. At first glance he was in his early twenties or thereabouts, but his hairline was much older and when he spoke, it was with a harsh, unattractive voice which thought the world owed it a living.

Finally, his gaze settled on Marlowe. 'Would you be Ned Sledd?' he asked in a rather confrontational manner, leaning forward and forgetting to lean back.

Marlowe took a while to answer, looking the man up and down. He was dressed from head to foot in rusty, dusty black and in a fashion which Marlowe had not seen on anyone's back since he was a treble singing in the Cathedral back in Canterbury. Only his gloves were in the mode of the time and they were works of art, finely stitched and with bugles and trim around the gauntlet which Marlowe envied on sight. Eventually, the poet spoke. 'Indeed, no. Not for ready money.'

Strange, who had grown used to Marlowe in the past days, snorted his amusement and smiled at the stranger, waiting for his reply. It was a surprise when it came. The man leapt at Marlowe and grabbed him by the collar, pulling him close so they were nose to nose. Marlowe squinted down at him, only an inch or two but it was an inch or two which mattered at times like these, then brushed him off like a fly.

'Touch me again,' he said, with a faint smile on his lips but not in his eyes, 'and it may be the last thing you ever do. But I would like to know who you are, to tell the Watch when they find you dead somewhere.'

'Shaxsper,' the stranger said. 'William Shaxsper. Son of John Shaxsper, the glover.'

'Ah,' Strange said, 'we've heard of him, from Sir William Clopton.'

'And it explains . . .' Marlowe waved a hand at the man's gloves. 'But it doesn't explain why you are looking for Sledd or why you tried to strangle me.'

William Shaxsper looked sheepish and reached out to tweak Marlowe's collar back into position. Then, he peeled off his gloves, folded them neatly and gave them to Marlowe with a flourish.

Marlowe was disconcerted for one of the few times in his life. 'No . . . I . . . these are too much. I didn't mean . . .'

'It's nothing,' Shaxsper said, reaching into the purse at his waist and drawing out another pair, if anything even more lovely than the last. 'I have plenty.' He shuffled his feet and pointed to a settle under the window. 'May we sit?'

'Of course.' Strange clicked his fingers at the landlord, who was still hovering. In a perfect world, these strangers would go away and take their troublesome ways with them, but failing that, they could at least spend some money in his inn. 'Landlord,' he said, 'three goblets of Rhennish, if you please.'

'I don't really drink wine,' Shaxsper complained. 'Ale, I drink, mostly.'

The landlord looked at Strange's expression. 'Three goblets of Rhennish it is, My Lord.' He took a few paces across the room and then turned back. He had been host to Edward Greville for a long time now and was learning the ways of the nobility. 'Er . . . we are a cash house, sir.'

'Of course you are,' Strange said with a wintry smile. 'And as soon as my steward receives your bill of sale, I am sure he will be delighted to give you some. Meanwhile, some sweet-meats with the Rhennish would be a wonderful idea.'

Shaxsper looked at Strange with admiration in his rather hooded and bloodshot eyes. No one had ever managed to get out of the Swan without handing over all they owed and then some to Thomas Dixon.

'So, Master Shaxsper – that is a very unusual name you have there, isn't it? Master Shaxsper . . .'

'Call me Will, sire.'

'May I?' Strange wasn't sorry. The other thing really was a bit of a mouthful. 'Will, Master Marlowe and I would love to know why you are looking for Ned Sledd.'

'He leads Lord Strange's Men,' said Shaxsper, the stars all but twinkling in his eyes. 'I want to join them, to be an actor.'

Marlowe caught Strange's eye. There was fun to be had here. 'Wouldn't Lord Strange be the man to contact, then?' he asked the strange Stratfordian.

'Lord Strange?' Shaxsper smiled in a superior way at Marlowe. 'He isn't real, you know. It's just a name that looks good on the posters. I've got one here, look.' He foraged inside his jerkin and brought out a tattered playbill from about a year before, advertising Lord Strange's Men in . . . but the name of the play was missing, left behind when the flyer was torn from the wall where it had been hastily pasted.

'It's a good name,' Ferdinando Strange said, thoughtfully.

'I've heard better,' Shaxsper said. He was feeling a little more comfortable with these men now that there was a table between them. The good-looking one was clearly some kind of madman. Shaxsper shared the failing of all short-tempered men, in that he assumed that everyone was shorter tempered than he was himself. The other one, with that peculiar mole on his forehead – a witches' mark if ever there was one – he was obviously rich, but then, anyone could become rich, given some luck. He, William Shaxsper, for example, intended to become very rich indeed. All he needed was a few bits of good fortune, made more likely by the some dozen or so talismans he carried under his jerkin. 'And while we are on the subject, may I ask your names, sirs?'

'With pleasure,' Strange said and extended a hand to Marlowe. 'May I introduce my very good friend and colleague, Christopher Marlowe. Master Marlowe is a scholar, poet and playwright, lately of Corpus Christi College, Cambridge. He is currently travelling with Lord Strange's Men and we hope that he will write us a play before the month is out.'

Shaxsper inclined his head and mumbled, 'Master Marlowe.' So, this was the opposition to be beaten before he could rise to glory. Not much to beat there. A scholar was bound to have a mouth full of long words and not an ounce of wit. Nobody went to the theatre these days to be shouted at in Greek. Somehow, Shaxsper couldn't see this over-educated popinjay making much of a scene involving a porter and a humorous vegetable. He smiled.

'Master Shaxsper.' Marlowe bowed in return. He forbore to add to Strange's list of all his different personae. 'And now, may I introduce *my* very good friend and colleague, Ferdinando Stanley, Baron Strange.' He looked Shaxsper in the eye, the one that seemed to be looking at him at that moment. 'Lord Strange is . . . correct me if I get this wrong, My Lord . . .

second in line to the throne, as set down in the late King Henry's will. That is right, My Lord, is it not?'

Ferdinando Strange inclined his head. 'Yes, yes, indeed. After my mother, I am the next in line. But we don't talk about it much. The Queen may yet marry and produce an heir.' His smile indicated two things; one, that this was rubbish and, two, that he believed it implicitly and it would be a good idea if they did too.

Shaxsper's mouth hung slack. The Rhennish arrived at that moment and he grabbed a goblet and drank it down. For an ale man, he could certainly quaff his wine.

Marlowe filled the silence. 'So, tell us about yourself, Master Shaxsper. Why do you want to join the acting life?'

Shaxsper ran his hand through his receding hair. 'I am twenty-one years old, Master Marlowe. I have a wife and three children here in Stratford. I was meant for more than this.'

Marlowe raised an eyebrow. 'Three children at twenty-one. By all that's holy, Master Shaxsper, that is really an achievement.'

Shaxsper waved a dismissive hand. 'The last two are twins, so it was not such a great achievement, Master Marlowe. And beside, although I love them dearly, of course, as I love my dear wife, they are not quiet children. Between them all, the crying, the shouting . . .' He pressed the heels of his hands into his eyes and took a deep breath. 'I just need to get some sleep . . . perchance to dream . . . and write my poems . . . to . . .'

Strange reached across the table. 'I have two children, Will. I don't notice them crying overmuch.'

Shaxsper raised his head and looked at the man as though he wanted to kill him where he sat. In a tight voice, he said, 'And how many servants do you have in your household, My Lord?'

Strange looked at the ceiling and did a small calculation on his fingers. Before he had finished, he looked at Shaxsper. 'Which house?'

'The ones with the children in,' the man said, through his teeth.

Strange finished his calculation and smiled ruefully. 'I can't tell you precisely, Will,' he said. 'My stewards manage that kind of thing. But I would imagine a hundred or so. We do have rather a lot of windows to clean, people to feed.' He gave a self-deprecating little laugh. 'You know how it is.'

'Not really,' Shaxsper said. 'We have a general girl to do the rough work. Other than that, Anne does everything herself. The twins do keep her busy of course, so I help when I can.'

Marlowe noticed a softening of the man's face when he mentioned the twins. 'Twins; that is a blessing for a man. Boys?'

'One boy,' Shaxsper said, his face alight. 'Hamnet, we have called him.'

'Hamnet Shaxsper.' Marlowe fought to keep any inflection from his voice. 'An unusual name.'

'One which will look good on the playbills, I thought,' Shaxsper said. 'I was looking to the future. Which will be good to us all, God willing.'

Strange and Marlowe carefully didn't look at each other, then Strange ventured a remark. 'So, you would leave your wife and three children to seek your fortune as an actor?'

'And poet. And playwright.'

'Of course. Those too. Well!' Ferdinando Strange slapped the table with both hands and stood, swigging the remains of his wine as he did so. 'We must be on our way back to Clopton. Do you have a horse, Master Shaxsper?'

'No. We had to sell the horse to pay the servant.'

'Don't worry, My Lord,' Marlowe said. 'If you can lead my horse, I will walk back to Clopton with Master Shaxsper. We can talk about poetry.'

Shaxsper looked at him through narrowed eyes. 'You know about poetry?' he asked, suspiciously.

'A little,' Marlowe conceded.

Strange, who had a copy of Marlowe's translation of Ovid in his library at home, smiled. 'Then all's well that ends well. I will see you back at the Hall. I expect Ned Sledd will be planning the performance, so don't dally, Kit.'

'We'll step lively, My Lord. Now, Will . . . may I call you Will? Do you have any poetry on you? In your head?'

As they left the inn, Thomas Dixon heard Shaxsper's high

and discordant voice begin to recite, words with which every patron of the Swan was heartily sick.

'"Pretty women we desire to bed, so that their beauty won't be dead. So when we get old and die, your children can keep green the memorie." That rhyme might need some work . . .'

'Let's think it through, Will, as we walk,' the landlord heard Marlowe say. 'To start with, how about that first line. What about "From fairest creatures we desire increase"? Not quite so . . . blunt, perhaps?'

No, thought the landlord. Still a load of horse shit, though. Why didn't men of that sort get a decent job, one which paid them, so they could pay him? He sighed, and went back into the scullery with the goblets, tipping each up to drink the dregs. No rest for the wicked, that was the only thing certain in this life.

'So what was Strange threatening, exactly?' Edward Greville was in his mews at Milcote, feeding live chicks to his goshawks.

'Nothing specific, sir,' Blake told him, unrolling parchment on the nearest desk and trying to avoid the flying offal. 'But he did mention Chancery.'

Greville paused, the helpless creature squirming and cheeping in his gloved hand. 'Did he now?'

Blake was still rummaging in his papers. 'I think, sir, we're on firm ground with the Lower Acres and probably that section of Arden spoken of in perpetuity. There is a codicil to the will of Sir Hugh Clopton, dated, as far as I can read it, fourteen forty-nine, but it formed part of the escheat . . .'

'Oh, do shut up, Blake!' Greville snarled and threw the chick into the air to be caught by the shrieking, squabbling hawks. One of them ripped the chick's throat with its murderous beak, then tossed back its head and swallowed the little bird whole. 'You and I know full well that if it came to court, I would lose.' He wiped his bloody glove in a napkin and threw it to a servant, before striding towards the door. 'The trouble with you lawyers is that you've all been lying for so long now you've started to believe your own hocus pocus.' He paused in the archway of the mews and clicked his fingers. A flunkey came forward with a goblet on a tray. 'Strange is one of the richest men in the realm and close to the throne,' he said, 'for all he goes about without a retinue and consorts with play actors. He can afford the best. And, with respect, Henry, that isn't you.'

He took a sip of the red wine and wandered across the lawn towards the great house. 'I don't mind admitting, Henry,' he said, 'I hadn't reckoned on Strange. If it were just old Clopton in my way, I'd have half the county by Lammastide. But Strange . . .' He tapped the silver-gilded goblet against his teeth. 'You said someone was with him at the Swan – some actor?'

'Probably, sir. I didn't ask. Seemed to fancy his chances, though.'

Greville looked at him. 'In what way?'

'Squared up to the lads. I think it quite shook them.'

'A sworder, do you think? A professional?'

Blake screwed up his face. All his adult life he had been weighing up men's characters, usually across a boisterous courtroom. 'Difficult to say,' was the best he could do in remembrance of the enigmatic face of Kit Marlowe.

'Well, it would make sense,' Greville thought aloud. 'Old Clopton's cleverer than I thought. He's got Strange on board to fight me in Chancery – where, at very best, it'll bankrupt me to take him on – and this fellow as a swordsman to handle the rough stuff.'

'He wasn't armed,' Blake told him.

'Was he not?' Greville mused. 'Was he not?' He reached the ornate doorway with its oak and its carved stone tracery. It swung open as another flunkey wearing the Greville livery bowed to him. 'Henry,' he said, turning to the diminutive lawyer, 'time, I think, that we were in touch with our friends.'

The colour drained from Blake's face. 'Oh, no, sir. No, really. I'm sure I can . . .'

But Greville's hand was in the air and Greville's mind was made up. 'Our friends, Henry,' he said, firmly. 'See to it.'

EIGHT

William Clopton's messengers cantered the length and breadth of the county that summer, thudding through the Forest of Arden, clattering under the great grey stones of Warwick and proclaiming their message in the Bull Ring in Coventry. There was a masque afoot at Clopton Hall and all were invited, high or low.

Men who knew Sir William assumed he had gone mad, that second childhood had come to him. Men who did not could not care less – there'd been no masques in Warwickshire for years. The Puritans had put a stop to the old Mystery Plays in Coventry and people missed them. Clopton Hall would be, just for a while, a place of magic. Men like Strange and Marlowe knew it was all a front; that an old, frightened and perhaps dying man was trying to recreate the gilded days of his own summer, when he had danced with Queen Catherine Parr under a floodlit sky.

No Clopton messengers came within a stone-bow shot of Edward Greville, but their horses' hoofs clashed over the cobbles in Guild Street and Waterside, blasting their trumpets along sleepy Scholars' Lane and throwing Clopton's rosebuds to the Puritan ladies of Stratford, who recoiled in horror and clutched their prayer books.

At the Hall that afternoon, it was all clash and carry. Like a general in the field, Ned Sledd directed his troops, hauling timbers and flats for the makeshift stage, hanging gilt-thread curtains and sweeping corners. The noise was pandemonium, the cross-saws of the carpenters and the tapping of their hammers vying with the lutes, flutes and hautboys of the orchestra, vainly trying to keep time. Stalls had appeared from nowhere in what had been the outer bailey in sterner times, enterprising townsfolk anxious to make money as well as merry at Clopton's masque. But by cock-shut time, the cracks in Sledd's well-oiled production machine were beginning to show.

The actor-manager's face flickered in the torchlights the crew had set up around the stage. And he was not a happy man.

'Twenty-four hours,' he said, solemnly. 'Twenty-four hours, Thomas, and you must play Britannia.'

'Hmm.' Thomas nodded in agreement. He certainly looked the part, his breastplate gleaming copper in the torchlight and his plumed helmet magnificent on his head.

'And how do you propose to do that?' Sledd asked him.

'Hmm?' Thomas was fiddling with his trident and prowling the stage, in accordance with the old theatrical adage 'If in doubt, walk about.'

'Give me your opening line,' Sledd commanded.

Thomas stood still, raised his trident aloft and steadied his shield. He cleared his throat. 'Yes, good St George, my man of men. What do you on the stroke of ten?'

There was a stunned silence.

Thomas cleared his throat again, looking nervously at Sledd. 'Well, it's your line now,' he hissed.

Mechanically and in a numbed disbelief, Sledd intoned, 'Why, good Britannia, queen divine, what time I have is at your shrine.'

Thomas raised the trident again to deliver his riposte, but nothing came out even though his mouth was open. In an instant, Sledd was up on the stage, hissing in the boy's ear, 'Your voice, Thomas.'

'What about it?' the boy warbled.

'It has broken. Nay, shattered.' He gripped the lad's shoulders so that both shield and trident clattered to the planks. 'You've been using that little pocky of yours, haven't you?'

'I . . .'

'Don't lie to me, sir. Who was the slut? I'll have her stripped and tied to the cart's tail.'

Thomas stood as tall as his corselet would let him. 'I can't tell you,' he said.

Sledd snarled at him. 'Honour among fornicators, eh? Well, you're out, young man. Collect your wages, such as they are, and I want you on the road by nightfall.'

'Master Sledd?' a female voice stopped him from felling

the boy on the spot. The actor-manager peered beyond the
torchlights' flicker to see Joyce Clopton standing there with
Marlowe.

'Mistress?' He half bowed.

'Do I understand you have lost your Britannia?'

Sledd glared at Thomas before replying. 'Aye, Mistress, I
have. And more has been lost besides.'

'I know the part,' she told him.

Sledd was appalled. 'Mistress . . . My Lady.' He let Thomas
go and came hurtling down the steps. 'Madame, you are aware
of the law?' He looked frantically from side to side. 'No
females may perform . . .'

'That applies to the London stage, Master Sledd,' she told
him, 'and to what is deemed by the Lord Chamberlain to be
a play. This is a masque and this is not London. I have heard
that Queen Anne Boleyn first appeared at court in a masque.'

'Yeah, Ned, you must remember that,' Thomas growled,
now that he had no need to hide his lack of octaves.

'Kit?' Sledd spread his arms theatrically.

'Don't look at me.' The playwright smiled. 'The lady is right.'

'Look . . .' Sledd was frantically rethinking the whole performance. 'Couldn't we do something else? I mean, *Rafe Roister
Doister*, for example. That always goes down well . . .'

Marlowe frowned. 'It's rubbish, Ned,' he said, 'from beginning to end. You know that. Anyway, it's full of parts for boys.'

'All right, then. Can you knock something up – er . . . a
shortened version of Dido, Queen –' he pierced Thomas with
a look and corrected himself – 'King of Carthage, perhaps?'

Marlowe looked at the man with disdain. 'You've hired an
orchestra here, Ned. And they'll have to be paid. Might as
well put them to use. And no, before you ask –' and he held
up a warning finger – 'I don't write musicals.'

The riders came in all through the night, in ones and twos.
Rain was coming from the south-west and the wind was already
howling in the elm tops as darkness fell. Clopton's steward,
Boscastle, was kept busy finding accommodation for them all,
placing them carefully according to their rank, itself based on
appearance. But one man confused him. He was of middle

age and middle size and his knapsack was stuffed full of herbs that trailed the ground from saddle height. He wore old fustian and spoke with an accent Boscastle had never heard before.

'Reginald Scot,' the stranger announced, easing himself out of the saddle. 'I hear there's a masque toward.'

'There is, sir.' Boscastle wrote down the name in his ledger. 'Where did you hear of it, may I ask?'

'On the road,' Scot said, beaming. 'On the road. I've heard fine things of Warwickshire theatre. Coventry – the mystery plays.'

Boscastle narrowed his eyes. 'Before my time, sir,' he said.

'Really?' Scot frowned. 'Well, well,' he dismissed it. 'Where am I sleeping?'

'In the barn, I fear, sir, for tonight.'

'A barn will suit me well,' Scot told him, hauling his saddle-bags off the horse. 'Know what these are?' He all but pushed the tendrils up Boscastle's nostrils.

The Cloptons' retainer sniffed them. 'Hops.'

'Ah.' Scot looked a little crestfallen. 'You've heard of them, then?'

Boscastle felt he had to explain. 'We *do* drink here, sir.'

'Yes, yes,' Scot said, 'but they don't grow, surely, in these parts?'

'Not in Stratford, sir, no. They come from the south, I believe. Kent.'

'Precisely,' Scot said, beaming. 'My county. Have you read this?' and he tugged a leather-bound book from the knapsack as well.

Boscastle squinted in the torchlight to read it – '*A Perfect Platform of a Hoppe Garden*. Is that how you spell it?'

'In Kent we do,' Scot assured him. 'A small volume, but my own.'

'Very nice, sir.' Boscastle smiled and clicked his fingers. 'Find a bed for Master Scot,' he growled to the lackey.

'Near the door, please.' Scot scuttled away with the man. 'The hops need all the fresh air they can get.'

It was a bleary-eyed Boscastle who signed in the next two arrivals. They came together, each man leading his horse up the gentle rise to the outer gate. It was nearly dawn now and the golden glow of the morning was warming the stands of elder and coppiced hazel that fringed the park. Boscastle shook himself free of his sleep and waved to the dismounted horsemen.

'Not too late, are we?' one of them asked. 'For Lord Strange's masque?'

'Indeed no, sir,' Boscastle told them. 'This evening. Have you ridden far?'

'No, only from Winchcombe,' the other one told him. 'It's no more than a day's ride as a rule, but my damned horse threw a shoe.'

'May I have your names, gentlemen?'

'I am Richard Cawdray,' said the first. 'From London.'

Boscastle wrote the name and sat poised with his quill for the second.

'Look,' the man said. 'Is this all really necessary? I mean we've just come to see a show, man, not to answer God's judgement.'

'A matter of security, sir,' Boscastle said. 'These are dangerous times, sir; I'm sure you understand.'

The stranger clearly didn't. 'Haywood,' he snapped. 'Simon Haywood. From Oxford. Any chance of a bite to eat?'

Boscastle could see another rider trotting forward out of the dawn mist and dripping slightly as he passed under the archway. 'Viands for these gentlemen,' he ordered a servant, 'and some wine. Eat first, gentlemen –' he smiled at them – 'and then we'll find you a bed.'

'*Two* beds,' Haywood insisted, looking his companion up and down.

The last horseman of the morning dismounted carefully. He too had been on the road for most of the night and every muscle ached. Boscastle noted the Colleyweston cloak, the plumed hat and the rapier, longer by far than the law allowed. If truth were told, he didn't *look* like a playgoer.

'Welcome to Clopton Hall, sir. May I have your name, for the record.'

'Certainly.' The stranger pulled off his glove as if to write it himself.

'Just say your name.' Boscastle dipped the quill into the inkwell. 'I have my letters.'

'Good for you.' The man smiled thinly. 'York,' he said. 'Nicholas York. From London.'

How confusing, thought Boscastle, but both men at that time of the morning were too tired for witticisms. 'Would you like your bed, sir? Or breakfast?'

'A bed,' York opted. 'I need to be fresh for Lord Strange's show. Tell me –' he paused as the servant bobbed to lead him to his chamber – 'is one Christopher Marlowe with Lord Strange's Men?'

Boscastle looked suitably vague. 'I don't know their names, sir,' he said unhelpfully. 'Seen one actor, seen them all.'

NINE

The Greville arms hung in the stillness over Milcote that morning as the Lord of the Manor lay dozing against a mighty oak. He had seen Blake, the lawyer, half a mile across the deer park, puffing and wheezing as he plodded up the road. Even so, he wouldn't give the man the satisfaction and kept his eyes closed as the lawyer arrived, sweating in the July heat.

'You look hot, Master Lawyer,' he murmured, crossing one elegant outstretched foot over the other. 'You shouldn't rush about so. A man might die of overexertion at your age and in your condition. But please, sit awhile and catch your breath.'

The lawyer stood panting, but lacked the flexibility to lower himself to the ground. 'I am perfectly fit, sir,' he protested, in the teeth of the evidence, 'but it is a long way from the Hall.'

Greville smiled a slow smile, opened his eyes and levered himself upright on one elbow. 'Yes, isn't it? Now, what news from the Maiden?' He shielded his eyes against the sun to look up at the lawyer, standing a respectful distance from his outstretched legs. 'Do sit down, man. It hurts my eyes to look at the sun.' He patted the grass at an arm's length away. 'Sit. Sit.'

Blake could see nothing would progress until he was seated, so bent his knees until they would bend no more and then flopped in an ungainly heap on the grass. Getting up would be another problem, but let the future take care of itself. He rummaged in his satchel. 'Well, with this masque nonsense,' he said, wriggling himself into a marginally more comfortable position, 'you can imagine that Clopton Hall is awash with visitors at the moment.'

'Anyone specific?' Grenville asked.

Blake shuffled his papers. 'We have a party from Coventry,' he said. 'Guildsmen on their annual outing. Sir George and Lady Wentworth.'

'The Buckinghamshire Wentworths?'

'The Maiden didn't say.'

Grenville waved him to continue.

'Er . . . a few of the Papist persuasion, perhaps not surprisingly, sir. I have a list somewhere . . .' He riffled through his papers again. 'Here it is.' He found it and held it out.

'We'll get to them anon.' Greville nodded grimly. 'Anyone . . . suspicious? The Maiden has a nose for these things.'

'Well, there's a hop grower, she thinks from Kent.'

Grenville frowned. 'And?'

'One named York will bear watching,' Blake said. 'The Maiden saw he watched everybody and his hand never strayed far from his sword hilt.'

'Hmm.' Grenville nodded. 'What of the sworder who was with Strange?'

'Ah, well,' Blake said, warming to his theme. 'We're on surer ground there. One Christopher Marlowe, a scholar and playwright.'

'A scholar?' Grenville scoffed. 'Well, there you are, Blake. Some harmless scribbler. And you say he squared up to the lads! You're losing your touch, man.'

The lawyer shook his head. 'Scribbler, sir, no doubt,' he said. 'But harmless? I'm not so sure.'

'Well, well. What of the poppet?'

A dark smile spread over Blake's face. 'That's already in place, My Lord,' he said. 'Somewhere it is sure to be found.'

Rain had spread across leafy Warwickshire by mid afternoon, threatening to ruin the squibs that Ned Sledd had carefully placed near to the edge of the copse to add that touch of authenticity as Guy of Warwick – played with due self-deprecation by Sledd himself – strode the little O to destroy the Dun Cow, leaving young Martin as St George with the lesser task of killing a dragon. The second hautboy was having difficulty too as the perpetual drip from the canvas awning had warped his instrument.

By evening, though, as Boscastle and Sledd's minions let the groundlings from Stratford in, it was fine again and Clopton Hall stood black and magnificent against the crimson of the sunset.

All was bustle and excitement. It had been years since many of the townsfolk had passed under William Clopton's great arch. Some disliked the man's secret religion. Others disliked his politics. They were all prepared to put that to one side however in respect of his ale, which flowed freely once the admission price was paid.

Anybody who was anybody was in the Great Hall, glittering with torches and candles where Sir William and Lady Joyce received their guests. At the door each one was given a vizard, a black mask to be held in front of their faces except when there was serious drinking to do or the galliard called for a change of hands. Boscastle, in fine form and in his master's best livery, announced each guest in turn and the great and good of the county hobnobbed with each other as if there had been no Reformation, no enclosures and as if they all sang lustily from the same hymn book.

Kit Marlowe wandered among the guests, his poet and playwright's ears pricked for a handy line.

'Is that Lady Wentworth?' he heard one dowager say. 'She looks a hundred. And that gown – my dear!'

'Good God and all the Saints,' he heard another gasp. 'Old Trumbull's brought his daughter with him. What a freak.'

'Are we to have any fireworks?' a woman asked in a braying voice which set Marlowe's teeth on edge.

'We are, Madame,' Marlowe answered her and bowed to kiss her hand. The lady shivered and smiled coyly behind her mask.

'Are you an actor?' she asked. 'I do so love actors.'

'The whole world is a stage, Madame,' Marlowe said. 'We men and women are merely players.' He nodded and moved on, not noticing Will Shaxsper in the shadows, scribbling something down furiously with a quill, resting the parchment on the back of the third flautist. The rest of the orchestra were striking up and he'd be missed in a minute, so he broke away to take his place on the dais.

'No, no,' Sledd hissed to him. 'Move further away, man. This bit needs to be kept free. For the procession.'

The flautist obliged. Nicholas York was sampling a particularly fine claret and chatting to Richard Cawdray. They both

knew London and Cawdray had had business recently in the
Custom House Quay – did York know it? Yes, indeed. He'd
recently been assistant to Sir Walter Raleigh wearing his
Comptroller of Wines hat. And Sir Christopher Hatton had
been kind enough to commend him. Having dropped names
for England, the two men drifted apart and York found himself
peering over his mask at the Lady Joyce, one of the few
women present who was showing her face. Enjoying the view
and the wine he was entirely unprepared for what happened
next as he felt the sharp prick of the tip of a dagger in the
small of his back. Instinctively, he tried to turn, but felt a
further jab and the loss of weight as someone slipped his own
weapon from its sheath.

'Not wearing your sword tonight, Nicholas?'

York did not need to turn to recognize the voice in his ear.
'Kit Marlowe,' he said, under his breath. 'What a pleasant
surprise.'

'If only that were true,' Marlowe said. 'Are you here for
the culture . . . or something more obvious?'

'If you'll oblige me by taking that pig-sticker out of my
back, I'll explain.'

Marlowe slid his dagger home and reversing the man's own
in his other hand, returned it to him hilt first.

'And it's York, by the way,' York said, 'at least for the time
being.'

Marlowe smiled and tapped the man's elbow by way of
greeting. He knew Nicholas Faunt of old, whatever he was
calling himself today. And he knew the man would have his
reasons. 'Were you looking for me?' Marlowe asked, taking
a goblet from a tray held high by a passing servant, 'or do I
flatter myself?'

'Walsingham has need of you,' Faunt said.

Marlowe paused before he sipped, then shook his head.
'No,' he said. 'I wasn't cut out to be an intelligencer.'

'I agree.' Faunt lowered his mask to smile at a passing lady.
'You're a projectioner. Born to it. You're a mover and a shaker,
Master Marlowe. You make things happen, just like me. I can
tell it's in your blood as it is in mine. We share a vaulting
ambition and it's pointless to deny it.'

'The theatre is in my blood, Master . . . York. That's my
life now.'

'So I believe.' Faunt sipped his wine, laying the mask to
one side. 'You're with Strange's Men. Although it took me a
while to find that out.'

'Yes.' Marlowe nodded. 'I saw you days ago.'

'You did?' Faunt frowned. 'Where?'

'On the road. You were following our wagons.'

Faunt chuckled. 'My dear Kit, I only got here this morning,
by the most circuitous of routes. If it was me you saw, it must
have been in Dr Dee's magic glass, or in another life. But
what price this? A mummer's play performed in the back of
beyond? Hardly what I call stardom.'

'We must all start somewhere,' Marlowe told him. 'Anyway,
this particular back of beyond is a veritable hornets' nest.'

'Oh?' Faunt was all ears.

Marlowe laughed and wagged a finger at him. 'No, you
don't,' he said. 'Stay and watch the show – you'll like the
fireworks. Drink your fill and make the acquaintance of any
of these ladies – preferably one without a husband present;
but then –' and he closed to the man, so close he could smell
the wine on his breath – 'then, in the morning, Nicholas Faunt,
ride on. Go back to Walsingham and tell him, no.'

A fanfare shattered the moment and the windows shook
and rattled with a sudden burst of coloured stars in the courtyard below. There were oohs and aahs from the assembled
company and everyone surged forward to the windows to
watch the fireworks whizzing and spiralling across the Clopton
lawns.

Faunt turned to Marlowe, but he was gone. He could have
been behind any of the masks in the room, but most had been
set aside as their wearers watched the pyrotechnic show. Faunt
smiled to himself and wriggled through the crowd to get to
the front. It didn't matter how sophisticated a person might
become, he thought, and he was very sophisticated indeed,
there was nothing quite like a firework show to bring a bit of
a lift to the spirits. Soon, he was oohing and aahing with the
rest.

Towards the back of the room, Marlowe found William

Clopton, watching the crowd watching the fireworks and looking, if not exactly happy, then at least more content than seemed usual with him. He turned to Marlowe.

'They seem to be enjoying the show so far,' he said.

'Everyone loves fireworks, Sir William,' Marlowe said, 'and Ned is really doing you proud tonight. But the play's the thing.'

'I'm sure you're right, Master Marlowe,' Sir William agreed, 'but before the play, I have one last surprise for my guests. We'll wait until the sparks have finished flying and then my steward will announce it. Can you see Joyce?' He sounded suddenly rather on edge and craned now one way, now another, trying to pick her out in the press of people over by the window.

'I saw her a few moments ago,' Marlowe reassured him.

'Was it her, though? It's hard to tell with all these masks. I wasn't happy about them, but she did insist.'

'Well, an unmasked masque would have disappointed many of your guests,' Marlowe said. 'From what I have seen, many of them are taking advantage of the anonymity to be . . . shall we say, friendly with their neighbours?' He smiled at Sir William, who looked back at him with his usual air of depressed puzzlement.

'Friendly with neighbours with whom they are not wont to be so bold.' Marlowe would have to spell it out next time, he could tell. There are only so many ways you can tell a man that his neighbours and guests were planning to use his house as a cover for a night of debauchery and he had almost run out of the polite ones already.

'No, I'm sorry, I . . .' The man's parchment cheek flushed with an uneven purplish-red. 'Master Marlowe, do you mean what I think you mean to tell me?'

Marlowe wasn't sure, but nodded his head. It was the simplest way, if this conversation was to move on at all.

'I had no idea . . . these people are respectable townsfolk . . . what can they be thinking?'

Marlowe put an arm around the old man's shoulders. 'It's better you don't know, Sir William,' he said. 'They will be discreet, they will have to be. And who knows, behind the masks they may well end up coupling with their own husband or wife, and then no harm done.' He looked up at the window.

'Look, the fireworks are over. Have your steward bring on the next surprise.'

'I feel a little unwell, Master Marlowe.' Sir William Clopton certainly didn't look too healthy, with a deathly white pallor settling upon his purpled cheek. 'Please announce my steward to my guests. Have them gather round.'

Marlowe stepped forward a pace, glad to move away from what had become a very difficult situation. He clapped his hands and the buzz of conversation died away as all faces, most behind masks again, turned to him. 'My Lords, My Ladies, all of Sir William's guests, please step this way for a special surprise from the renowned kitchens of Clopton Hall. Please gather round but make way for Sir William's steward and his great surprise!'

There was a smattering of applause and the guests moved closer to the trestle table which had been set up down the middle of the room. With a stately step, Boscastle came through the big double doors, flanked by two maids. They all carried covered platters, which they placed carefully on the table in a place already cleared in readiness and then the maids stepped back. Boscastle, with the perfect timing of an old retainer, lifted the left-hand cover with a flourish and the people gasped in admiration. On the dish, set against the silver and gleaming like gold in the candlelight which filled the room, was a perfect rendition of the town of Stratford, made of glossy pulled sugar. The river which ran through the fairy tale town had a sprinkling of crumbled loaf sugar to show where it tumbled over the weir and the buildings were exact, down to a tiny weathercock on top of the church spire. Everyone craned forward to see and to exclaim at the amazing workmanship. Just outside the door, in the darkened corridor, the pastry cook wept happy tears.

Turning to his right, Boscastle whipped off the right-hand cover to reveal this time another view of the nearby country-side, this time of the woods and deer park around Clopton, but carved this time entirely out of loaf sugar, except for the tiny deer and promenading people, which were made out of glossy caramel. Those close enough to see could pick out details such as the ruffs around the tiny figures' necks, which were made of icing. The pastry cook was beside himself with delight at the applause and the cries of amazement. He hugged himself with anticipation. The central platter contained a model of Clopton Hall itself, made entirely of pulled and spun sugar. Its glossy walls were surrounded by the thinnest threads of spun toffee, pulled over and over on two wooden spoons and laid with care on the whole, so that the house looked as though it were surrounded by solidified sunshine. He held his breath, listening for the sounds from inside the room. He heard the rustle of Boscastle's best livery. He heard the chink as the cover touched the platter's edge as the man lifted it aloft. He heard . . . a scream. That can't be right! He rushed in through the doorway, heedless of protocol and pushed Boscastle aside. If the fool had spoiled his creation he would kill him where he stood.

The creation certainly was spoiled, but not by Boscastle, who stood as though frozen, the heavy cover of the silver platter quivering in his still upraised hand. In the middle of the spun sunshine and many chimneys of Clopton Hall, lay a grotesque doll. It lay on its back, with its limbs splayed out, as though dropped from the sky to plummet to its death on the sharp-tiled turrets of the house. Through its chest was a wicked thorn, curved and vicious, with what looked like blood staining the laced jerkin and square collar of the shirt. It had dark horsehair sewn roughly on to its overlarge head and on the forehead was a mole. In many ways it was a tribute to the model maker's art that everyone around the table knew that it was a poppet made to represent Ferdinando Stanley, Baron Strange, who even now stood at one end of the trestle table, staring at it in horror.

Marlowe was at the far end of the room from his new friend and he immediately started to make his way around the back of the pressing crowd to get to his side as soon as possible. Out of the tail of his eye he saw Faunt, on the other side of the trestle, do the same. They reached Strange almost together and elbowed people aside to stand one on either side of him. Strange flinched at the touch of Faunt's hand on his arm, backing away into Marlowe and grabbing at his wrist.

'Kit,' he said, through dry lips. 'Who is this? Did he make that thing?'

Faunt kept silent. He knew that Marlowe wouldn't lie.

'No, My Lord. This is . . . a friend, Nicholas York. He is here to help you.'

Strange looked Walsingham's right-hand man up and down and gripped Marlowe's wrist even tighter, leaning back to put all his weight on Marlowe's chest. 'He's lying to you, Kit. His name isn't York, it's . . . I can't remember. I have met him before. In London. At court. His name is . . . his name is . . .' He turned to look over his shoulder at Marlowe. 'He is called . . .' And without turning his head again, he slid down to the ground.

'Step back,' Faunt said, to those standing near him who were showing a lamentable tendency to gawp. 'Give him air.' He looked up at Marlowe. 'You know him better than I, Kit, although he is right, poor wretch, we have met now and again. Is he fainting through fear? Is he hysterical?'

Marlowe thought back to Strange's fall from his horse, his fear of the woman with no eyes and wondered whether this might be the reason for this faint now. But he thought not, on balance. 'No, I think he is poisoned. Smell his breath.'

Faunt leaned forward. He wrinkled his nose. 'Almonds?' he said, looking the poet in the eye. 'Can almonds poison a man?'

'No,' Marlowe said, 'but I remember when I was a boy, a woman in Canterbury murdered her husband by grinding up cherry stones into his porridge. He took ill and died weeks later. She nursed him devotedly, of course, with nourishing food, which was killing him by inches. She was discovered when the maid finished up his last bowlful and fell ill almost at once. She didn't die, but said that the porridge tasted of almonds, which of course weren't in the recipe. Were almonds served tonight?' He half rose from his crouching position near Strange's head. 'Is the cook here?'

'The pastry cook is here,' Boscastle said, giving the man a malicious little push in the small of the back. There was no love lost between these two at the best of times.

'Well,' Faunt said, unable to resist taking over the questioning. 'Did any almonds go into the food tonight?'

The man shook his head.

'Cherries?'

'The cherry season is over, My Lord,' the chef said, addressing his answers to Sir William Clopton, out of habit. 'We have some bottled, but we take out the stones and anyway, we didn't serve them tonight.'

Around the table, people stood aghast, holding their stomachs in readiness for the onset of poison, but none came. Then, the mutter began and soon swelled across the room. It was the poppet which had felled Lord Strange. No one knew how, but it had done its dreadful work. Here and there the voice of reason was raised, that the poppet had a thorn through its breast and Lord Strange was not stabbed. That it was stupid superstition. But the story grew and took hold and was growing in certainty even as Marlowe and Faunt lifted Ferdinando Strange to his feet and half walked, half dragged him from the room and up the stairs to his bedchamber.

Ned Sledd didn't like the way the evening was going. He particularly didn't like the expression on William Clopton's face. The old man was clearly terrified.

'The show must go on, though, surely,' he said.

Clopton stopped in his march from the solar. 'Are you mad?' he whispered. 'Finish it. Now. Give them their money back. I want everybody out of my house.'

Joyce was at his elbow, trying to pour oil on troubled waters. 'Father, people have travelled for miles . . .'

He spun to face her, eyes wild and staring. 'Ferdinando is lying in there –' he flung his arm behind him in general approximation of where the bedchamber was – 'and for all I know he'll be dead by morning. There will be no masque.' He glanced down and realized he was still wearing his costume of feathers and spangles over his doublet. He tore it away and carried on walking.

'At least,' Joyce called after him and he turned. 'At least . . .' She closed to the old man and leant her forehead against his shoulder and spoke softly so he had to bend to hear. It brought back the intimacies of her childhood and he became more disposed to listen. Joyce was a clever daughter. 'Let those who have come a long way stay tonight. Tomorrow is soon enough for them to go.'

Clopton hesitated, then turned his head and kissed his daughter's ear. 'Very well,' he said. 'First thing in the morning.'

In the same clusters as they had arrived at Clopton Hall, so they left, the ones that had come on foot being the first to leave. Most of the groundlings hadn't seen or even known for certain what had happened. And that made it worse. They handed in their vizards at the gate as Boscastle's people saw them all out.

'I've always said it,' one of them commented ruefully, 'the Devil is loose at Clopton.'

'I've never seen anything like it.'

'There's a curse on the Stanleys, that's well known.'

'What about the rest of us?'

'How do you mean?'

'Well, it was the food, obviously. My money's on the fish. Not natural. Here we are as far from the sea as you can get and they serve us codfish. Don't tell me they served it with that much nutmeg except to hide the taste. It was off, mark my words. Not natural.'

And so it went. The great and the good of the Stratford groundlings robbed of their St George, their Guy of Warwick and their Britannia. There had been rumours that Lady Godiva herself would ride bareback in every sense of the word through the Clopton courtyard, but as soon as they realized that she would be played by some boy, as like as not, most of them lost heart. Only one or two had still been interested.

In the solar, as the lights burned blue and the candle flames guttered in the wind rising from the west, Kit Marlowe sat with Will Shaxsper on either side of an empty grate. The household had officially retired for the night, in that Sir William had gone to bed leaving strict instructions that he should be woken in the event of any change in Lord Strange's condition.

Marlowe held the poppet in his hand, staring at it.

'Must you do that?' Shaxsper asked him.

Marlowe looked up. 'Afraid of dolls, Master Glover?'

Shaxsper shook his head. 'I've seen this before,' he said softly. 'No good will come of it. Put it down, Master Marlowe.'

'That's not a bad idea,' a voice boomed from the darkness and a man appeared, dressed for the road.

Marlowe was on his feet, hand on his dagger hilt, in one movement. Although he hid it better, he was as jumpy as the rest. 'Who are you?' he demanded.

'Forgive me for the interruption,' the traveller said. 'I just had to see that . . . thing . . . for myself. May I?' and he held out his hand.

Marlowe passed the rough doll to him and waited.

'I am Reginald Scot,' he said, 'and I have some knowledge of these things.'

Now Shaxsper was on his feet. 'Don't let him touch it, Kit,' he hissed. 'Get it back.'

'Kit?' Scot looked up at the taller, darker man and smiled. 'Would that be Kit with the Canstick?' he asked.

Shaxsper gasped. 'Tom Tumbler,' he said, and he crossed himself. 'Boneless . . .'

'And the Spoorne,' Scot went on, still smiling, 'the Mare, the Man in the Oak. Not forgetting the Puckle, the Firedrake, Hob Gobblin . . . oh, and Robin Goodfellow, of course.'

Shaxsper had turned quite pale. 'Who are you?' he whispered.

'I told you,' Scot said.

'No, no.' Shaxsper shook his head. '*What* are you?'

Scot threw the rag doll on to the table and crossed to the fireplace. He pointed to a ewer and said 'What does a man have to do to get a drink around here?'

Shaxsper seemed frozen, rooted to the spot but Marlowe did the honours. Scot wafted the wine under his nose.

'Checking for poison, Master Scot?' Marlowe asked.

'Ah,' Scot said, wagging a finger at him, 'the first sensible thing I've heard all night. Tell me, Kit with the Canstick, are you by any chance a university man?'

'I am.' Marlowe nodded. 'Cambridge.'

Scot beamed. 'Oh, bad luck. Oxford. Hart Hall.'

'Corpus Christi, and the name is Marlowe, not Canstick. Just for the record. Although some have called me a demon.'

Scot chuckled and sipped his wine. 'You're the playwright,' he said, 'with Lord Strange's Men.'

Marlowe nodded.

'And you, sir?' The hop grower looked at Shaxsper.

'I'm a playwright, too,' he said.

Marlowe smiled and poured more wine all round.

'Really?' Scot frowned. 'How unlikely. You have the air of a burgher, sir. And local, by your accent. Here without your wife and children, I imagine.'

Shaxsper was on his feet, his quick temper, already simmering, come suddenly to the boil. 'Have you been following me, sir?' he shouted in Scot's face. 'Someone is at my back, I feel it. Is it you?'

Scot stepped back a pace and put a calming hand on Shaxsper's chest. 'I follow no one who is not up to no good,' he said. 'I assumed the wife, Master . . . Glover, is it?' He cast a questioning glance at Marlowe.

'The name's Shaxsper,' the Stratford man shouted.

'Ah.' Scot looked knowing and stepped back another pace. 'You are travelling incognito. A wise move for a man running away from home.'

Shaxsper looked as though he would explode. 'I'm not running away from anything or anyone,' he bawled. 'I . . .' He suddenly seemed to run out of steam and collapsed back in his chair, all passion spent. 'I am a glover by trade. I have a wife and three children. I come from Stratford but . . .' He looked up at Scot with his slightly popping and divergent eyes. 'I need to at least try to be a playwright. I need to go to London, just to find out if I am any good.' He looked down at the floor despondently.

Scot clapped him on the back in a cheery fashion. 'And are you any good, Master Shaxsper?' He looked at Marlowe as he spoke, who shook his head just twice and made a rueful mouth.

Shaxsper shrugged.

'I am a little curious,' Marlowe said, to break the mood. 'How did you know about the three children?'

'I didn't know it was three,' Scot admitted. 'But there is a shiny line on Master Shaxsper's breeches about so high –' he gestured with a downturned palm – 'from the ground, the height of a two or three year old child's nose. I know when my own Elizabeth was small, I bore such a badge of honour. Then, on your shoulder, another well-cleaned patch, where a baby might posset its milk after a feed. I confess I never had such a mark, leaving such moments to the wet nurse and my wife, but times have changed since then, perhaps. You are one of the new breed of men, Master Shaxsper, perhaps, who care more for their children.'

'Twins,' muttered Shaxsper to the floor. 'A lot of work, twins.'

'Well.' Scot spread his hands and looked at Marlowe modestly. 'I was right, but perhaps only be accident.'

Marlowe looked impressed. 'I am very impressed, Master Scot,' he said. 'I am an observant man myself, but had not noticed the marks on Master Shaxsper's clothing, except to wonder why he looked so . . . so . . .'

'Even so,' Scot said, and with a deprecatory cough continued with the conversation as though Shaxsper's outburst had never happened. 'Do I detect a hint of Kent in your voice, Master Marlowe?'

'Canterbury.' Marlowe smiled. 'And call me Kit, Master Scot, do. But without the canstick, if you don't mind. And your accent needs no magic to identify it. Maidstone, at a guess.'

'Correct,' Scot said, reaching out for the doll again, seeming drawn to it.

'Look.' Shaxsper had put up with this old boys' act for as long as he could and the doll was making him feel very uneasy. 'Just what the Hell is going on here?'

'Ah, Hell,' Scot said. 'Very perceptive of you, Master Playwright. That's exactly what you're supposed to think.'

'Whereas you think attempted murder,' Marlowe said.

Scot did not answer. 'May I see Lord Strange?' he asked.

'No,' Marlowe told him. 'Sir William has put an armed guard on his door.'

'That'll do no good,' Shaxsper said. 'The Devil knows no locks.'

Marlowe rested his back against the fireplace. 'With charms

I drive both sea and cloud,' he said. 'I make it calm and blow aloud. The viper's jaws, the rocky stone, the force of earth congealed in one . . .'

Scot chimed in, '. . . I make the souls of men arise. I pull the moon out of the skies.'

Shaxsper was even more rattled now than he was before. 'What's that? Some spell?'

'No, Will.' Marlowe crossed to the man, his voice calm and kind. 'It's the Roman poet, Ovid. Fifteen hundred years ago he wrote of the power of witches.' He looked into the Stratford man's eyes. 'It's just a poem. It's the sort of thing they don't let university scholars read these days. I assume that's true of Oxford, Master Scot?'

'Sadly, yes. And that's Reginald, by the way. Now, look, er . . . Will, is it?'

The glover-playwright nodded. If this man had forgotten his surname, all to the better. He didn't like his knowledge, the way he scoffed at nature and at God.

'The doll,' Scot went on, 'is the likeness of Lord Strange, I assume.'

Shaxsper nodded, and pointed vaguely to his forehead, his throat and finally his chest. The wicked thorn was still embedded in the doll in what was meant to be the location of the heart.

'It's just a toy,' Scot said, 'a piece of mysticism and nonsense, designed to frighten little children.'

'As is Kit with the Canstick,' said Marlowe, 'and Boneless.'

'And all the others,' Scot continued. 'Fustian. The sort of stuff you playwrights deal in.'

'But . . . Robin Goodfellow, surely,' Shaxsper said. 'He's real.'

'Puck?' Scot raised an eyebrow. 'Spoiler of milk and scatterer of soot? He who can girdle the earth in forty minutes? Come on, Will. Where have you been living all your life?'

'Here,' Shaxsper shouted. 'Right here in Stratford. And I've seen what the Devil can do. I want no more of it. I've a family. You can keep your plays, Kit. And Master Scot, your explanations. Lord Strange was as fit as a flea before he saw that poppet. And now Death waits in his chamber.' He looked at them both, then snatched up his extra pair of gloves and his bundle of poetry tied with a bow and was gone.

Marlowe refilled Scot's goblet.

'Does he?' Scot asked. 'Does Death attend Lord Strange?'

'I'm no doctor,' Marlowe said. 'Sir William sent for one hours since, but the local medical men are like Master Shaxsper. They come to heal the body but fear only for our souls.'

'And you, Kit Marlowe.' Scot looked at him steadily. 'Do you not fear for yours?'

Marlowe smiled and answered, 'If there was a Devil, I'd be afraid of him. If there was a God . . .'

Scot's mouth opened but he said nothing and Marlowe turned away to look out of the window. In the silent courtyard below, the once-flaming torches were out now, wisps of smoke rising from them like ghosts in the near-dawn. Little, creeping winds blew the ribbons fluttering around Sledd's stage and all that was left of the orchestra were abandoned chairs at rakish angles in the grass.

'You've come a long way from Maidstone to watch a masque,' Marlowe commented after a while.

There was another pause and then Scot gave a low chuckle. 'I had heard that there were good fishermen in Canterbury,' he said. Marlowe turned from the window with a smile, and a cocked and questioning eyebrow. Scot could see that he was going to have to tell the man a few more facts. 'No, you've guessed aright. The masque would have been an hour's relaxation, nothing more. I'm a hop grower, seeking to introduce the plant into this leafy county.'

Marlowe leaned back on the sill, his back resting on the window transom and looked out again on to the dark court. 'And I'm the Pope's arse wiper,' he said to the night. He turned his head to Scot. 'Try again.'

Scot gave him a look of surprised innocence which fooled nobody. He hauled a leather-bound book from his knapsack. 'Here's proof,' he said. '*My Hoppe Platform*. Not bad, though I do say it myself.'

Marlowe looked at it and thumbed the pages. 'What about the other book you carry?' he asked.

'How did you . . .?' Scot didn't like to be surprised by any man, especially one from Canterbury and Cambridge. But he complied anyway and pulled out a much older volume, the leather scarred and worn. It was in Latin.

'*Malleus Maleficarum*,' Marlowe said, reading the title aloud. 'The hammer of the witches.'

'Do you know it?' Scot asked.

'I know *of* it,' Marlowe told him. 'Rather like Ovid, it's not exactly on the reading list at Corpus Christi.'

'It should be,' Scot told him. 'If only to remind us all of the vicious nonsense spouted by the Papist church.'

Marlowe frowned. 'I didn't have you down for a Puritan, Reginald.'

'Oh, I'm not. Until I see what wicked rubbish leads to in Christ's kingdom. The tortures. The murders. I've seen things in Germany, Kit . . .' His voice trailed away. He cleared his throat. 'I am in Warwickshire researching for the next edition of my latest book. *A Discovery of Witchcraft*, it's called. It came out last year, but it wasn't really ready, to my mind. The publishers have promised to put in my new material, when they print more.'

'It's a good title.' Marlowe nodded, although, good title or not, he doubted the next printing would ever happen. He had dealt with publishers himself and knew them for a tricky bunch. 'But why Warwickshire?'

'Place is riddled with it. Or rather, the fear of it.'

'You don't believe it, then?'

'Of course not.' Scot snorted. 'Will Shaxsper does.'

Marlowe chuckled. 'He has small children,' he said. 'Probably frightens them to sleep with tales of things that go bump in the night and got a bit carried away by his own imagination.'

'Oh, there are witches, all right.' Scot was warming to his theme. 'Poor, deluded souls who seek an explanation for the great cruelty of this world with the supernatural. None of it's real. And all of it's condoned by the church of Rome.'

'And the Church of Elizabeth, as I understand it. Chelmsford?'

'What do you know of Chelmsford?' Scot asked. 'You couldn't have been much more than a tot in your hanging sleeves.'

'It was still the talk of the Cambridge taverns when I was there.'

'Yes,' growled Scot, 'Mother Waterhouse and her talking cat. You couldn't make it up.'

Marlowe turned to face the man. 'The doll is real,' he said and snatched it up. 'In the likeness of Lord Strange. The velvet doublet, the square-cut collar, the mole on his forehead.'

'So?'

'What does Will Shaxsper believe?'

Scot sat on the settle and crossed his legs. 'He believes that the poppet *is* Lord Strange. That the doll was made by *malefica*, a black witch.' He looked at the image in Marlowe's hand. 'It is ripped across the belly. Is that where Lord Strange's trouble is?'

Marlowe nodded. 'He complained of pains there, yes, as we carried him to his bed.'

'Because he is a believer, too.' Scot shrugged. 'Such nonsense can only work if you believe in it. Ovid's Greek witches could pull down the moon. Ours can kill Lord Strange.'

'And in the real world?'

'Not my department,' Scot said, getting up and collecting both his books. He paused. 'But I've got a feeling it's yours.' He tucked the books away and extended a hand. 'It has been an education, Kit,' he said.

'Likewise, Reginald.' Marlowe shook it. 'Are you for the road?'

'Yes, I'm making for Meon Hill.'

'Meon Hill?'

Scot tapped the side of his nose. 'There are more witches under Meon Hill than trees in a forest, so I'm told.' He paused in the doorway. 'And you know, Kit, rather like Master Shaxsper, I believe everything I'm told.'

TEN

No one. Absolutely no one was to come to Lord Strange that night, and the two armed men on his door were there to see that Sir William Clopton's orders were carried out. If Marlowe had been Kit with the Canstick, he would have drifted like candle smoke through the keyhole. If he'd been Boneless, he'd have shifted his shape and slid under the door. As it was, he was Kit Marlowe and he dropped heavy coins into the men's purses while they studiously looked the other way.

Ferdinando Stanley lay like a corpse on the high tester bed, bedecked with the brocaded Clopton arms. He who travelled with no servants desperately needed one now. Ned Sledd and Nat Sawyer had stripped the man of his day clothes and wrapped him in a nightshirt tied to the neck. But no one, not even Ned and certainly not Nat had the nerve to spend the night in that pain-wracked room. After all, they were troupers and both of them had a stage to de-rig and musicians to pay off. Gate money had to be returned and the gunpowder carefully moved out of harm's way.

Joyce Clopton had offered to stay with the shivering, rambling lord, but her father wouldn't hear of it and she was shooed away. The casement had been locked, the door bolted on the outside and the guards placed. Marlowe checked the window, its sill sickly smelling with fennel. He checked the fireplace, black and empty. On the table alongside the bed lay a goblet of water, which he sniffed and tasted briefly on the tip of his tongue and a Bible, black and comforting in Latin and Greek.

The candle was burnt down to a stub and there was a winding sheet of wax pinning it to the table. The room was full of the small noises that a man makes even when he is unconscious, tiny clickings of tongue on palate, a sibilance of air in the nose. These noises were always present, but there was something about a death chamber which made them louder, echoing in the silence between each laboured breath. Picking up the candle, Marlowe dressed its wick to make it burn more brightly in its last minutes and peeled back the coverlet to see what a dying man could tell him, though he had no powers of speech.

Strange's breathing was laboured and his colour ghastly. His eyes were half open but he seemed to see nothing. He had clearly not moved since he had been put to bed and Marlowe felt the man's wrist to find a pulse. It was there, but barely and the playwright covered the man up again and sat in a corner, waiting for the dawn to bring the room to life with its dove-light.

The crowing of the cock made Lord Strange stir. He opened his eyes wide and Marlowe was sitting on the bed beside him, holding his outstretched hand and cradling the patient's head.

'Marlowe,' Strange mumbled, trying to make his tongue work. 'Marlowe, is that you?'

'It is, My Lord,' Marlowe said, standing up and releasing the man's hand. 'Welcome back.'

Strange frowned up at him and struggled into a sitting position. 'Oh, Kit,' he whispered, his voice rasping and harsh, 'I have spent such a night.' He gasped in memory of it. 'I saw her, Kit.' He clawed at the playwright's sleeve. 'The woman with no eyes. I saw her again. Here at the Hall.'

'When was this?' Marlowe asked.

Strange seemed nonplussed by the question. 'I can't remember,' he said. 'Was it . . . before . . . or . . . was it a dream?' Suddenly, he sat bolt upright, his arms rigid in front of him, his fists tightly balling up the coverlet, his knuckles white. 'The poppet,' he hissed, through clenched teeth. 'The poppet with my face.'

'A doll, My Lord,' Marlowe said softly, patting the man's hand. 'A child's toy, nothing more.'

Strange looked at him. 'It was a Devil's doll,' he said as though the weight of the world lay on him. 'Put there by a witch. And a thorn was through my heart. Help me up, Kit. I must go home, while I still can.'

'Sir –' Marlowe studied the struggling lord – 'You are not well enough . . .'

'Help me or not, as you will,' Strange barked and coughed with the effort of raising his voice. 'But with or without you, I'm going home. If I'm to die, I'll do it in my own bed.'

The camp that had been building over the last few days broke up the next morning. The canvas and the ropes came down and the braziers were stashed away.

'Well, that's it,' Sledd said, hands on hips. 'The party's well and truly over. Oxford it is.'

'What about His Lordship?' Thomas asked. He wasn't sure Sledd was still talking him to him now that his balls had dropped and he was staring Other Employment in the face.

There was a commotion at the west door and Lord Strange was helped down the steps by Marlowe.

'Here he comes,' said Sledd, 'but I don't like the look of him.'

'And he's our meal ticket,' Thomas muttered. 'Lose him and we lose all that sponsorship.'

'Heart as big as the great outdoors, Thomas, that's you. Anyway, I'm not talking to you, as I'm sure you recall. I've got to find another female lead now because of you answering the call of nature. And it's precisely because of our imminent loss of sponsorship as you put it that we'll have to hit Oxford. Got to make some money somewhere until we can find a new lord as stage-struck as this one. Know anything about the Earl of Northumberland?'

Thomas just shrugged.

'Well, there's a surprise,' Sledd muttered. 'When we reach Oxford, you're on the thunder box. Although why I should give you a second chance, I don't know. My Lord!' And he trotted off to where Strange was being helped into a carriage. William Clopton was fussing around, as was Joyce, but, in the event, it was Marlowe who took charge.

'My Lord, I believe you met this gentleman briefly last night,' he said quietly as Nicholas Faunt bounded into the carriage.

Strange recoiled. 'Liar!' he shouted, disoriented. He plucked at his cloak, trying to hide his face.

'A mere subterfuge, My Lord,' Faunt calmed the man. 'You

are right; we have met before, in London. I work for Sir Francis Walsingham.'

Strange frowned and blinked. 'Walsingham?' he repeated.

Faunt nodded. Strange, bewildered and half delirious though he was, assessed the situation. Faunt was armed to the teeth, with a rapier, dagger and the butt of a wheel lock under his cloak. If he worked for Walsingham, he worked for the Queen and that was good enough for Strange. He was finding focusing difficult, but by closing one eye and looking across the bridge of his nose, he could see the man clearly enough and he did seem familiar.

'Master York will accompany you, My Lord,' Marlowe said loudly, stepping down from the carriage. 'Driver,' he called up to the man, 'Her Majesty's palace of Nonsuch and don't spare the horses.'

'Wait,' Strange gasped, sticking his deathly pale face out of the window.

Faunt had gripped his sleeve and brought his mouth close to the sick man's ear. 'Another subterfuge, My Lord,' he breathed. 'We are going north to your estates. The driver knows that. Whatever actually happened last night, we must accept that someone here means you harm. The less they know about your *actual* destination, the better.'

Strange turned panic-stricken eyes to him, but didn't move his head. Faunt's hot breath was still cooling in Strange's ear when he heard another voice calling his name. The voices were bothering him this morning and it was all a bit too much. He wrapped himself closer in his cloak and closed his eyes.

'My Lord Strange!' Sledd was still trying to barge his way through the Cloptons and Marlowe.

'Not now, Ned.' Marlowe turned to face him. 'His Lordship is not well.'

'The Devil,' Sledd grunted.

'Yes.' Marlowe nodded. 'Very likely.'

And the carriage rolled back a little before the driver hauled on his reins and whipped his horses on.

'That this should happen in my house.' William Clopton shook his head as he watched the coach rattle under the archway and out of sight.

'Master Marlowe.' Joyce left the old man at the door and crossed to the playwright. 'They tell me you spent the night in Lord Strange's room.'

He closed down his face and looked at her, giving away nothing.

She smiled and led him away, out of her father's earshot. 'Don't worry,' she said. 'A guard that can be bought by a poet's purse can also be bought by the lady of the house. That was brave.'

'No more, My Lady, than you intended to do, or so I hear.'

She paused in her walk, then burst out laughing. 'I'm afraid we are both guilty of over-bribery,' she said. 'I shall have to dock Ogden's wages; the man is earning far too much.' Then, her smile faded and she looked anxiously over Marlowe's shoulder to where her father still stood, watching through the archway as if he could still keep an eye on the departing coach, long out of sight. 'What did you discover?'

'About the black arts?' Marlowe asked her.

She shrugged. 'About any arts,' she said.

He looked around him. Cawdray and Haywood were standing by their saddled horses, talking to Sledd. Lord Strange's Men – and women – were hauling canvases and timbers on to wagons to be ready for the road. 'Before I went to Strange's chamber,' he told her, 'I went to the Great Hall.'

'What for?' she asked.

'To see if I could find Lord Strange's cup.'

Her eyes narrowed. 'You suspect poison,' she said, nodding.

'Let's just say I believe it more likely than the power of an evil charm.'

'The pastry cook is prostrated. His model in sugar had taken him days to make and to have it reduced to the pillow for a poppet has quite unhinged him for the moment.'

'An extreme reaction,' Marlowe remarked. 'Perhaps we should look closer at the pastry cook.'

'He is a sensitive soul,' she said, dismissing the cook's temperament with the wave of a hand. 'I have seen him take to his bed if his Easter buns don't rise properly. He is no poisoner. Did you find the cup?'

'One among so many? No. It was always an outside chance

and, anyway, Boscastle is an excellent steward and had already issued his orders. Every cup, every plate, every knife was washed and dried and put away.'

'Who do you think was responsible?' she asked, with hardly a tremor in her voice.

Marlowe smiled at her and shook his head. 'Half Warwickshire was here last night, My Lady,' he said. 'And men like Lord Strange have many enemies.'

'My father is heartbroken,' she said. 'To think that a guest in this house . . . well, what with his other troubles, the shame of this could kill him. I must go and try to get him to take a little breakfast, Master Marlowe. If you will excuse me?' and she dipped her head in farewell and walked back to the old man. As she took his arm, he hardly acknowledged her and allowed himself to be led away. As Marlowe watched them he was aware that more than one man had been led to the gates of death the previous night. He bowed to her retreating back.

'Kit,' Sledd called as the playwright crossed the courtyard to where the other men were standing. 'Master Cawdray here feels we have cheated him.'

'Oh?' Marlowe raised an eyebrow.

'I don't believe in hocus pocus, sir,' Cawdray said. 'I came to see a play. I hope His Lordship will mend.'

'We all do,' Sledd echoed. He, above all others present, had hopes that His Lordship would mend; the Late Lord Strange's Men was a bit of a mouthful for the handbills. 'I've told Master Cawdray, Kit, that we're on our way to Meon Hill to get some rehearsals in. And I've promised him the best seat in the house on our opening night in Oxford.'

'Gratis,' Cawdray remarked, with a smile.

Sledd sketched a bow. 'Of course,' he agreed. 'Gratis.' The word was wrenched out through his gritted teeth.

'I hope we won't disappoint you, sir,' Marlowe cut in quickly, so that Sledd didn't end up papering the entire house with Cawdray's friends and relations.

'I'm sure you won't,' Cawdray said, tucking his toe into his stirrup. 'Any company with the great Ned Alleyn in it can never disappoint.'

Marlowe drew breath to answer, but Sledd's heel pressed down on his toe stopped him in his tracks. He settled for a muttered agreement, though it was hard to bear. 'The great Ned Alleyn,' he said; he was a play short because of that man.

'Too kind,' Sledd gushed. 'Too kind.'

They rode south-west as the sun climbed in the heavens, taking the old drovers' road through the Cotswolds, the low hills pale and shimmering in the July heat.

'It's good of you to put me up, Simon,' Richard Cawdray said as his roan calmly negotiated the iron-dry ruts of the road.

'My pleasure, dear boy,' Hayward said. 'At the agreed price, of course.'

Cawdray smiled. 'Of course.'

'I never knew a man so keen to see a play.' Hayward squinted sideways at him, knowing full well that his agreed price for the stay at Winchcombe was little short of usurious.

'I love it,' Cawdray said. 'I never miss a performance at the Rose or the Curtain when I'm in London.'

'Do you go there often?' Hayward asked him.

'Not any more.' Cawdray's smile had faded. 'Not since . . .' His voice tailed away.

'I don't mean to pry.' Hayward shrugged, looking around to find another topic of conversation.

'No, no,' Cawdray said. 'It's all right. My wife loved the theatre, too. She saw in it a kind of magic. The lights, the music, the actors . . . She could lose herself in it, she said, in all that. Now she's dead.'

Hayward jolted a little in the saddle. 'I'm sorry,' he said. There seemed little more to say. The tale was clearly a sad one; Cawdray was no age. Middle thirties, perhaps, hardly more. 'Sweating sickness?' he ventured. 'Ague?'

'No.' Cawdray was staring straight ahead. 'She took her own life.'

They rode on for a while. Hayward hated a silence as he hated the Devil. 'Children?'

'Only the one who died in her womb,' the widower replied, shutting his mouth like the gate of a tomb.

'That's the road to Long Compton.' Hayward seized on the

geographical feature like a drowning man on a straw. 'It leads
to the Rollrights and to Meon Hill. That's where Strange's
Men are going, isn't it?'

Cawdray nodded. 'I believe so.'

'That's what I don't understand about these damned actors,'
Hayward said. 'You'd think they'd want to put up at an inn
or something, say at Moreton or Chipping Norton. What the
attraction is in camping in some bloody field, I don't know.'

Cawdray smiled. 'I asked about that,' he said. 'According
to them, it's all to do with the Muse, apparently, being at one
with God's nature.'

'And nothing to do with saving money, of course,' Hayward
said.

And both men laughed as they rode on to Winchcombe.

'God's nature, my arse!' Ned Sledd slapped his boot top with
his riding whip. 'Come on, lads. How hard can it be?'

'Talking of arse,' Nat Sawyer grunted as he took the strain,
'if you got off yours and helped us lift, it'd be a whole lot
easier.'

'I have . . . people,' Sledd told him. 'We actor-managers do
the thinking. You lot do the wheel changes.'

'Well –' Martin wheezed with the exertion – 'Kit's got his
shoulder to it, and he's a genius.'

'Dear boy,' said Marlowe, in unconscious imitation of
Edward Alleyn and although Martin was easily ten years older,
'how nice of you to notice.'

The cart had died a little south of Ettington and it was
only Thomas's quick thinking that had saved two chests of
costumes crashing into the ditch that drained the road. Now
everybody, except old Joseph, who couldn't, and not-so-old
Sledd, who wouldn't, were raising the wagon while the
women tried to fit the spokes, strapped and nailed, back into
position.

'All right,' said Sledd, to whom every minute lost on the
road was a loss of money, 'we may as well have our dinners
here. Liza, bread and cheese, if you please. Perhaps we can
catch the odd coney by tonight. Hello, who's this?'

A solitary horseman was trotting along the road, wheeling

around the parked wagons and reining in alongside the collapsed cart.

'Master Shaxsper,' Sledd hailed him. 'I thought we'd seen the last of you.'

'Yes.' Shaxsper swung out of the saddle. 'So did I. Look . . .' He closed to Sledd and Marlowe. 'I was a little hasty back at Clopton. It's a fault of mine, I'm afraid, shortness of temper. Well, call me old fashioned if you like . . .' He paused, but nobody did.

Sledd, however, clapped a friendly hand on his shoulder. 'Master Shaxsper, we're none of us sure exactly what happened back there . . . with Lord Strange, I mean. But we are his Men –' he stood up proudly, striking a pose in a theatrical tradition – 'and we owe it to him to carry on.'

'Where are you going?' Shaxsper asked.

'Meon Hill,' Sledd told him. 'To rehearse. And then, on to Oxford.'

'Meon Hill?' Marlowe could have sworn that Shaxsper's naturally waxy complexion had gone several shades paler still. 'The Rollright Stones?'

'Yes,' said Sledd. 'Do you know the place?'

Shaxsper nodded. 'I'll be frank, Master Sledd,' he said. 'I had a row with my Anne earlier. Oh, it's not the first time and it won't be the last. I've made up my mind to join Lord Strange's Men if you'll have me. But the Rollrights . . .'

'As I understand it,' Sledd said, 'they are simply a circle built by ancient peoples, long ago. A natural amphitheatre, I've been told.'

'No.' Shaxsper was grimly serious. 'No, nothing like that.'

There was a silence, punctuated suddenly by a crack as the repaired wheel broke again and a burst of blasphemy from Thomas and Nat in the finest tradition of choral speech.

'Do you intend to follow us back to London, Master Shaxsper?' Sledd asked him.

'Indeed,' the glover said, looking at Marlowe. 'And to write for the stage.'

'Well,' Sledd said with a smile. 'A word of advice, then. Shaxsper. Shaxsper. It's a little . . . odd, isn't it? Rather . . . brutish and short. As though there's a syllable missing and, not to beat about the bush, a bit foreign sounding. If you're going to make a name for yourself, I'd better start by making one for you. How about . . .' He looked around for inspiration and his glance fell on one of the wagons where the women were setting about making dinner. He tried a few words silently, just to see how they sounded in his head, then said, 'Bacon? No? Hmmm . . . Ham, then?' This was met by a snort of derision from most of the troupe and Sledd climbed on to his high horse and jingled the bridle pettishly. 'All right, then, if you are going to deride my best efforts, let it be Shaxsper and see how it goes down in London.'

Liza looked up from sawing bread against her bosom with a fearsome looking knife. 'What about Shakespeare, Ned? That doesn't sound quite so . . .' One of the other women nudged her and giggled. Liza nudged her back and carried on, 'Well, Master Shaxsper, we think Shakespeare doesn't sound quite so *rude*.'

Shaxsper, who had never seen the comic possibilities in his name, although Nat Sawyer had compiled four obscene couplets based on it within their first five minutes of acquaintance, stood silently, thinking.

'Shakespeare!' Sledd declaimed. 'It has a ring to it, all right, don't you think?'

'Shakespeare,' Shaxsper repeated, then smiled at the company at large. 'Yes, yes I like it.'

'Done, then,' Marlowe said. 'Now, Master Shakespeare, how are you at changing wheels?'

Sir William Clopton sat in his favourite chair by the fire in the solar, soaking up what remained of the heat of the day from the ancient stone. Joyce sat opposite him, trying to look calm but giving the game away with her hands, tightly interlaced, one finger over another and her brow, which was furrowed and taut. She had had Boscastle send someone to light the fire; although she was warm enough, even overwarm on this summer's evening, her father's hands were cold and trembling. His eyes were closed in his waxen face and his lips moved silently, saying his rosary without the benefit of beads. Every now and again, he twitched and shook and moved his head slightly from side to side, but never stopped his unending wheel of prayer. Eventually, she could bear it no longer.

'Father?' she said, gently. 'Father, wake up. We must talk.'

He opened one eye and looked at her and she was taken back to games of hide and seek in the park of Clopton, all those years ago when she was just a tiny girl and Sir William was still hale and hearty. She almost expected him to jump up and shout: 'Boo!' But it was not a hale or hearty Sir William who spoke.

'Why?'

'Why talk? Surely, we must talk over what happened to Lord Strange. What is happening to us, here, with Edward Greville on the prowl.'

Her father shut his eyes again. 'I meant, why wake up? I want to sleep until I die.'

Joyce felt her heart shrink into an icy ball and she was on her feet and at his side before he knew she was moving. She fell at his feet and buried her head in his lap. 'Don't,' she muttered. 'Don't speak of leaving me, Father. I will be all alone.' She felt his hand rest on the top of her head, but it did not caress her, it just lay there like a dead thing.

'You will marry,' he said, dully. 'You will soon forget your old father and the mess he left behind.' The words came slowly, and were only clear to her, who had lived with him every day of her life.

She left her head in his lap, and gently stroked his knee. 'Father,' she whispered, 'Father.'

She lay in his lap, with the fire crackling behind her for who knew how long, before a cramp in her leg made her stir. His hand slipped off her head and slapped down on his lap, palm up, fingers uncurled and didn't move. She drew back so the light of the fire fell on his face. The man she knew had gone, transformed into a blank mask, as blank as the vizard he had worn only the night before. Only his eyes betrayed that there was a living man inside the shell.

Joyce was her father's daughter, through and through and she did not shout, panic or scream, although every nerve told her to do all three. She knelt at her father's feet for a few minutes more, stroking his lifeless hand. Then, she walked to

the door of the solar and stepped out on to the landing.
Pulling the door half shut behind her, she called for her father's
steward. Boscastle would know what to do.

They looked like an army. They sounded like an army. To the
people of Clopton Hall, they *were* an army. The flag of the
Grevilles lifted and floated wide on the breeze and the solitary
drum kept time.

Boscastle turned away from the sight to the terrified faces
clustered round him. 'Fetch Lady Joyce,' he growled to one
of his people and the lad was pleased to be gone. Heart
thumping, he dashed across the peacock lawns and up the
curve of the stairs, his pattens clashing on the stones. But he
didn't reach his master's door, because Lady Joyce was already
on the landing.

'I know,' she said curtly, to his ramblings. 'It's all right,
John. I've seen them.'

She glanced through the casement on the turn of the stairs,
as she hurried to join her household. From there, she could
see her people, the Clopton people in knots of two and three,
instinctively drawing together around Boscastle. On the slopes
that rose to the dark woods beyond, where the elders gave
way and the oaks began, Greville's men were advancing on
Clopton. This, she imagined, was how it must have been in
her great-grandfather's day when the families of York and
Lancaster clashed in deadly sway across English fields and
good men went down before the relentless ranks of roses, red
and white. Yet this was now, today, the year of her Lord 1585.
Could it be, as the Jesuit priests had told her, that good Queen
Bess was just the Jezebel of England after all?

She crossed herself at the foot of the stairs and her heart
jumped as she saw John lift a halberd from the rack in the
hall. 'No, John,' she said. 'It's not going to come to that.' She
straightened to her full height and smoothed down her bodice.
'I expect Sir Edward has heard of my father's indisposition,'
she said, 'and has come to pay his respects. Put it back, John,
there's a good lad.' And, hesitatingly, the boy obeyed.

Boscastle hadn't gone armed in years. But today, at least
for the last hour, he wore his old sword, the one his dad had

used to good effect against the Scots at Solway Moss. He'd already counted his menfolk. Eleven of them young enough and fit enough to hold their own. After that, the Clopton servants were women and children. And even the eleven had never actually *fought* before. They'd all had scraps, no doubt, in hayricks and farmyards the length of the county, when fists and clogs came into play. But this would be different. Straining his eyes against the glare of the noonday sun, Boscastle had counted more than thirty men, in jacks or brigandines. One or two of them wore helmets. At their head, Edward Greville was in full field armour, an expensive piece he'd had imported from Milan.

'My Lady.' Boscastle nodded to Joyce as she swept into position alongside him. He had served the Cloptons all his life, as had his father before him, since just after the Solway fight, in fact. He was only a young man when the girl was born and he remembered the parties and the hunts and the music. It was Boscastle, not old Sir William, who had taught the girl to ride.

She glanced down at the broadsword hilt bobbing at his hip. 'There'll be none of that,' she said, secretly longing for the altogether more promising dagger of Kit Marlowe. 'Not today.'

Edward Greville clashed under the Clopton arch in a storm of echoing hoofbeats and halted his bay, standing in the stirrups to view the ground. At a nod of his head, his armed horsemen broke into two, half to his left, half to his right and formed a semicircle of death around the Clopton servants. A little girl began to cry until her mother hushed her, burying the child's tear-streaked face in her skirts.

'Sir Edward,' Joyce Clopton called out in a clear, strong voice, 'you are frightening the children.'

Greville unhooked his helmet and lifted it off, passing it to a lackey on his left. He steadied the horse as though to dismount.

'No,' she said, 'no need to get down. You won't be staying that long, surely.'

He paused as his foot left the stirrup but no mere woman was going to deflect him from his purpose, by God, and with

an arrogant jump he reached the ground. Another lackey ran
to hold the animal's bridle and Greville closed to Joyce. 'I
have heard your father is unwell, My Lady,' he said softly.
'May I see him?'

'No, Sir Edward, you may not. Not if you were the last
man alive.'

His scowl turned to a smile. 'This is simply a courtesy call,'
he said. 'One local landowner to another.'

She tapped smartly on the damascened breastplate with her
knuckles. 'Do you always go so heavily armed to pay your
courtesy calls?' she asked. 'Or is it true what they say?'

The scowl had returned. 'What do they say?' he asked and
immediately wished he hadn't.

'That Sir Edward Greville is so feared for his life that he
sleeps surrounded by crumpled paper in his chamber in case
someone should sneak in on him. That he goes to the jakes
armed cap-a-pie.'

She saw the muscles twitch in Greville's jaw and knew the
risk she was taking. So did Boscastle and he instinctively
moved towards her, making sure his sword arm was free.
Greville snapped his fingers and a portly man wearing the
livery of Lincoln's Inn was grateful to climb down from the
saddle. Never a natural horseman, Henry Blake was far happier
on his own two feet.

'I had hoped to deal with Sir William in person,' Greville
said as Blake held his satchel in front of him, ready for business. 'But as that seems impossible . . .' He gestured towards
the front door. 'Shall we, Lady Joyce?'

'Whatever business we have to discuss,' she said, 'can be
conducted here, in the open. In the honest light of day.'

'Very well,' Greville conceded. 'Blake. You know my
factotum?' he checked with Joyce by way of introduction.

'I know your creature,' she said, looking down her nose at
the reptilian lawyer, busily ransacking his satchel for the necessary papers.

'By an escheat dated 1544 and another for 1469,' Blake
began, reading from the Latin, 'Clopton Hall and all the movables thereof are forfeit to the lord of the manor of Stratford,
viz and to wit, Sir Edward Greville . . .'

'Show me that!' Joyce snapped. Blake passed the parchment scroll across, vaguely astonished that the woman could read Latin at all. She read while Boscastle steadied the scroll.

'This is nonsense,' Joyce said, 'legal hocus pocus. In what sense can one landowner demand the property of another without a mutual agreement, either by cash or marriage?'

'Marriage,' Greville said with a smile, closing to the woman. 'The idea had crossed my mind and since you force me to conduct such delicate business here in my . . . in your father's courtyard, I must, I'm afraid, dispense with the usual formalities. I had come, Lady Joyce, to ask your father for his daughter's hand in marriage. But as things stand . . .' He smiled at the astonished look on her face and bent his head towards hers, his nose pointing to the jut of her breasts. 'We are people of the world, Joyce, you and I, not country clods. We don't have need of banns and courtship and ceremony. And time is pressing –' he glanced down – 'as my codpiece is reminding me.'

There was a ripple of coarse laughter from his men behind him and no one was quite ready for what happened next. Joyce brought her left hand back with force and slapped Edward Greville around the face. He staggered backwards and three or four swords shot clear among his horsemen. Boscastle's blade gleamed in his hand too. Steadying himself, Greville held up his hand to calm the moment. He tasted his own blood on his lip and snarled at Joyce. 'Very well,' he said. 'Master Blake here assures me that I have the right to take Clopton Manor, if, as now seems likely, it does not come to me by any formal arrangement, on one condition only.'

'And that is?' Joyce was too furious to realize the risk she was taking and her voice was still strong, her head high.

Greville wiped his lip with the back of his hand and saw the blood smear the laces at his wrist. 'And that is that all recusants' lands are forfeit to the Crown.' He flung his arm behind him towards Stratford. 'The Clopton pew in Trinity Church has been empty this many a long year, lady,' he said, 'because your father – and, no doubt, you – are of the Papist faith.'

The rumbling that had been growing among the Clopton people ever since Greville arrived now broke out into shouts and curses, men and women screaming at the intruder. But Joyce held up her hand for quiet and they obeyed.

'As Lord of the Manor of Stratford,' Greville went on in the new silence, 'I claim Clopton in the name of her glorious Majesty, Elizabeth.' And he crossed as near to Joyce Clopton as he dared. 'And all the movables thereof.'

ELEVEN

Meon Hill lay stark under the summer sun. The fields of the Midland Shires shimmered in the heat of the noonday. And the farmers, long waiting for this for their harvests, whetted their scythes and smiled to each other. The circle of the seasons was complete, once again. Time, come Sunday, to give thanks to the Lord.

Etty Barham sat on an old tree stump staring out across the rolling hills. She had done this ever since she was a girl and had talked to herself under the moon. Her father, when she was little, had taken off his belt and strapped her – she had the weals across her back to this day. But then, on a day like this when the birds sang in the meadow stillness, she had looked at him, whispering under her breath the words she knew but could not remember learning – '*Eheich, iod, tetragamaton elohim, el elohi gabor. Tzabaoth, Tzabaoth. Eheich.*'

Her father had stopped in his tracks, his blood frozen, his mind gone. He had fallen, writhing to the ground, chewing the dust as he clawed to bring back his fleeing soul. But it was all too late for him and by cock-shut time he lay in his burial shroud. No one ever took their belt off to Etty Barham again.

She sighed and went on stroking the warm plumage of the plover in her lap. That was all so long ago and she could barely remember it now. She who lived by herself, who knew the winding roads and the lonely call of the wind. What was it they called her in the village? A hedge witch? No, she was more cunning than that. Her children scampered around her, the rats that scuttled in her thatch, the toad that sat bloated and sullen, slowly blinking its golden eyes, by her hearth; the earthworms she nibbled through the night. She was never lonely.

They came to her for charms, for spells. At night, when their neighbours couldn't see them – the men whose wives wandered to other men; the lame who couldn't walk; the blind who couldn't see. Those who had lost their way; those who wanted blood; those who believed in an eye for an eye. They all came to her and she gave them what they wanted.

But now was a different time. The summer of the weather, the summer of storms. It was nearly Lugnasadh and she had miles to go. All must be ready, all carefully prepared. She stroked the half-tame bird one last time and then snapped its neck.

Henry Blake sat in Sir William Clopton's chair in Sir William Clopton's Great Hall and smiled to himself. Standing in front of him were the entire staff, all of Clopton's people. Blake sensed the air in the Hall, the mood of pure hatred; but then, he was a lawyer of Lincoln's Inn and he was used to that. He noted that none of the men had taken off their caps and all of them, even the children, scowled at him as if the Devil himself was in their chamber.

One by one, Blake's clerk read out the names and one by one they sullenly answered. There was no 'sir', no deference. But then, Blake couldn't expect any. What had Greville called him – his factotum; his jack of all trades. And the Lady Joyce had translated that as 'creature'. Marvellous!

'Sarah Williams,' Blake said, repeating the name the clerk had just read out. No one stirred. 'Is Sarah Williams here?' he asked.

'She is not on the staff,' Boscastle told him, from the far end of the room, 'and she is known as Merriweather.'

'Not on the staff,' Blake repeated, 'yet her name is on the list.'

'Of those to be fed and cared for,' Boscastle explained. 'No more.'

'How touching.' Blake smirked mirthlessly.

'Dorothy Gilligan,' read the clerk, his quill poised.
Silence.

'Dorothy Gilligan,' he said again.
Again, nothing.

'Not another defaulter?' Blake said loudly. 'Is she another grace and favour, Boscastle?'

'No,' the steward told him. 'She is a maid of the kitchen. And should be here.' He was looking round at his people, but none met his eye.

'You are in my father's chair, creature!' A voice shattered the moment and all eyes turned to the stairs. Joyce Clopton stood there, imperious in her gown with ermine trim. In three strides she was at Blake's elbow. 'Stand up, you toad, when a lady enters the room.'

Henry Blake wouldn't have known a lady if one fell on him, and it had been many a long year since that had happened. He was shamed in front of Greville's men and those of Clopton Hall and he rose to his feet with an awkward smile on his face. 'Some of these people seem to be missing,' he said, tucking his thumbs into his belt.

Joyce looked at her father's staff, Boscastle at their head like an ox in the furrow. 'What is that to you?' she asked.

As if to a child, Blake explained. 'By law, Sir Edward Greville has taken possession of this estate and the movables thereof . . .'

'Movables?' Joyce spun to face him. 'Movables, you clod?' She snatched up a goblet on a side table with the Clopton arms stamped on it. '*This* is a movable,' she said and threw it at him, gashing his forehead as he was far too surprised to get round to ducking in time. '*These*—' she shrieked, and then, calming herself, went to stand in front of them. 'These are my people.'

Blake batted aside the fussy attentions of the clerk. 'No longer,' he called out to her. Then he half turned to the man trying to staunch the blood from his temple. 'Where is Dorothy?' he hissed. 'Where is the Maiden?'

The clerk frowned. He had no idea what Blake was talking about. He put it down to the blow on the head.

'Well.' Blake cleared his throat and resumed his seat. 'To proceed.' The clerk took up his quill again.

'Boscastle,' Joyce whispered in the man's ear. 'Where are Dorothy and Merriweather?'

And all the steward of the Cloptons could do was shrug.

The wagons arrived at the Rollright Stones after much patching and swearing just as the day was beginning to cool. The sweat from their labours was sticky on everyone's brow and the little breeze that sprang up as they turned from the main road on to the track to the stones was like a blessing and everyone turned their face to it, brushing their hair back to feel the benefit.

'My word, that feels nice,' Sledd said to Thomas, as he pulled on the reins of his horses. He slewed round in his seat and looked at the boy. He didn't look any different from the old Thomas, perhaps a slight whiskering of the upper lip, but that was probably there all along. Sledd knew you couldn't keep nature at bay for ever. What was it he had been told when he himself was a boy actor? It's sad when a lad's voice broke, but sadder if it never did. He flung his arm around the boy's shoulders and gave him a squeeze. 'Forget the thunder box I promised you,' he said. 'I might let you have a crack at a part in this mummers' rubbish we're filling in time with. But don't push your luck – no name on the handbills, nothing like that.'

'Of course not, Ned,' the boy agreed, a smile splitting his face from ear to ear.

'And a pay cut.'

'That'll be hard to do,' Thomas said, evenly, 'since I haven't been paid since last Christmas. I was learning the trade, you said, so I shouldn't expect a wage as well.'

Sledd nodded and smiled. 'That's true enough.'

'So,' Thomas said, with the air of one pushing his luck just one tiny inch further than its leash would reach, 'now I'm not learning any more, I get some money. Right?'

'Wrong. Now, get down and start pitching the tent for the women. It feels a bit weird up here, I don't want them in the open tonight.'

Thomas jumped down from the wagon and looked around. The track had brought them out on to a flat plain, with a circle of weathered stones immediately in front of the wagons. To his left, one large stone was standing alone, and ahead and beyond the circle there seemed to be another group of stones. Tucked under the lee of the last group, there seemed to be a small hut, with smoke coming out of a hole in the roof.

'We aren't alone, Ned,' Thomas hissed, pointing to the shed.

'Well,' Sledd said, glancing in the direction of the boy's finger, 'I don't think we'll be outnumbered by whoever is in there, boy, do you think? You couldn't swing a cat in there.'

'Why would I want to swing a cat in here?' a voice behind them suddenly asked.

Both actors spun round, but there was no one there.

'Who said that?' Sledd hissed to Thomas.

'Me,' said the voice, 'over here, in the hut by the Whispering Knights.'

'If that's you, Nat . . .' Sledd roared.

'If what's me?' Nat Sawyer appeared round the end of a parked wagon, his bed roll over his shoulder and a pipe of tobacco between his teeth.

Thomas plucked Sledd's sleeve. 'Over there,' he whispered. 'Look.'

From the doorway of the hut, an arm had emerged and at the end of it, a finger beckoned. The finger was crooked and gnarled, with a nail hooked and sharp like a talon.

Sledd looked askance at it for a moment, but it didn't stop its slow gesture, which seemed to pull on him so he had to approach. As his feet seemed to drag him over the grass, Sledd looked over his shoulder, trying to catch someone's eye, someone who would help him, but everyone seemed oddly busy examining the ground at their feet.

Finally, he reached the door of the hut. The arm had been withdrawn, but he could see a figure inside, huddling over a roaring fire in a fireplace almost as big as the room itself. Sledd screwed up his eyes against the glare of the flames. The heat hit him in a wave; it was like looking into Hellmouth itself. The creature inside did not turn as he approached the door and he certainly didn't want to go in uninvited. It just didn't look like the kind of place where that behaviour would be acceptable.

'Come in.' The person beside the fire turned to him suddenly. 'Don't stand there with the door open. Were you born in a barn? There's a terrible draft.'

Sledd looked back over his shoulder, to the sight of his troupe all fanning themselves and turning their faces to the breeze to try to cool themselves down after the hottest day they could remember for years. He opened his mouth to speak, but thought better of it. He went in, dragging the plank which served for a door to behind him.

There was very little room inside the hut and the heat from the fire meant that the choice for Sledd was even more limited. He took a seat on a small stool over in the corner, furthest from the hearth. The woman sitting by the fire turned to look at him and he was surprised to see that she was not what he had been expecting. The skinny arm that had beckoned him could surely not belong to this woman, who was one of the fattest he had ever seen. Feature rolled into feature and taken overall she looked like something which had melted, like a candle which had been added to and burned over years, decades even. Where a foot showed under the ragged hem of her dress, it was overlaid by running fat. He looked around for the other person, although Heaven knew where he or she could be hiding.

'There is no one else in here, Master Actor,' the woman said. 'I will not keep you long in my little home. People would talk to see you here alone with me. A lady must watch her reputation. So listen well and do not interrupt me. You should leave this place while you can. The stones are not welcoming to those who come uninvited.' She looked at Sledd from under sagging brows. 'I know you will not take heed of anything I tell you, but I will tell it all the same. Don't try to count the stones; it can't be done. Don't speak a secret near the Whispering Knights; although they whisper, they cannot keep their counsel and words spoken here echo around the world. Respect the King Stone. Don't look for me again, for I won't be here.'

Sledd nodded, then shook his head. He wasn't sure whether he was agreeing with something or not.

She looked at him again and shook her head with a sigh. They were all the same, all those who blundered into the sway of the Rollrights. 'How many come with you to the Stones?' she asked him.

Sledd started to count on his fingers, his eyes cast up to the sod roof over his head.

Her sigh this time was deeper. 'Master Actor, just hear this.

Leave a copper coin for every man, woman and child who is
with you at the foot of the stone which watches, and all will
be well. Now, leave me. You are making me feel the cold.'
She threw another log on the fire and huddled over it, rubbing
her hands together. He could almost hear the fat sizzle. He
edged past her and out of the door and it took all of his actor-
managerial skills not to run like a scalded hare across the grass
to the wagons.

'No one there, Ned?' Marlowe asked, sitting on the tailboard
of a wagon eating a pear.

'Why do you ask?' Sledd said, wiping the sweat from under
his eyes.

'Well, you just peered in at the door and then came back.
I thought you would have gone in if there was someone there.
Thomas said he could see an arm, but it just looked like a
shadow to me.'

Sledd swallowed hard. 'There was a woman in there, as
fat as a maggot. She had a fire burning, red and hot as Hell.
She told me some things . . . I can't remember them, but I
will in a minute. Just let me sit down, I don't feel too well.'

Marlowe hopped down from the cart and beckoned to one
of the women. 'Ned's not feeling quite the thing,' he told her.
'Fetch some water, will you? I'm just going over there, to
investigate that hut, or whatever it is.' He strolled off across
the grass, the slanting shadows from the stones pointing the
way.

Closer to, there wasn't a hut at all, it was just a trick of
the eye because of how the old stones leant on each other.
Marlowe could tell that there had once been a fourth stone
and perhaps even a roof, but there was nothing there now. In
the corner, just visible as the shadows lengthened, there was
some ash from a fire, but when he touched the ashes, they
were cold. He stood up straight and looked around him, then
back towards the wagons. With a final glance back at the
ashes, he brushed his fingers on the stone and walked slowly
back to the circle.

In the grove just up the hill, the fat woman turned her head
on her great neck and spoke to her companion. 'He'll take
watching, that one.'

'Right enough, Sister. He's as tricksy as Lucifer. We must watch him as hawks will watch a mouse.'

'No, Sister,' the fat woman said, with a nod which set her chins vibrating silently. 'We must watch him as a mouse watches a hawk.'

'Eerie, this place, isn't it?'

Ned Sledd spun at the sound of the voice, but at first he couldn't see anybody. Just the shafts of the dying sun from behind the stones that hurt his eyes and he looked away, dazzled. 'Who is it?' he snapped. 'Who's there?'

'Scot,' came the reply. 'Reginald Scot. We met at Clopton Hall.'

Sledd relaxed. Rehearsals had not been going well and he wasn't at all sure that the Rollrights were a good place for a mummers' play to be practised. It was no more an amphitheatre than he was – the acoustics were all to buggery for a start, you couldn't hear someone standing next to you, but you could hear a whisper a hundred feet away. And that damned old hag tending her fire had set his nerves on edge.

'Master Scot –' Sledd extended a hand – 'if I didn't know better, I'd swear you were following us.'

Scot chuckled. 'You delude yourself, Player King,' he said. 'No, something else entirely has brought me to Meon Hill.' He sat down on a stone and began to ease his boot which was chafing his ankle. 'Master Shaxsper.' He nodded to the glover-turned-actor, seeing the same worried look on his face he'd read at Clopton. 'So glum, sir?' he asked.

'Glum?' Shaxsper straightened. Sledd was trying the man out as the Turkish Knight and he was beginning to regret it. Only in half costume as he was, Shaxsper cut quite a comic character in his turban and didn't seem to know quite what to do with his scimitar. 'No, sir, just cautious.'

'All right, everybody.' Sledd clapped his hands. 'We'll take a break. Thomas, work on your timing. You missed Joseph's cue for the thunder.'

'That's because he didn't give it,' Thomas explained, ever the professional.

'Well, well. Will –' Sledd threw a look at Shaxsper – 'we all know the Turkish Knight isn't exactly real, but try to do *something* with the accent, will you? You sound like a Warwickshire fishwife.'

'I'm a playwright!' Shaxsper reminded him, but Sledd wasn't listening.

He sat wearily down next to Scot. 'Do they have fishwives in Warwickshire, Master Scot?' he asked, swallowing heartily from a leather bottle.

'Not my county,' Scot told him. 'But I know of these stones, though.'

'You do?'

'That one over there, the tall one standing alone.'

Sledd followed the man's pointing finger. 'What of it?' he said, in an airy tone, trying to put the memory of the woman and her hellish fire behind him.

'That's the King Stone,' Scot said. 'What day is it?'

'Er . . . Wednesday, I think.'

'No, no. I mean the date.'

'Um . . .' Sledd's calendar was in one of the wagons so he couldn't be sure. 'July twenty-second, isn't it?'

'The Feast of St Mary Magdalene,' Scot murmured.

Sledd looked at the man. He tried to steer clear of religion and politics, finding that the two were a dangerous concoction in the theatre. And in these insane times both of them could kill a man. 'Is that important?' he asked.

'It might be.' Scot nodded. 'We'll find out come midnight.'

Sledd frowned. 'Midnight? You're talking in riddles, sir.'

'At midnight,' Scot said softly, drawing closer to Sledd as he told his tale, 'on the feast days of certain saints, just as the nearest church clock strikes, that stone becomes a man. Or a king, to be precise.'

Sledd blinked and broke the other man's hypnotic spell. 'Rubbish!' he scoffed, but his eyes flicked to where the hag had bent over the flames in her hut, over in the lee of the Whispering Knights.

'"Seven long strides you shall take, says she,"' Scot said, suddenly declaiming and making Sledd jump, '"And if Long Compton you can see, King of England will you be."'

'What's that?' Sledd asked. 'John Lyly? Nicholas Udall?' It wasn't Kit Marlowe; that much was certain.

'It's an old wives' tale,' Scot told him. 'There may not be too many fishwives in Warwickshire, but they make up for the lack in *old* wives. You can take my word on that.'

On a whim, Sledd stood up and took seven long strides to the west. He looked out against the purple clouds that crossed the dying sun to the black of the land that lay beneath. 'I can't see a damn thing,' he said. 'Not a solitary light. Ah, well, there goes my claim to the throne.'

'Not necessarily,' Scot called to him. 'Long Compton's to the north. You're looking in the wrong direction.'

They laughed and Sledd felt the hold of the old woman grow a little weaker. Reginald Scot seemed more rooted in reality than most men, but since Sledd made his living by pretending to be someone else and lived with others who did the same, that might not be so amazing after all. Whatever the reason, Sledd felt a little safer with Scot around. 'Join us in our evening repast, Master Scot,' he offered. The way to a man's heart is through his stomach and if he could catch him in a quiet moment, when his belly was full of food, he might be able to find out the truth about these stones.

'I would love to, Master Sledd, but, surely, your purse is a little light, what with what happened to Lord Strange . . .'

Sledd dismissed his politeness with a wave of the hand. 'The weight of my purse is not relevant, Master Scot. I don't know who owns these lands, but whoever they are, they are light a few coneys tonight. You look like a rabbit stew man to me. Can I tempt you?'

Scot looked out at the darkening land, then at Sledd. 'I won't argue with you, Master Sledd. It smells delicious already.'

Joyce Clopton sat by the side of her father's bed as the day died softly in the west. He had always liked this time of day, when all the birds were flying home to their nests and the night animals met the day ones briefly as they went about their business. He liked to listen as the house quietened, as the timbers shifted in the brick, as the tick of the cooling slates echoed down into the spaces of the house. And now he was dying, going home for the last time. In a perfect world, the priest would have performed the anointing of the sick, but, in the absence of the priest, her father was as yet unshriven. The bread and wine waited at his bedside for the viaticum, the last communion, which in extremis anyone could give for his soul's comfort, but Joyce could not bring herself to give them yet. To give them would be to admit that all hope had gone. Since he had left her in all but body less than twenty-four hours before, Joyce seemed to have hung on his every breath, each one drawn, it seemed, from a great distance inside his body. They came less often now and each exhalation was a sigh. There was a tap at the door.

'Mistress?' Boscastle put his head round the door and whispered. He was at that age where death was not looking over his shoulder yet, but he had seen many people die. He had known Joyce since she was born and knew that she was as stubborn as her father, and as soft hearted. He didn't want to leave her alone with the dying man but also didn't want to intrude. He was a perfect servant in every way. 'Mistress, go and rest. I will sit with your father for an hour or so. You can come back then.'

Even in the twilight of the room, her eyes flashed back at him. 'We don't have an hour or so for me to go and rest. But I would be grateful for your company.'

The steward picked up a stool from just inside the door and carried it to the other side of his master's bed. He had so much to tell her, to ask her, but this was not the moment. As soon as this old man stopped breathing, neither he nor Joyce had a home at Clopton any more. Blake had approached him, asking him to stay on as steward, but he could no more serve Edward Greville than he could fly. His answer, in measured, steward's tones, had made Blake blench and the clerk snort with suppressed laughter. No, homelessness was in his future, all right.

The room seemed full of the old man's breathing. Boscastle found himself counting the cycles of ragged indrawn breaths and the silences, as a frightened child might count the seconds between lightning and thunder, to tell how many miles away the storm might be. Boscastle knew that Death was not miles away from this room. He was standing at the foot of the bed, watching and listening for his moment to intervene.

'Mistress,' he said, reaching across his master's coverlet to touch her hand. He nodded to the bread and wine. 'I think . . . if you want . . .'

She looked up at him, her eyes brimming with tears. 'So soon?' she asked, her voice low.

He nodded.

She stood up and took up the sliver of bread. Boscastle slid his arm under Sir William's neck and lifted him a little, the baronet's head heavy on his shoulder. The man's daughter bent over him, making the sign of the cross and muttering the benediction under her breath. She touched the crust to his lips and then, with another genuflection, put it into her own mouth and swallowed it. In the silence as she prayed, there was another long and shuddering breath from her father.

'Quickly,' Boscastle said. 'Oh, mistress, the wine. Quickly.'

She snatched it up, spilling a little on the sheet in her haste and touched it to her father's mouth. His eyes opened and he looked up at her. 'Joyce,' he murmured, sipped the wine, swallowed it and died.

With the rasping breathing stilled, the room seemed to ring with silence. Boscastle gently let the old head slip back on to the pillow and closed the tired eyes. He pulled the sheet up over his face, tucking it in with deft movements. Soon, he would rouse the women who would come and do all that was needed to make the old man decent for the grave.

He looked up, to offer words of comfort to Joyce Clopton. She stood there, almost as if she herself had been struck down. Tears ran down her cheeks and dripped off her chin, but she made no sound. 'My Lady . . .'

She held out a hand, palm out, as though to ward him off. 'No kind words, Boscastle, if you please,' she said. 'I don't think I could stand it.' She backed off, away from the bed, towards the door. 'I just can't take another thing. He isn't dead. He wouldn't leave me. If I don't see him, he isn't dead. Don't speak.' Her voice rose with every strangled phrase and

Boscastle instinctively moved round the bed to comfort her. But she was quicker than he was and she was out of the door before he could reach her. He stood on the landing and heard her frantic feet beat a tattoo down the wooden stairs and then the slam of a door. He moved across to the long gallery which marched the length of the house and watched her ghostly figure run like the hounds of Hell were after her across the park, until she disappeared into the elder copse at its edge.

Lord Strange's Men spent most of the next morning arguing about what to perform. They could drop Lady Godiva for a start, because nobody in Oxford would have heard of her. Because of Thomas's tumble in the hay, he wouldn't make a convincing Britannia and Oxford would never allow a woman on stage even if, at this last, dying moment, Sledd could find one. Could he perhaps become Gog or Magog, Hengist or Horsa – possibly, at a pinch, King Arthur? Then, there was the whole audience dimension to consider. The townsfolk would probably accept any old nonsense as long as it had a clown, a bit of tragedy, at least one duel and fireworks. There always had to be fireworks. But the scholars? If any of the university men came along, they'd expect something altogether more highbrow. Aristophanes? Sledd had heard the name some-where. Could Kit Marlowe help? He was a scholar. Couldn't he knock his Dido into shape? Hadn't he been waffling on at dinner the other day about this Tamburlaine fellow? Sledd could play him with one hand tied behind his back. He wouldn't even have to bother with an accent; who would know how the man sounded, all this time and all those miles from when and where he had lived, because he was real, according to Marlowe.

But, all morning, Kit Marlowe had said 'No!'

Reginald Scot sat with Marlowe near the Whispering Knights as a warm breeze from the south floated over the linen line the women had put up. The man was sitting cross-legged, scribbling furiously in his pocket book, dipping his quill into an ink pot balanced precariously on one knee.

'Friend Shaxsper's not half bad, is he?' he said, nodding to the stage area where the ex-glover was going at it hammer and tongs with Martin, steel banging on steel.

'Not like that,' Martin said. 'You've got to make it half believable, Shaxsper.'

'Well, how then?' Shaxsper snapped, slicing high into the air so his fencing partner had to duck.

Marlowe smiled. 'Indeed not,' he agreed, 'though how he'd fare in some dark alleyway, I'm less sure.'

'Vicious life, acting?' Scot enquired, seeing the purple fury in Shaxsper's face.

Marlowe looked at him and tapped his paper. 'Not as vicious, I'll wager, as witchcraft.'

Scot chuckled. 'The old crone,' he murmured, 'the keeper of the stones.' With other men, Scot would have had to hiss a hurried, 'No, don't look.' But Marlowe had instincts of another sort and he kept his eyes on Scot's paper.

'What about her?' he asked.

'What do you make of her?' Scot asked.

Marlowe marshalled his thoughts. 'She's here and there,' he said. 'She certainly was in the company last night, because the rabbit stew didn't seem to go round the way it should have done and there is a lot of her to feed. Ned was certainly very scared by her; his bluff act might fool some people, but it didn't fool me, nor you, I would guess.'

Scot inclined his head in agreement.

'She seems to have a skill at blending into the background, which for one of her size is quite incredible. I am quite good at seeing through subterfuge, and yet I find I must look at her from the tail of my eye to see her clearly at all and if she sees me looking at her even askance, she moves away.'

'So,' Scot asked him, 'would you say she has magical powers?'

Marlowe chewed his lip. He had seen some things, not all of them explicable in the normal way, but taken overall, magical powers were not the kind of thing you expected to find in an ignorant old woman the size of a small cart, out in the middle of nowhere. 'I think she knows people, and how to move them about in their own heads to suit her purposes. She can bend the unwary to her will.'

Scot looked at him and smiled. His expression was suggestive of someone whose dog has just performed the trick they had been years perfecting. 'You are an interesting man, Master Marlowe, and one day I will find out more about you, but for now, I want to find out more of this old crone of the stones. If you questioned her about who she is and what she does here, what would she tell you, do you think?'

'I don't need to question her. She stays here to gull travellers out of a few paltry pence. She told Ned to put a coin for each one of us at the stone that watches.'

'Could he work that one out?' Scot said, leaning forward over his paper, ink dripping on to his boot.

Marlowe moved his hand aside, not out of care for the man's attire, but for his own. 'Ned is not stupid, Reginald,' he said. 'He is a little over dramatic, perhaps, and sometimes a little over zealous, but he has kept this troupe fed and watered and on the road safely these many months and a stupid man couldn't do that. In this case, he would probably have worked it out, but he noticed Nat Sawyer behaving somewhat inappropriately for the amusement of the women. It involved a carrot and the stone with a hole in – it gave Ned all the clue he needed.'

'Did he leave the money?'

'He says not.'

'But, did he leave the money?'

'Of course. But that doesn't make him stupid, just careful.'

Scot looked over at the rehearsal. Sledd had Martin by the throat and seemed to be trying to shake some lines into him. It was impossible at this remove to tell if it was having any effect. He turned back to Marlowe. 'But, say for a moment, just to please me, that you had to find out something which she knew and would not tell you. How would you go about it?'

Marlowe had a persuasive tongue and rarely had to use more than that to find things out. He knew there were other methods, which he tried not to think about too much; one of those dread engines might well be his future. He shrugged.

'Well,' said Scot, tiring of the chase. 'You could use one of these . . .' He rummaged in his knapsack and pulled out a steel bodkin, five inches long with a deadly point.

'Pretty,' said Marlowe, drawing back a little.

'I got it in Bamberg,' Scot told him. 'It's a witch pricker.'

'So . . . threaten the old girl with one of these and she'll tell you anything. You might need a longer one for the lady in question, though.'

Scot smiled again. 'That's not exactly how it works,' he said, and lunged at Marlowe with the pricker. The poet, sitting cross-legged almost knee to knee with Scot, had no time to react and the spike thudded into his doublet a little above the heart. He grunted with the impact and his hand was already behind his back reaching for his dagger. But there was no pain. No blood. Nothing.

'Sorry,' said Scot, sitting back again in the upright position and taking his bodkin with him. 'Just proving a point, you might say. Or the lack of one.' He pressed his finger against the bodkin's tip and it slid up inside the hilt. 'Ingenious, isn't it?'

Marlowe took the thing. 'Well, I'll be damned,' he said.

'Around here,' Scot said, 'that's very likely. You felt no pain, then, when I stabbed you?'

'None,' Marlowe said. 'Just the pressure of the blow.'

'And you're not bleeding?'

Marlowe frowned and smiled at the same time. 'Do you want me to look?' he asked. 'Is this another trick, Master Witch Finder?'

'I'm not a witch finder,' Scot said grimly. 'And yes, what men call witchcraft is entirely trickery. It's an illusion. Smoke and mirrors. Let me paint you a different picture. Imagine the crone under interrogation. She's stripped naked, bound hand and foot. She can't move, but she can see, and she can feel. If I were a witch finder, I'd ask her about her familiars: her cat, her dog, even the lice that crawl in her hair. Did the Devil send them? Does she suckle them? And if so, from where? Where is the Devil's mark, the witch's tit? Her own nipples? No, they once gave milk, but not blood. A mole then, like Lord Strange's, but somewhere on the body, hidden under her clothing. But nothing is hidden now, remember? She's naked, shamed and ridiculed and exposed to the gaze of men. I find such a mole. I tell her that if that is the Devil's mark, she will feel no pain as I prick her. There will be no blood. And lo . . .' This time, Scot jabbed the bodkin into his own chest. He looked at Marlowe and made the sign of the cross. 'The Devil is in you, mother. Look, look, how you did not cry out; how you do not bleed.'

He glanced across at the old woman for the first time, stirring her cooking pot on a fire built behind the Whispering Knights and singing softly to herself. 'Irrefutable evidence of damned witchcraft,' Scot said, 'and they'd hang her for it. Can you see her, Kit, her wretched old body creaking in the wind?'

But Kit Marlowe wasn't looking at the miserable old woman of Scot's imagination, twirling at the rope's end. He was squinting into the sun, trying to make out what was causing the flashes of light on the slope of the hill to the north. The flashes were bright, halting, intermittent and below them, in the heat of the July day, Marlowe could just make out a horseman. The horseman he had thought was Nicholas Faunt when they were on their way to Clopton.

'What's that, Reginald?' he asked. 'Those lights flashing over there?'

Scot half turned and focused his eyes through the heat haze, watching as the lights flickered once more and vanished. 'That's Meon Hill, laddie. Better you don't ask.'

TWELVE

The golden day had gone, leaving a sky of purple and amber, like the bars across a fire in a cottage home. All day, Sledd had put his cast through their paces. St George, the Dragon and the Turkish Knight it would be and Kit Marlowe had rustled up a quick prologue to give the whole thing a bit of a lift.

Will Shaxsper read it tolerably well, despite endless suggestions on how it could be improved. Old Joseph was ready to kill for the part, standing at Shaxsper's side and reading over his shoulder like some drunken echo.

'"Now see the rolling hills of golden thread,

Now see great England's heroes stand,

St George of red cross fame; a knight apart

The greatest knight of all this sacred land." Deathless, dear boy.' Joseph was in raptures. 'A mighty line indeed.'

Marlowe cringed. It was far from his best and, to be fair, his mind was on other things than iambic pentameter. But with Oxford beckoning in two days time, it would have to do. He was lolling against a wagon wheel idly strumming a lute to some half-forgotten tune when Thomas shouted from the elder stand to the north, 'Riders coming. Our way. To the north-east.'

Sledd and Scot were on their feet first, crossing to the stones and the road that lay beyond. Martin was with them, then Shaxsper and the others.

'Kit,' Sledd called to him. 'You'd better come and see this.'

A little procession was winding its way up the slope of the hill towards them, torches guttering in the breeze. The watchers at the stones heard the thud of the horses' feet and the creak of a wagon.

'It's a funeral,' said Thomas, trying to make out the details.

'And it's coming our way,' said Shaxsper, crossing himself out of habit.

The horse at the head of the solemn procession was ridden by a lady, trailing black weeds of mourning, fluttering gently in the currents of cooling evening air. By the horse's head and carrying a torch, a tall, sombre-looking fellow, wearing an old sword, kept even pace with the ambling animal. Behind them was a bier on wheels, draped with a flag that Marlowe knew. 'Those are the Clopton arms,' he said, 'and that is Sir William Clopton's funeral cortège.'

The others stood rooted to the spot, but Marlowe dashed between the stones and ran down the hill towards them. The lead horse halted, snorting and tossing its black-bridled head.

'My Lady.' Marlowe bowed. Joyce Clopton sat sidesaddle, her face pale in the half moonlight against her sepulchral black.

'Kit,' she said quietly. 'Oh, Kit!' And he helped her down, cradling her in his arms as Boscastle steadied the horse. 'I'm sorry,' she said, all the pain of her upturned world trickling down her cheeks. 'I had nowhere else to go.'

And he held her at arm's length.

Dawn was glowing as a distant cockerel heralded it, from somewhere to the south where the sleepy Cotswold villages were stirring. Joyce Clopton had fallen asleep, finally and her head lay on Kit Marlowe's chest. He looked beyond her and saw the worn-out faces of her people. They lay in huddles under the wagons with Lord Strange's Men, wrapped in cloaks and snoring softly in the morning. There were only a handful of them, those who were diehard loyalists, who had served the Cloptons all their lives. Those who had no kin or friends in Stratford; those not wedded to the stone and the timbers but to the heiress of Clopton herself. Only Boscastle sat upright against a wagon wheel, wide awake and watchful.

Marlowe eased the girl down so that she lay on the blankets on the ground and he laid his Colleyweston cloak over her shoulders. He crossed the grass in silent strides and sat down next to the Clopton's steward.

'A sorry scene, this,' he said.

'Aye, sir.' Boscastle nodded. 'And one I never thought to see.'

'What are Lady Joyce's plans, Boscastle?' Marlowe asked. 'Do you know?'

'The day before yesterday, I found her wandering the elder woods at Clopton,' the steward said. 'Singing to herself, she was, a song of the nursery, Master Marlowe, from when she was a little girl. I don't mind telling you –' he looked the man in the eye – 'I cried a little too.' He cleared his throat. 'Men aren't supposed to do that, are they?'

Marlowe smiled. 'Good men do.'

'She spoke of taking her father's body to the south-west. The Carew family are distant cousins. George of that name and Lady Joyce were betrothed at one time.'

'Were they?' Marlowe asked. He knew there was many a slip when betrothals happened early.

Boscastle smiled at the memory of it. 'There was nothing formal. She was seven, he a year older. She came running to me in the old woods, dragging this hapless, confused boy by the hand and said "Boscastle –"' his voice became higher in his fond mimicry of her – '"Boscastle, congratulate us. We are betrothed."'

'So she had a mind of her own even then,' Marlowe said, laughing.

'Oh, she did,' Boscastle said, remembering. 'They'd kissed, you see. Joyce and George. And to her, that was it. A promise of marriage. She was going to have twenty children, apparently.'

'And George?'

Boscastle chuckled. 'George didn't look too keen. A bit bemused by the whole thing, if you ask me.'

The pair fell silent as Boscastle's smile faded and his face darkened into a frown. 'But the south-west is far away,' he said. 'And they'll be coming.'

'They?' Marlowe asked. 'Who?'

'Did Lady Joyce not tell you? About Greville, I mean?'

'She did,' Marlowe told him. She had blurted it all out through the tears as they lay under the stars beyond the Whispering Knights. 'But I assumed that once she'd left Clopton . . .'

Boscastle chuckled grimly. 'It must have slipped her mind,'

he said. 'It may be a sacrilege, Master Marlowe and I own it was my idea if anyone is to be damned for it, but in the coffin with the master is what we could gather together of the family gold and silver – by Sir Edward's rights, his.'

'And the movables thereof,' Marlowe said, quoting the fatuous law.

'Indeed, sir,' Boscastle said. 'Now, mercifully, I don't know Sir Edward Greville very well, but I do know he's a greedy bastard who doesn't like being cheated. That lawyer of his . . .'

'Blake?'

'That toad'll reckon up what's missing soon enough and his High and Mightiness will be on the road to get it back. We didn't exactly disguise our tracks. Everybody remembers a funeral on the road. All they'll have to do is ask.'

Marlowe stood up to look over the wagon at the road snaking into the morning, to the north-east. 'If you're right,' he said to the steward, 'how much time do you think we have?'

Boscastle looked around him at the pitiful remnants of the Clopton people, at the large number of women with Strange's Men. 'Not enough, Master Marlowe,' he said. 'Not nearly enough.'

'A funeral, sisters,' one of the women hidden in the small stand of trees said, licking her lips with a pointed and blackened tongue.

'Yes,' said one of her companions, leaning against a tree to scratch a recalcitrant louse biting her back. 'But why here?' She rummaged in her ear and inspected the results. She carefully harvested the wax from under her fingernail into a small bag hung around her waist.

'I know the woman,' a voice said from ground level. 'It's her father in that coffin.'

The first speaker, the keeper of fire and stone at the Rollrights gave her a look. She knew that they were all sisters under the skin, but sometimes these newcomers got above their station, speaking out of turn. The conversation had been going nicely widdershins round the circle, as it should, when she had spoken. Still, she was young. Another thing to hold against her, to hug to her heart until it festered into some nice helpful hatred.

One of the other women sniffed the air, like the Beast Glatisant. 'Long dead?' she murmured to the girl.

'Days, one day. I'm not sure. I left before he died, but he had the mark on him so I know it must be him. There's no one else she would hawk round the countryside, that's sure.'

The woman sniffed again and frowned. She was also new to the company and relied on her other senses more than the rest, being without sight. The smells emanating from the women around her would have confounded the most talented hound, so perhaps that was why she was getting no smell of corruption. She liked a bit of corruption and if the corpse was far advanced, there were rich pickings to be had; fingers, hands, even locks of hair could all be put to good use. Never mind, she told herself, if he wasn't ready for harvesting yet, time would soon solve that problem. She had listened from a distance to the conversation between the hawk and the woman in the night. Although she hadn't said as much in words, her voice was telling all with ears to hear that she wouldn't be leaving his side in a hurry, given half a chance.

The fat keeper of the stones shifted her weight from one foot to another and spoke to the rest. 'I don't know about the rest of you, but I need to have a sit down. Shall we gather by the King Stone? It makes a nice centre for a circle.'

'Won't they see us?' the young woman asked.

Another, who hadn't spoken so far, said, 'Cloak of invisibility.' She rolled her eyes and clucked her tongue. She got fed up with those sisters who wouldn't use the powers He gave them. The old one she travelled with, for example. Wouldn't fly to save her feet, not for anything.

Her travelling companion spoke softly, the voice of reason. 'Not everyone has your skills, my dear,' she said. 'Why don't we just sit over there on that nice bank, well into the trees? Then we won't have to worry about our cloaks slipping from our shoulders and giving away our presence.'

The blind woman had never acquired the skill of invisibility, having no way of knowing when the trick had worked, so she nodded in everyone's general direction and held out her hand to be led through the shrubby trees to the bank. They sank down on to the moss and began to talk together in low voices, but every now and again, the eyeless woman raised her nose and sniffed the air.

No corruption yet. But with a thrill in her heart she knew that something wicked was coming their way.

They looked like a black cloud at first, a smudge on the bright gold of the corn fields. Their spear points glinted in the sun and the little camp on the hilltop fell silent.

'No, no, Will,' Martin was saying, 'that's cut two. You want cut three now. Up, parry and . . .' But he was scything thin air with his broadsword because William Shaxsper was standing yards away, his scimitar trailing on the ground and he was staring at Meon Hill.

The black cloud was moving down it now and Shaxsper groaned. He crossed to Sledd and Marlowe who were standing by the wagons. 'I know that flag,' he said. 'It's Lord Greville.'

'Sir Edward Greville,' Joyce Clopton corrected him. 'The man has enough airs and graces as it is.' She had recovered herself having slept and having poured out her troubles to Marlowe. She was the heiress of Clopton now and estate or not she intended to honour the name. One by one the heads came up, the women mending costumes and darning stockings, the men who had been hammering flats into place. All of them were staring at the little army reaching the valley floor below them.

'Who are these people?' Reginald Scot had abandoned his notebook and joined the others.

'Let's just say they haven't come for our autographs,' Marlowe told him. He glanced at Shaxsper. Perhaps the time had come to see if he could use that sword for real.

'Kit, Master Sledd,' Joyce hissed to them. 'It's me Greville wants or at least what's in my father's coffin. We shouldn't have imposed, shouldn't have come. We still have time. It'll be half an hour before they reach us. Boscastle, harness the horses.'

'One moment, My Lady.' Marlowe stopped the man in his tracks. He turned to the camp, all of them watching, waiting, uncertain what was happening or what to do. 'These are the men who stole Lady Joyce's home,' he said, raising his voice.

'The home where you and I were made welcome just days ago. Sir William's barns gave us shelter, his beds gave us rest. We drank his beer and his wine, ate his food. Some of us –' and he glanced sidelong at Thomas and Nat – 'enjoyed other things at Clopton.' Only Thomas blushed. 'Now, this jackanapes Greville has come to take Sir William's body itself.'

There were shouts and cries from everybody.

'He can't do that!

'That's sacrilege, that is!'

'The sick bastard!'

Only Marlowe heard Nat Sawyer mutter, 'Not really our problem, my opinion.' He noted the reaction but said nothing. Time enough to get even with the little squirt later.

'No!' Joyce shouted. 'No, Kit, you don't understand. Greville's after . . .'

He stopped her with a finger to his lips and a raised eyebrow. '. . . after all, no more than a man,' he finished for her.

Sledd was not at all sure about this. 'We've got women here, Marlowe. If there's to be fighting . . .'

It was a woman who spun him round. Little Liza, barely reaching to the man's ruff. 'Now, see here, Ned Sledd. I've been with you now . . . how long?'

'For ever,' Sledd groaned.

'With Lord Strange for nearly two years. And with you, masterless man as you then were, for over five before that. All of us women have fetched and carried, cooked and cleaned, nursed and tended. We've let you have us when you can't find a strumpet and we've wiped up your vomit and put you to bed when you're any side up with drink. So –' she wagged a finger at him – 'don't use us as your excuse.'

To a man – and woman – Lord Strange's Men burst into applause and whistles. Marlowe clapped a hand on Sledd's shoulder. 'I thought you told me you didn't have a Britannia, Ned,' he said with a laugh. 'Well, you've got one now.'

Joyce Clopton's eyes were red and wet as the camp exploded to life around her. With Marlowe as general and Sledd his second in command, the wagons were rolled end to end to form a bulwark on the ridge in front of the Stones and each

man and woman grabbed what weapons they had to hand and
stood shoulder to shoulder.

On the slope below the Rollrights, Greville's column halted.

'They mean to make a fight of it,' their captain said, standing
in the stirrups and squinting under the rim of his burgonet.
He glanced across at Henry Blake sitting uncomfortably on
his bay. 'You'll excuse me for saying this, Master Blake, but
at times like these I can't help wishing that Sir Edward was
here.'

'Sir Edward obviously assumed you could handle the job,
Paget,' the lawyer snapped. This was not his idea of a good
time. *He* had found the Clopton coffers light by a considerable
sum. *He* had put two and two together and realized that Lady
Joyce had smuggled the coins and gold out. And now *he* was
supposed to get it back. Why couldn't Greville do it himself,
or at least leave it to Paget? Blake didn't do rough stuff.

'It's them players, Captain –' one of the horsemen nudged
his animal forward – 'from Clopton Hall. What are we waiting
for?' And the watchers at the Stones heard the scream of steel
as he drew his sword.

'Reginald,' Marlowe murmured to the man on his left. 'Liza
has made it pretty plain where Lord Strange's Men stand in
all of this . . . whatever Ned thinks of it. The Clopton people
are committed, out of duty or love. But you . . . this isn't your
fight. Things could get nasty.'

'My work's not finished yet,' Scot told him, putting his
notebook now in his satchel at his side, 'and I refuse to leave
until it is.'

Marlowe smiled. 'Will?' he said to Shaxsper standing to
his right. 'You've got a wife and children.'

The glover-turned-Turkish-Knight stared at the column on
the hill that was fanning outwards to form a battle line. 'I also
have a father,' Shaxsper said. 'A good man who is afraid to
leave his house in Stratford because of Sir Edward Greville. I
knew there'd have to be a reckoning one day. I just wasn't
expecting it to be here or now. Fighting with these odds is
always madness, but let's form up and see if we can put some

method in it.' He thumbed the edge of the Turkish Knight's scimitar. 'This is as dull as the play it is part of,' he said, ruefully.

'Then turn it round and use it as a bludgeon,' Marlowe advised him. He was secretly impressed by the man. Gone was the skittish hothead afraid of Boneless and Kit with the Canstick. In his place stood the Turkish Knight, bold and resolute, his eyes calm, his scimitar at the ready, albeit upside down. But perhaps Master Shaxsper was only afraid of the shapeless things that lurked in the dark, things to terrify the soul.

Along the ridge, where the Clopton people stood, Boscastle was at the front, his old sword drawn, his legs apart as though to balance its weight. Next to him stood Lady Joyce, unarmed and silent, watching as a knot of horsemen broke away from the formation below and came trotting up the hill towards them. Next to her, young John gripped the halberd he'd brought with him from Clopton Hall, just in case, the smooth wood of the handle strangely comforting to him, as if the house itself was with him in spirit, protecting him as it always had.

The knot of horsemen halted a little below the ridge. Marlowe looked across at Joyce and they both stepped out of their makeshift lines and walked towards Greville's flag. Boscastle fell into place behind his mistress and Marlowe, glancing over his shoulder, saw that Sledd was at his back. But it came as something of a surprise to see that the man they faced was not Edward Greville.

'What do you want, lawyer?' Joyce asked the man, sitting awkwardly on his horse, which snickered and caracoled as if it knew it had an incompetent on its back.

'What is rightfully Sir Edward Greville's, madam,' he told her, 'the movables of the manor of Clopton.'

'He has them,' she said, her head held high. 'Would he steal my father's body too?'

The lawyer looked flustered for a moment, glancing nervously at Paget. For the first time he saw the black-suited figure of Marlowe and noted that he was wearing a sword at his hip, a fancy weapon of Spanish make, its quillons curling like quicksilver. He looked like the kind of man who could handle himself in any situation, with tongue or dagger and he hoped that Paget had marked him out for his own personal attention. Just because the pale man standing in Marlowe's ranks was holding a sword the wrong way round, Blake felt it would be a mistake to underestimate this rabble. That was William Shaxsper, if he remembered rightly, the glover's son from Stratford.

'If I may check the coffin, My Lady . . .' he began.

'You may not, sir!' she told him flatly.

'Master lawyer.' Marlowe stepped closer so that he stood by Blake's horse's head. He reached out slowly and cradled the animal's soft muzzle, calming it by stroking its nose and breathing gently into its nostrils. He looked up at Blake. 'You are on Warwickshire soil, sir. And your men are armed. You realize that, in itself, is a violation.'

'A violation?' Blake repeated. If this upstart was going to debate the law with him, he would lose. Or at least, *should* lose. Blake played for time. 'A violation of what?'

Marlowe spread his arms wide, letting the horse go. 'The edict of the Lord Lieutenant,' he said. 'Ambrose Dudley . . .' He could see the confusion growing in the man's eyes. 'You know,' he said, leaning forward with a smile playing in the corner of his mouth, as though humouring an idiot, 'the Earl of Warwick.'

A nervous laugh escaped Blake's lips. 'Come, come, sir. You'll have to do better than that.'

Marlowe lowered his arms and closed to the horse's head again, leaning forward. 'That's why he's not here, isn't it?' he murmured. 'Sir Edward. That's why he hasn't come himself. Doesn't want to mix it with Ambrose.'

The lawyer straightened in the saddle, pressing down in the stirrups and was rewarded by the startled horse flicking its tail and stamping its feet. He grabbed the pommel of the saddle to regain his seat. 'Ambrose? You are very informal, sir, for a play actor or whatever you are.'

Marlowe beckoned him closer and despite himself Blake leant forward in the saddle, still keeping a firm hold on the pommel with both hands. Paget's horse had backed away, out of range of the lawyer's animal's flying hoofs. 'I am your worst nightmare, Master lawyer. I was at Cambridge with

Ambrose Dudley's son. Oh, it's childish I know, but I still call him Uncle Am when we're alone.'

Blake sat upright, smiling his victory. 'I happen to know,' he said, smugly, 'that Ambrose Dudley doesn't have a . . .'

But he was too slow for Marlowe. The poet had grabbed the lawyer's rein and hauled it round hard so that the horse's head slewed to one side and the animal lost its footing on the slippery, tinder-dry and wind-blown grass. As it hit the ground with a thud, Blake was thrown clear, but landed badly on his shoulder and lay there, whimpering with pain.

Joyce couldn't help herself. She burst out laughing and there was a rapturous applause from the hilltop. There were even a few smiles in the ranks of Greville's men, because, as they had often agreed between them when speaking of the lawyer, nobody liked a lickspittle who lies for a living. Blake's horse rolled upright and trotted away, flicking its mane, alarmed by the sudden noises. But Blake himself just sat there on the grass, nursing his dead arm to his side and feeling decidedly hard done by.

'Keep it in!' shouted Sledd in the time honoured tradition of actor-managers the world over. 'With pratfalls like that you should take up the stage, Master lawyer. Do you play the tambour too?'

Paget's sword was in his hand and he was about to spur forward to tackle Marlowe when Boscastle grabbed the halberd he had brought with him, just in case, and levelled it at the man's face. 'Not wise, Captain,' he grunted. And Paget steadied the rein, holding his horse in check. He knew what weapons like that could do to a man, ripping through flesh and bone.

'What I forgot to mention,' Marlowe said, leaning over the rocking, crying Blake, 'is that Uncle Ambrose is on his way here, now. Lady Joyce thought you might come calling so I took the precaution of sending a messenger by my fastest horse. What did we ask for, Ned, two hundred horse?'

'Three hundred, Kit,' Sledd said, falling into the mood of the moment with the skill of a born ad-libber. Anyone who worked with Joseph could roll with anything that came out of anyone's mouth. 'But I did think that that was a *little* cheeky of you.'

Marlowe laughed. 'What time is it, Boscastle?' he asked the Clopton steward.

The man squinted behind him at the sun. 'One, sir,' he said. 'One of the clock.'

'Right,' said Marlowe, muttering to himself and counting on his fingers, 'so . . . in a little over twenty minutes, His Lordship should be here with three hundred heavily armed retainers. Yes, I know it smacks of a private army, but we can't be too careful, can we, in these topsy-turvy days? Captain,' he called to Paget, standing back a way now that things seemed to have taken a rather strange turn, 'you have precisely twenty minutes to void the field. After that, I can't be responsible for what may happen.'

Paget signalled to his lackeys and they hauled Blake to his feet before wheeling away and starting back for their own lines.

'Kit?' Joyce Clopton waited until the men were out of earshot. 'That business about the Earl of Warwick . . .'

'Begging your pardon, My Lady,' Sledd cut in as they turned to trudge back up to the Stones. 'That was some of the finest horse shit I've ever heard. Oh, beautifully done, I grant you that. But Master Blake may have been a little miffed before. Now he's really mad. And when he stops crying, I don't reckon our chances.'

'Such ingratitude.' Marlowe shook his head. 'I buy us an extra twenty minutes *and* provide a good laugh into the bargain and you call it horse shit. Come, Lady!' He took Joyce's arm ostentatiously and turned his back. 'Let's get away from the nasty man.' And they all laughed as they negotiated the rise. All of them except Ned Sledd. He was a man who understood that revenge was not always served cold. Sometimes it came in red heat and then it could burn anyone in its path.

Two women watched from the edge of the trees.

'Did you see how I made that horse fall over?' the older of the two said, smugly.

The younger one thought it had been her black thoughts that had caused it, but there was enough tension in the group to cause more so she just raised a shoulder and grunted in agreement. 'But it was me who put his shoulder out,' she said. 'See?' And she held out a forked branch, now pulled apart like a wishbone.

'That was a very nice touch,' the other said, patting the girl on the shoulder and grimacing to the imp that sat on her shoulder. The imp smiled back knowingly and rolled its eyes in a secret message, just between the two of them. She smiled back. She didn't feel alone these days, not since he had come along.

They watched for a while as the lines reformed, however raggedly.

'Will there be a fight?' the younger one asked.

'Hopefully.'

'Death?'

'And destruction. Rich pickings for us. We will get there before the ravens.'

The two rubbed their hands together and giggled cruelly.

Further back in the shadows of the trees, Merriweather sighed. What had come over the young these days? Nothing but doom and gloom. At that age she was out picking flowers at dawn to find her own true love. An eyeball held no attraction for her then or now. She shook her head and went back to the bank where her sisters were still sprawled, those whose joints would let them. No good could come of this, whatever He might say.

The twenty minutes crawled by like years and Greville's riders showed no sign of moving on. Clearly Marlowe's bluff hadn't worked. Nor could he really hope that it would. Again and again in those twenty minutes, Joyce Clopton begged him to let them go, but his words were wise enough. Bedded down behind their wagons and the Stones, they stood *some* chance. On the open road, they'd be cut to pieces and Sir William Clopton's body would be rolled into a ditch, along with that of anybody else who tried to defend it.

Besides, Marlowe knew his Caesar. Time and again he had read, in the King's School cloisters by the Dark Entry, of how a tiny Roman cohort held a high ridge against the hordes of the Gauls. He chose to forget in that moment that the Romans were the finest infantry in the ancient world, hardened veterans who were armed to the teeth. Then he looked again at little, battling Liza with her wheel-lifting biceps under her chemise and he took heart.

'Here they come!' It was Thomas the lookout and in that moment Ned Sledd's heart took wing. In his incipient panic, the lad's voice was as high as a lark's. Perhaps that was the answer, then. Terrify him every night before he goes on and all will yet be well.

Marlowe, Sledd and Scot stood alongside Joyce and her Clopton people. Will Shaxsper, who had sensibly used the past few moments exchanging parries and ripostes with Martin, rested his chin on a wagon edge and watched them come on, images of his browbeaten father and his uncomprehending, horrified wife flashing in his brain. Boscastle, with his recent experience of those men counted twenty, all of them armed, all of them mounted. Obviously Greville had not expected much resistance from the ragbag little column that left Clopton with their forlorn load and he thought twenty should cover it. Boscastle had three good men besides himself. In Lord Strange's company there was Sledd, Martin, Nat and the lad, Thomas, who could probably handle themselves. Oh, and that frightening little woman with the shoulders. Marlowe was a given. So too, probably, was Scot. And Will Shaxsper, the glover's son, might make a decent fist of it. Old Joseph was struggling to buckle on some ancient armour from the props wagon and it was already getting the better of him.

He saw Lady Joyce cross herself. And Will Shaxsper too. Kit Marlowe did not. And neither did Reginald Scot.

Marlowe noticed that Henry Blake was not advancing with the cavalry line. He sat some hundreds of yards back, his right hand tucked into his gown.

'They've got no guns at least,' Sledd grunted to him.

'No, but we have,' Marlowe suddenly shouted.

'Kit?' Sledd instinctively dashed after him as he rolled away from the makeshift barricade. 'Kit? What are you doing?'

'The gunpowder, Ned,' Marlowe yelled. 'The fireworks. Ever seen a horse that can stand still for them?'

Sledd slapped the man's shoulder. 'Why didn't I think of that?' he asked.

Marlowe looked at him straight faced and said, 'You've led a very sheltered life, Ned,' and the two men set to, hauling their firing piece into place, Sledd frantically wrestling with the tinder box while Marlowe rammed the linstock into the ground.

'Too high, too high!' Sledd shouted, 'it'll frighten our horses too and they'll trample the camp.'

Marlowe wrenched the linstock lower, clawing at the metal frame until his fingers bled. The noise behind them told both men they were too late as the thud of horses on the hillside grew deafening and the shouts and curses of Paget's men rained in on their ears. Nat Sawyer just happened to be running backwards as he took the first blow from the flat of a sword, as its owner dragged it from its scabbard. The comedian had always been a believer in the power of timing to get the laugh and this time it had saved his life. The blade slapped him round the head and he pitched backwards off the wagon. It was the best stage dive he'd ever done but there was no appreciative audience to applaud him, just armoured riders with their blood up hurtling against the wagons of Lord Strange's Men. Sawyer landed under the wagon, his head ringing and opened one eye cautiously. With no one to see him or pass judgement except his own conscience, which had been dead for years, he crawled away further into the darkness of the barricade and waited for it all to be over. You've done your bit, Natty, he thought to himself.

Boscastle still had his halberd in his grip and he poked upwards, catching a horseman in his chest and wrenching the weapon round to slice the tendons of the man's arm. He screamed as he left the saddle and rolled in the Rollright dust.

Joyce snatched up the fallen man's sword and stood defiantly, waiting for her turn. Three horsemen leapt the wagons together in the centre, somehow holding their seats as the animal's hoofs clipped the flats. Props and scenery crashed to the ground and Martin was hacking about him with St George's sword. Will Shaxsper was with him, the stage enmity of Christendom and Islam forgotten as they traded blows with the milling riders.

'Forget it!' Sledd roared at Marlowe. The moment for

terrifying the enemy had gone and now it was every man for himself. Little Liza had leapt upwards and was hanging around a horseman's neck, taking vicious bites out of his right ear as he tried to fling her off. John and another of the Clopton lads had floored another horseman and were busily kicking him into unconsciousness by the Whispering Knights.

Sledd was doing his best to protect his wagons with their precious cargo of stage paraphernalia. Thomas had dragged Liza's quarry out of his saddle and now just stood back while she proceeded to haul the man about the arena by his hair, calling him names only some of which were familiar to the boy. Marlowe made for Paget, his rapier flashing as he thrust for the man's doublet. Paget wheeled his horse and parried for his life. He felt a stinging pain as Marlowe banged the fancy quillons off Paget's sword and he saw in disbelieving horror one of his fingers fly with them. He was about to pull back to try and regroup his isolated horsemen when a horn rang out, shivering through the cries of horses and men.

It grew louder and more insistent and was sounding from the north-west. 'I told you!' Marlowe yelled above the crash of battle. 'The Earl of Warwick. Good old Uncle Am!'

And Paget's spent force, bloodied and bowed, hauled back on their reins and slunk away.

The horns were still braying from the far side of the hill and when a mere two riders appeared. Everyone was secretly glad they had approached from Paget's blind side or the fight would still be raging.

'Caesar's cavalry!' shouted Marlowe and reached across and poked Sledd in the ribs. 'Thank the buggering echo in these hills, Ned. Not good for rehearsals, but damned useful to us today.' Sledd grinned and nodded, slumping against a wagon to get his breath. Marlowe sheathed his sword and stepped forward to welcome the newcomers.

The horsemen cantered into the circle of stones and brought their foam-flecked horses to a stop. It was Richard Cawdray and Simon Hayward, out for a gallop on a bright afternoon.

'Gentlemen.' Joyce Clopton crossed to them and they both bowed in the saddle. 'You are very welcome. You may have saved our lives today.'

'Ah, it's nothing.' Cawdray slid out of the saddle. 'Simon said his horn would come in handy. We saw you were having a little difficulty from a couple of miles away. What's happening here, exactly?'

Marlowe took the two men by the arm and led them away from the circle. 'How long have you got?' he asked them.

THIRTEEN

The sun had all but disappeared over the Warwickshire fields when there was a stir from the remnants of Paget's men skulking along a line of pollarded trees above the brook.

'Horsemen coming!' Thomas sang out, still watchman, having by far the best eyes in Lord Strange's Men. 'White flag.'

Everybody crowded to the wagon sides, improvised weapons at the ready again.

'I knew it wouldn't fool them for long,' Sledd muttered to Marlowe. 'Nice try, though, Master Cawdray.'

The huntsman nodded.

'Ho, the camp!' a voice called out in the gathering darkness.

'That's Edward Greville,' Joyce Clopton said to Marlowe. 'I'd know that devil's voice anywhere.'

'What do you want?' Sledd shouted back.

The knot of horsemen under the flag of truce shifted and a lone rider nudged his horse forward. 'Lady Joyce,' the voice cried. 'I would speak with Lady Joyce.'

While the watchers on the ridge tried to work out what this new ploy was, Joyce ducked under the guide rope and stepped outside of the wagon circle. It was Marlowe who stopped her. 'Not wise, My Lady.' He reached out and took her arm. 'Better you stay here. Ned? Fancy an evening stroll?'

'Why not?' Sledd shrugged. 'What's a life to lose, when all's said and done?'

'Liza,' Marlowe called, 'can I borrow your apron?'

The camp follower hesitated. 'I will get it back, won't I, Master Marlowe?'

'As I continue to live and breathe,' he said to her with a smile. He drew his sword and tied the apron around the point, waving it in the air as he and Sledd sauntered down the hill. Half turning, he said to Scot, 'Keep Lady Joyce company, Reginald.' And to Shaxsper: 'You too, Will.' The glover-turned-actor looked less brave now that the darkness gathered.

Greville steadied his frisky mare as the flag-bearers reached him. 'I wanted Joyce Clopton,' he growled.

'Many men do, I am sure,' Marlowe said. 'What is your business?'

'Who are you, popinjay?' Greville snapped.

'I am Christopher Marlowe, playwright. And you?'

The horseman straightened in the saddle. 'Sir Edward Greville, Lord of the Manor of Stratford.'

'Then you're trespassing on the Earl of Warwick's land,' Marlowe told him, as aware as Greville of the pecking order among the gentry.

'Trespassing, my arse!' Greville spat on the Earl of Warwick's turf. 'I have a lawyer here with a dislocated shoulder and a captain of my household with a finger less than he started out with this morning, and all because of you.'

'Take it to the Court of Chancery,' Marlowe told him.

Greville narrowed his eyes and looked the poet up and down. 'You're the sworder, aren't you? The man who came looking for me at the Swan with Strange. How is His Lordship, by the way?'

'Exceedingly well,' Marlowe said, 'and under the protection of the Queen by now, at Nonsuch.'

'How very sweet,' Greville said, his voice dripping acid. 'Rather like old William Clopton, under the protection of his maker.'

'Indeed,' Marlowe said. 'I suppose you have come to pay your respects, have you?'

'No need,' Greville said. 'I've done that already. When I came across his makeshift grave at Clopton.'

Sledd looked at Marlowe, then back at Greville. He couldn't resist a glance back up the hillside to his waiting people. 'His body's with us,' he told Greville. 'Up on the hilltop, in a coffin with a pall and everything.'

The Lord of Stratford looked at the men and stifled a laugh. 'Is it?' he asked. 'That was the question I wanted to put to Lady Joyce herself.'

'Unavailable,' Marlowe said and folded his arms. 'Lady Joyce is not receiving visitors today.'

'What's going on?' Sledd asked. The conversation seemed to have escaped from him and he wasn't quite sure how.

'It's quite simple,' Greville said, shifting in the saddle. 'Sir William Clopton died – sad, but inevitable. His daughter, incomprehensibly, blamed me and was driven to distraction by his death. She knew she'd have to abandon her home, but she couldn't bear the thought of the old man lying anywhere but Clopton, so she had him buried in the deer park, no doubt –' he scowled at Marlowe – 'with the full rites of the Papist church.'

'So . . . let me get this right,' Sledd said. 'That coffin is empty.'

'Oh, no.' Greville chuckled mirthlessly. 'I dug up the old bastard's body, just to make sure nothing else had been buried with him. Blake found the treasury rather short, you see. No, what is in *that* coffin –' he nodded to the wagons and stones on the ridge – 'is the gold and silver of the Cloptons, which is, by rights, mine.'

'Don't you mean the Queen's?' Marlowe asked. 'The forfeit property of a recusant? I'm sure Master Blake will have told you the law, even if you didn't know it already.'

'The Queen's, then,' Greville acknowledged. 'But I shall protect it on her behalf.'

Marlowe closed to the man's horse so that the white flag dangled near his face. 'You'll have a hell of a job trying,' he promised. 'This conversation is at an end.'

And he turned on his heel to trudge up the hill, Sledd floundering with as much dignity as he could muster in his wake.

'How much are we talking about, Kit?' he whispered when he'd caught the poet up. 'In the coffin, I mean?'

'Who steals my purse, steals trash,' Marlowe told him, 'or in this case, Lady Joyce's purse.'

'Yes, yes,' Sledd muttered. 'We know all that, but I'm seriously out of pocket here. With Strange gone, hopefully temporarily, and the damage those bastards did to the props wagon earlier . . .'

'I'm sure Her Ladyship will reimburse you, Ned.' Marlowe untied the apron from his sword point and passed it back to Liza.

'She'd better!' Sledd stormed, breaking away from Marlowe's side and marching off in a temper towards the King Stone.

'What did Greville say?' Joyce asked Marlowe as he sheathed his sword and accepted a cup of wine from Will Shaxsper, who then showed signs of lingering on the edge of the conversation. Marlowe thanked him with a nod and waited, face impassive until he moved away. Then he turned back to Joyce Clopton. 'He wants what's in the coffin,' he said.

'My father's body?' she said, in high dudgeon. 'How could he ask such a thing?'

Marlowe put down the cup on a wagon step, where it was quickly appropriated by Joseph, who was still feeling the after effects of shock, as he told anyone who would listen. He still had a rusty helmet on his head. Marlowe grabbed Joyce firmly by the shoulder and led her into the dark beyond the wagons. 'Not the body,' he said, shortly. 'The gold.'

She gasped and pulled herself away from him. She wanted to run, but she didn't know where to go. 'You looked!' she hissed at him. 'You told him. You traitor.' She pulled her head back to spit in his face, then burst into tears instead.

'I didn't look because I had no reason to doubt that the coffin held your father's body. You are the liar here, My Lady, not me, don't forget. Does Boscastle know what you did?'

'Of course he does,' she snapped. 'Who do you think dug the grave?' She suddenly grabbed Marlowe's hands, squeezing them tightly. 'How did Greville know?'

There was only one way to tell her and that was straight with no embroidery. 'He found the grave.'

'Oh my God.' Joyce crossed herself. 'You don't mean he . . .?'

'No,' Marlowe said, shaking his head. Better by far that Joyce Clopton never heard the truth. Greville had not gone into detail, but he was unlikely to have reinterred the old man with full honours. Marlowe did not like to think of the fate of his body now. Personally, he had no strong views on how a body should be treated after death; after all, it was just meat by then. But there was such a thing as respect for your fellow man and he was certain that Edward Greville was woefully short on that particular trait. 'Don't worry. He found the fresh-turned earth and questioned some of your people at the Hall and put two and two together. He doesn't miss much, your Sir Edward Greville, I'll give him that.'

'He's not *my* Sir Edward Greville,' she reminded him. 'And if I were a man, I'd give him six feet of the Earl of Warwick's land. I have asked you before, Kit Marlowe, to kill Edward Greville. I have less to offer you now, but I ask you again; will you do it?'

He looked at her, the little lost girl, the disinherited Lady, the icy heroine all rolled into one. 'A stab in the dark?' he said quietly. 'That's really not my style.'

It had been one hell of a day. Not everyone had been injured in the brawl with Greville's men, but most of them had a story to tell in which wounds featured even if the marks had now miraculously healed. The supper round the fire had been scanty; time enough in the morning to repack the wagons properly and find out what food and other bits and traps remained unbroken. For now bread and cheese would suffice. Cawdray and Hayward had some pie packed up in their saddlebags, which they nobly gave to the women to share. They had ridden off at dusk, to the comfort of a nearby inn, so there would be pie enough for them, and anything else they fancied too. Hayward might be a huntsman but he drew the line at sleeping under the stars in the company of potential vagabonds and thieves. Cawdray, rather stage struck, would have happily stayed, but as a good guest he went with his host, waving regretfully over his shoulder. Nat Sawyer's story was lurid, redolent with sweat flying, hand-to-hand combat and death being looked squarely in the face. No one had seen him crawl under the wagon and so most of the troupe listened agog. Sledd was sulking wrapped in his cloak by the King Stone and although he had accepted some food from Liza, he wouldn't talk to anyone. He was feeling very hard done by. Marlowe and Scot had talked and talked the subject of the battle to death, along with the coffin full of gold and the perfidy of women in general, and witches in particular. It was hard to get Scot off his hobby horse once he was firmly astride. Marlowe put an extra guard on the coffin and gradually the camp fell asleep, once Joseph had run out of scurrilous catches to sing, in drunken discordance.

The dark was intense outside the ring of wagons. The women in the trees had stopped watching once the campsite had fallen asleep and soon they were sleeping too, wrapped in their cloaks or curled up in the roots of a tree, according to their preference. The self-appointed keeper of the Stones slept propped against one of the Whispering Knights, one eye half open but even so dead to the world. The various whistles and grunts of dozens of sleeping people filled the night and drowned out the smaller sibilances of mole, vole and weasel as they went about their varied business in the grass and ground of the Rollright Stones.

A darker darkness detached itself from a wagon and crept across the space between the stones, searching the rolled-up bodies on the ground, peering at them one by one in the moonlight. Sometimes, the figure knelt beside one of the sleepers, head bent, as though listening to a secret. But always, the secret proved not the answer, and the figure moved on. It slipped between two wagons and disappeared into the night. There was a muffled oath and a clatter of conversation, which died away into silence again. The camp slept, fitfully or like the dead, according to their taste, until dawn broke, with the promise of heat already in the sun as soon as it broke cover over the crest of the hill.

Slowly, the sleepers woke and found their bumps and bruises had not been improved by a night on the cold, hard ground. Nat Sawyer had a lovely black eye, from his one and only blow sustained in the fight, but it gave verisimilitude to his story and he flaunted it like a badge of courage. Everyone was soon at their various tasks, appointed since they had gone on the road, things to pack, rubbish to bury, heads to count before the wagons could roll towards Oxford and a chance for Lord Strange's Men to strut their hour upon the stage.

There was of course the complication of Lady Joyce and her Clopton people, and the fact that Edward Greville would trail her to the mouth of Hell to get what he wanted. So it was agreed, at least to Marlowe's satisfaction, that she would stay with the cavalcade for safety and at Oxford throw herself on the mercy of the town. After the bloody nose Blake and Paget had been given it was unlikely that the Lord of Stratford would try anything again, at least in broad daylight. So now, it was all hands to the wagons and the Devil take the hindmost.

And it may have been the Devil who screamed that morning as the cocks began to crow in the distant, still-slumbering villages. The sound scraped through everyone's brain like a nail on slate and all heads swivelled to its source. Liza came scampering across the flattened, yellow grass, holding up her skirts with one hand with the other held like a flag of truce above her head. Her eyes were wide with terror and her face turned up to the sky, mouth red and wide in her scream. The horses shifted and whinnied in panic and everyone in the camp started off to meet her.

Thomas, who had been on watch on the ridge, woke up with a start at the terrifying shriek and for a moment wondered where he was. He instinctively tightened his grip on the pike in his hand and looked down to the line of birches where he knew Greville's men were still camped. There was no movement there. There were no fires on that already warm day and the horses held their lines. Nobody seemed to be standing, except Thomas's opposite number, who threw his halberd across his chest in a movement designed to repel cavalry. He had clearly heard the scream, too.

The keeper of the Stones was not surprised to hear the scream. These people had been treating her precious circle as if it were a village green since they had arrived. They had tried to count the stones. They had not respected the stones. The pennies on the watching stone had been three ha'pence short. She heaved herself to her feet and walked towards Liza, now in the middle of a group of women, pointing frantically behind her to the King Stone. She was babbling, but the keeper didn't listen. She just kept up her rolling gait in a dead line to the stone. She and Marlowe got there about neck and neck. They looked down at what had made Liza scream and run.

Ned Sledd lay below the stone, his bedroll pulled back, his britches still on and his doublet rolled up under his head. But his eyes were open, staring at the puffy clouds which scudded far overhead and his shirt front was spotted dark brown with his blood. Buried deep in his throat was a silver-handled bodkin. And it was one Kit Marlowe had seen before.

He was still squatting by the body, holding the dead, cold hand of Ned Sledd when the keeper of the Stones suddenly spoke. She turned to the approaching crowd of Lord Strange's Men and the Clopton people. Her voice started low, and rose in tempo and timbre as she declaimed her rhyme to the sky.

'Rise up, stick,' she muttered, 'and stand still, stone, for King of England be you none. You and your men hoar stones shall be. I myself, an elder tree.' And she suddenly pushed her way out of the circle of gathering spectators and was gone, skimming across the smooth grass like a galleon in full sail.

'And who appointed you Constable of the Stones?' Simon Haywood wanted to know. He and Cawdray had ridden into a scene sadder than the saddest tragedy Lord Strange's Men had ever offered to an audience. Everyone was weeping, Marlowe included, and even Scot was not dry eyed. The morning had progressed in a series of short scenes, each one more harrowing than the last, from the discovery of the body to the laying out and now Marlowe had commandeered Sledd's wagon in an effort to create some kind of order out of the undoubted chaos. By midday, as the fierce July sun burned on to the Rollrights, the women of Strange's Men had stripped their leader, washed his wound and laid him in a plain linen shroud, the one they usually used for the Ghost should there be one in any play they were putting on. Most of them had not stopped crying all day and even the guard, doubled now to watch Greville's men, did so through the blur of their tears. The Player King was gone. And there was no one now to lead Lord Strange's Men.

'I have some experience in these things,' Marlowe said. He was under the canvas awning, where the heat of the day had not yet penetrated and the only sound was the occasional snort and whinny as a horse shifted in the lines and shooed away the flies with its tail.

'Have you, by God,' said Hayward, testily. 'I feel I should ask from what side of the bar, Master Poet, have you experienced an investigation into murder?'

'If you have questions to ask me, Master Hayward,' Marlowe said, keeping his temper in check with extreme difficulty, 'I would ask you to wait until we can speak more privately and at more length. I had asked to speak to Master Scot, so if you please . . .' He extended his arm, his palm outstretched to show the way to the outside world of tears and loss.

Hayward spluttered and said, 'You expect me to wait my turn? What are you, boy? Twenty? Twenty-one? You may be some damned hack with a pretty pen, but I own three hundred acres. You can go to the Devil.' And he turned to leave.

'I can't make you stay,' Marlowe called to him, 'but if you leave, we'll all assume the worst.'

'What . . .?' a furious Hayward spun round on him, feeling for his dagger at his back.

Richard Cawdray stepped under the awning, dipping under its flapping edge. 'Simon, Simon,' he said, holding the man's sleeve. 'No need for all that. Master Marlowe is just trying to find out what happened to his friend. He didn't mean . . .'

'You can *all* go to the Devil!' Hayward roared and strode across the grass to stand, arms folded and chin raised defiantly, at the edge of the stone circle.

Cawdray and Marlowe watched him in silence. Then Cawdray spoke. 'We're all a bit on edge today, Master Marlowe. I'm sorry.'

Marlowe nodded and Cawdray stepped out of the shadow into the sun and went to stand next to Hayward, his hand on his shoulder, his head bent to him as he spoke some words which eventually seemed to calm him.

'Sorry, Kit –' Reginald Scot popped his head around the awning – 'you wanted to see me?'

Marlowe held up the bodkin in his right hand. It still had traces of Sledd's blood on it.

'Ah.' Scot's bonhomie vanished. 'I wondered when you'd raise that. Bit of a ticklish issue, isn't it?'

'Your weapon found embedded in the neck of a dead man?' Marlowe murmured. 'I'd say so, yes.'

Scot sighed and sat down heavily, cross-legged on a props chest. 'Shall I put my case?' he asked.

'I wish you would,' Marlowe said.

Scot cleared his throat, as though he were facing the Assize or the Star Chamber. 'I didn't know Ned Sledd, other than passing the time of day with him. Was anything stolen, from the body, I mean? Money? Trinkets?'

'Not that I can tell,' Marlowe said. 'Would robbery have been your motive, then? I didn't have you down for a thief.'

'Nor a murderer, I hope.' Scot's sudden guffaw had no mirth in it. He saw that Marlowe wasn't smiling. 'If I had killed the man –' Scot leaned forward, earnestly – 'would I have been so foolish as to leave my weapon in the wound?'

'I don't know,' Marlowe said. 'I believe I was the only one you had shown it to. Perhaps you thought I wouldn't remember.' He suddenly threw the bodkin to Scot who fumbled and dropped it. 'Show me how it works,' Marlowe ordered. 'The last time I saw it in use it couldn't actually have hurt anybody.'

'Ah.' Scot held it aloft between them. 'Ordinarily, when used as a pricker, no. But if you just . . .' He pressed in a catch, hidden in the chasing on the handle. 'It becomes just an ordinary dagger, albeit with a thin blade.' He pressed gingerly on its tip and the blade held firm. 'See?'

'I didn't know that,' Marlowe said thoughtfully, 'even though you had shown it to me.'

'So, what are you saying?' Sledd asked, peering at him in the wagon's shade. 'That I must have killed him? Look at this handle.' He held it out towards Marlowe. 'The catch is not obvious, but it isn't really hidden very well either. A child could find it. I don't see why you assume I killed Sledd.'

'But it would be useful if you said you did.'

'What?' Scot frowned. Marlowe wasn't making any sense.

'From what I saw of the wound, it was driven home with some force,' he said, 'with the strength, I assume, of a man. Although –' he smiled despite the grimness of the situation – 'having seen Liza in action, I'm not so sure. But if it was a man, it could be you, Will Shaxsper, Simon Hayward or

Richard Cawdray. It could be Boscastle or the lad John from Clopton.'

'Well,' Scot sighed, 'that narrows the field.'

'But there's a problem with all of them.' Marlowe was half talking to himself. 'As you said, you didn't know Sledd. Neither did they. Why kill a total stranger? And in such a risky situation? There were men on watch, high alert thanks to Edward Greville. It was a chancy thing to do.'

'Sledd's men, then,' Scot said. 'You, Kit Marlowe –' he was quietly enjoying turning the tables – 'the only other man in the camp who knew about that bodkin *and* where I kept it. Then there are the others. You know them better than I do. Rivalries? Jealousies? Somebody's name higher than another on a playbill? Personally, I wouldn't turn my back on any actor living.' There was a pause. 'Or dead.'

'They might squabble,' Marlowe conceded. 'They might behave as though they would stab each other in the back given the slightest provocation, but in fact Lord Strange's Men are as tightly knit a group of people as you would wish to meet in a day's march. The only one without a scruple was Edward Alleyn, from what they say, but I hardly met the man.' Marlowe's face clouded over just at the thought of Alleyn and his purloined play. 'But we are overlooking one other possibility, of course.'

'Ah.' Scot smiled grimly. 'I thought you'd get around to that.'

Marlowe looked under the canvas to where Strange's Men sat in a circle around the shrouded body of their leader and to the King Stone beyond. 'The spot where Ned lay last night is nearest of all to Greville's camp. Depending on the alertness of our people, any one of them could have crept up the hill and done the business.'

Scot was shaking his head. 'Not with my bodkin,' he reasoned. 'What would be the point? It would double the risk of his being caught, having to ransack my tent first – and there was no sign of disturbance there, by the way, I checked. No.' Scot leaned back against some flats. 'No, that wasn't the possibility I had in mind.'

'Oh?'

'Think back,' Scot said. 'To Clopton and Lord Strange. The thorn through the poppet. The blade through the throat of Ned Sledd.'

Marlowe sat upright. 'You mean, this is witchcraft?'

Scot shook his head. 'No,' he said, 'but it may be murder in the name of witchcraft.'

Marlowe looked at the man for long seconds. Then he leaned forward and whispered to him, 'Play along, if only for a good actor's sake,' and he suddenly lashed out with both feet, thudding into Scot's chest and sending him crashing off the wagon. He leapt out after him and knelt beside the startled and winded hop grower, his dagger point pricking his throat. 'This is the man who killed Ned,' he shouted to the camp. 'Look –' he held up the bodkin – 'he has admitted that this is his.'

The company had formed themselves around the fallen Scot now, their faces dark with hatred.

'Kit . . .' Scot knew all about the mob baying for the blood of the guilty, even if the guilty were innocent. But he had never actually been on the receiving end before. He felt boots crash into his ribs and hands claw at his shirt before Liza clouted him round the head with a griddle pan.

'Hang him!' somebody shouted and they all took up the line. Only Joyce Clopton hung back. Only old Joseph was still manning the barricades, watching Greville's camp.

'No!' Marlowe's sword was suddenly in his hand from nowhere and he banged Liza's pan out of her hand so that it thudded to the ground some feet away. 'No, we'll have no more deaths here,' he growled, facing all of them down. 'We'll tie Master Scot to the cart's tail and take him to Oxford, to the Assizes there. The authorities will hang him come Michaelmas.'

There were mutinous mutterings, but there was no fight left in Strange's Men and Marlowe knew he had won the day. As they manhandled Scot to the furthest wagon and lashed his wrists together in front of him and then to the rear running board, Marlowe knew he had bought himself a few days.

'So, sisters,' the keeper of the Stones reported back to the women waiting in the trees, 'they have gone at last.'

There was an awkward shuffling of broken-down boots and finally Merriweather spoke for them all. 'Did you . . . help the man at the King Stone, sister?'

The fat woman's eyes narrowed further in their puffy sockets. 'Help?' she hissed.

'Help him . . . move on?' Merriweather persisted. She had personally never killed anyone, but she knew people who had. Nice people, who just had their reasons.

'No, I most certainly did not!' the fat woman snapped. 'He would be the last one I would want rid of. He was a credulous man but with no malice in him. There were plenty in that camp that deserved that fate before him.'

The blind woman stepped forward. 'I could smell bitterness and anger,' she said. 'There was one in that number who smelled like an ants' nest when the spade strikes it. If any living man did this, it was that one.'

'And which one was it, sister?' the youngest one of the party asked.

'You may not have noticed, sister,' the blind one said, her voice dripping honey over the vinegar, 'but I don't happen to have any eyes.' There was a silence. Then, she added, more kindly, 'But I would know him if we met again. By his stench.'

FOURTEEN

I t had been a difficult conversation but Joyce Clopton had
eventually agreed to let them carry the body of Ned Sledd
on her father's bier, in her father's coffin, on a bed of more
gold and silver than the actor-manager could have hoped to
earn in a lifetime.

They travelled at walking pace, the back riders changing
every now and then to keep watch on Greville's men who
followed them at a wary distance. Kit Marlowe was no general,
but he knew how vulnerable their little column was on the
open road without the wagons as a barricade and without Ned
Sledd to lead them. Simon Hayward knew the ground well
and suggested they keep to the main highway with its villages
and its people. All day the sun was bright in the cloudless
blue and summer had at last come to the Cotswolds. That
Hayward and Cawdray were still of the party had come as a
surprise to everyone, not least the men themselves. Hayward
was intent on making sure that no one tried to pin the murder
on him in his absence. Cawdray was still waiting to see his
play and it would take more than a dead actor-manager to
stop him.

Marlowe trotted up and down the line, pulling his horse in
alongside one wagon, dismounting to amble with those on foot,
talking all the time and, although they didn't know it, asking
key questions. Martin was driving Sledd's wagon, dragging the
quickly exhausted Reginald Scot in his dust as they rattled
through Chipping Norton with its mellow, yellow houses and
on through the gentle dip of the Glyne Valley. The grey stones
of the Hoar barrow stared down at them, as if wondering why
they had been so mad as to leave the shelter of the Rollrights,
their sister stones to the north-west.

Smocked labourers in their fields saw them go and tugged
off their caps to mark the passing of a funeral on the road.
And the rooks, black against the sun, bickered and fought in

the tall elms. Thomas sat hunched on the second wagon's tail, surrounded by costumes and women who patted him. The tears were tumbling down his cheeks still as Marlowe rode alongside. For seconds together, the lad could put aside his loss and then it would sweep across him brand new and searing, all over again. He knew he would get used to it one day, but he knew it would be no day soon.

'He was the best of us, Kit,' the boy said, 'The Player King. We shan't see his like again.'

Marlowe nodded.

'And the worst of it is, it's all my fault.' He buried his head in his hands.

Liza yanked him hard around the neck, her idea of a cuddle. 'I keep telling him, Master Marlowe, but he don't listen.'

'How is it your fault, Thomas?' the poet asked.

'I was asleep,' Thomas shouted as if God Himself did not know. 'I was on guard duty and I fell asleep. Any of those bastards from Greville's camp could have slipped past me in the dark.'

'But Scot's confessed, Thomas,' Marlowe lied.

The boy frowned up through his tears. 'Has he?' he asked.

Marlowe shrugged. 'As good as.'

Thomas shook his head. 'Makes no sense,' he said, trying to rationalize it. 'What had Scot got against Ned? You don't kill a man for no reason.'

'If that's true,' Marlowe said, 'then Scot is a liar and the killer has to be one of us.'

He watched Thomas's face change, darken with the realization of it. 'No,' he said, sniffing. 'That's not possible. We all loved Ned.' He looked around as if waiting for someone to challenge that statement. No one did. And he buried his face in his hands again, missing the man who had taken him in as a child, taught him to curtsy and how to wear a stomacher and farthingale. Greater love has no actor-manager.

Marlowe reached out an arm and patted the boy. 'Look after him, Liza,' he said and hauled his rein back so that the wagons rolled past and he turned the animal to amble with the riders at the back of the column.

'Damned hot, Marlowe,' Hayward grunted, trying to ease

his ruff. 'Look, I'm sorry about earlier, at the camp, I mean. We're all a bit on edge.'

Marlowe nodded. 'Think nothing of it, Master Hayward. I never thanked you properly for riding to our rescue like that. Happy coincidence, wasn't it?'

Hayward reined in and his horse halted. Marlowe did the same. 'All right,' Hayward said, 'let's have this out in the open once and for all. How long have you been with Strange's Men?'

'About two weeks,' Marlowe told him.

'And before that?'

Marlowe turned his animal's head and the pair rode on again. 'Before that I was a scholar at Cambridge.'

'So you don't really know Strange?'

'No. I never met the man until two weeks ago. The troupe was on its way to Stratford and I came upon them on the road. I had met Sledd before, in Cambridge last year.'

'Sledd handled the finances, did he?' Hayward asked.

'I really don't know.' Marlowe frowned. 'From what I saw, that might have been Lord Strange himself.'

'Yes,' Hayward growled. 'What do you make of that, Marlowe?'

'Of what, Master Hayward?'

'Come, come, sir.' Hayward eased his stiff neck from its position, watching the riders in the distance. 'You're a university man and I assume you weren't born yesterday. First the troupe's sponsor is taken peculiar and then the troupe's leader is murdered. If I didn't know better, I'd say somebody had it in for Lord Strange's Men, wouldn't you?'

'Greville's not with them.' Will Shaxsper was certain. He was at the rear of the column that afternoon as they trotted past Glympton with its little church and cluster of thatched roofs.

'I think you're right,' Marlowe said with a nod. 'I wonder how Captain Paget is feeling now he can't pick his nose so easily.'

'Was it one of them, do you think, Kit?' Shaxsper asked. 'One of Greville's people who killed Sledd?'

'If you look carefully ahead, Will,' Marlowe said, humouring the man, 'you'll see a certain Reginald Scot tied at the cart's tail. His bodkin was found in Sledd's throat, after all.'

'You don't believe that, do you, Kit?' Shaxsper asked. 'I mean, it's so obvious, isn't it?'

'Do you play cards, Will?' Marlowe asked. 'Cent? Lansquenet?'

'Sometimes,' Shaxsper said.

'The double bluff.' Marlowe tapped the side of his nose. 'Scot leaves his obvious weapon for us to find, so that we'll think just what you think. "Too obvious." It must be somebody else.'

'Murder will out,' Shaxsper said grimly. 'Beware the smiler with the knife.'

'That's rather good.' Marlowe smiled. 'Chaucer, isn't it?' Marlowe had passed too many clandestine quotes off as his own to be fooled by one as obvious as that one.

'Umm . . . is it?' Shaxsper asked, all hurt innocence, inwardly furious that Marlowe had his measure.

'It is.' Marlowe tapped the man's elbow. 'If you're going to be a success in London, Will,' he warned him, 'don't be a borrower – or a lender if it comes to that. Write your own stuff, there's a good boy.'

'Joseph.' Marlowe had to raise his voice over the rumble and rattle of the wagon. 'How goes it?'

The tragedian of Lord Strange's Men was in his element, three sheets to the wind on some of the choice Malmsey that Boscastle had smuggled out of Clopton Hall. The fruit of the vine had always made old Joseph lachrymose, but this evening, as the sun's shadows lengthened ahead of them on the road as they wound through the cornfields to Woodstock, he was positively awash in tears.

'I can't get poor young Ned out of my mind,' he bellowed in what to him was a stage whisper.

'A great loss,' Marlowe agreed.

'Yes,' Joseph sighed. 'Especially as I am responsible.'

Marlowe urged his horse closer so that his left leg was jammed against the cart's side. 'What do you mean?'

'Yes, you're right. Or at least as clean as you can be on the road all the time,' Joseph said, agreeing with something only he had heard and Marlowe had to pause a moment to work out what it could be. 'But we were talking of my terrible responsibility,' the old man boomed.

Marlowe could tell the best he could do in this conversation was to hop and skip along and hope to be dancing the same dance once in a while. 'How are you responsible?' he asked, enunciating each word like bells.

Joseph looked backward, then forward and at one time down at the ground as he momentarily lost his balance. He hugged the Malmsey bottle to his chest for comfort. 'I saw him last night,' he said.

'Ned?'

'No, no.' Joseph shook his head and closed his eyes. 'His murderer.'

'You did? When was this?'

'Last night,' Joseph said, wondering what sort of idiot they had writing plays these days.

'Who was it?' Marlowe could hear nothing now but his own voice rising about the thud of his own heart. People down the column were turning to look.

'Well, that's just it.' Joseph's face was a picture of helplessness. 'I don't know. It was late. I was . . . tired.' He glanced down at the bottle. 'It may be that I had had a spot to drink, to keep out the cold, you know, the damp ground . . . I couldn't focus. He fell over me to start with, in the dark, between the wagons and when I asked who goes, he said, "Where's Ned?" I told him, I said, "Over there, by the King Stone."'

'And that's where he went?' Marlowe asked. 'This murderer of yours? Towards the King Stone?'

'No.' Joseph tried desperately to remember. 'No, he went the other way, towards . . . the other way.'

'What did he say, Joseph?' Marlowe asked him, leaning in as far as horse, jolting wagon and Joseph's breath would allow. '*Exactly*, now. Word for word.' His heart fell as he suddenly realized that 'word for word' and Joseph had parted company long ago. Even so, for a moment at least, hope sprang eternal.

Joseph had not always seen eye to eye with Ned Sledd but he had been as fond of him as the rest of Lord Strange's Men, perhaps more so, as he could see himself in him, before the drink and age had done their dread work. So he really tried as hard as he could to remember the night before, which, as far as his memory was concerned, might just as well have been a decade ago. Joseph was waiting for the moment when distant memory was clear as day; he couldn't remember anything at all before breakfast and that only applied until about midday. Then it was anything before dinner.

'He said . . .' His face was screwed up with the effort of remembering. 'He said "Where's Ned?" He might have said something else, but I didn't catch it. People mumble these days, don't you find? Well, anyway, I said . . .' His eyes widened and his face reddened as it all came back to him. 'I said, "Where would you expect a man like Ned to be? By the King Stone, of course." Oh, God –' and his voice rumbled deep with sorrow – 'I sent him to his grave. I may as well have thrust that bodkin into his throat myself. And the throat, of all places! That golden voice, those syllables that soared aloft like . . . like . . .' He glanced around for inspiration. 'Pigeons!' It didn't sound right, but a swig of the bottle soon sorted that out.

'No, no, Joseph.' Marlowe patted the man's sinewy arm. 'It was probably just a dream. You were tired. You may have had a drink and we had all had an exciting day. The mind plays tricks. Don't worry. We'll find out who killed Ned. I promise.'

And he hauled on the rein again, leaving the old man to wrestle with his demons.

At first she had protested. Then, when he countered each of her arguments one by one, she just stood defiant and alone, looking first at Marlowe, then at Boscastle. She knew they were right. And it would only be for a short time. And Boscastle would be with her.

'Would the queen want a disinherited Papist under her roof, Kit?' she had asked him.

'The Queen knows all about what it feels like to be disinherited, My Lady and she has not been under the roof of Woodstock Manor for more years than we have been alive, you and I. They say her steward there is a kindly man. He

has, I am told, daughters of his own and his wife will not turn
away an orphan of the storm.'

She looked at Boscastle again and knew a male conspiracy
when she saw one. He read her mind. 'Our people will be
safe enough on the road, My Lady,' he said. 'But you and . . .
the coffin . . . will be safe in the manor house. And I shall be
at your side.'

He saw her father in her briefly, before age and sadness had
taken him, a bear of a man who knew his own mind and would
not be crossed. Her eyes smouldered just like his.

'Very well,' she said. 'But only until such time as the
authorities in Oxford can disperse the rabble at our heels.'

'We'll have to be quick and we'll have to be careful,'
Marlowe said. 'Boscastle, can you have the bier limbered by
midnight at the back of the Woolsack? There's a quiet lane
that will lead you out of sight of Greville's men. It will have
to be just the two of you; more will attract notice. Can you
do it?'

Boscastle nodded. 'Leave it to me,' he said.

'What about Master Sledd's body?' she asked. 'Surely, his
people . . .'

'. . . would want it given a decent burial,' Marlowe said.
'They have nowhere to call home, no churchyard where their
dead are laid. Ask the steward at Woodstock to lend some
earth to a good man and make sure he is laid in it with respect.
He will live forever where anyone forgets a line.'

'We'll do that,' Joyce said. 'And we'll make sure he has a
marker, for if his people ever pass that way.'

'He'd like that,' Marlowe said. 'Make sure you spell it right
– he was very proud of that double dee.'

'Kit . . . this isn't your way of getting rid of us, is it? You're
not abandoning us?'

'Of course not,' he said. 'Once we're in Oxford, I'll send
word to the magistrates. We'll be back in three days at most.'

She looked into those dark dancing eyes. 'Three days,' she
said. 'Or I'll go toe to toe with Edward Greville myself.'

The candles fluttered against their reflections in the window
panes like so many moths, sending magical lights radiating

around Richard Cawdray's room. He and Simon Hayward had taken rooms at the Woolsack, anxious to have soft beds after a hard day on the road.

'What do you make of it, Master Cawdray?' Marlowe sipped his wine. 'Scot and Ned Sledd?'

'Bizarre.' Cawdray shook his head. 'Quite bizarre.'

'He said it could be witchcraft,' Marlowe told him.

'Who?'

'Scot. Obviously trying to muddy the waters. He's guilty as a pikestaff.'

'What will you do with him?'

'Well, tomorrow, I'll pass him over to the town constable, if they have one. If not, we'll take him on to Oxford. Tell me, how long have you known Simon Hayward?'

'Er . . . we met on the road on our respective ways to Stratford. I do so love the theatre, you see. That's why I particularly wanted to see Lord Strange's Men in action. The great Ned Alleyn in particular.'

'Except that the great Ned Alleyn isn't here, of course,' Marlowe remarked.

'He's not? I thought . . .'

'If you had found us earlier, say two weeks ago, you'd have met him then. He left, though.'

'Left?' Cawdray raised an eyebrow. 'Dramatic differences?'

'Theft,' Marlowe said, crisply. 'He stole my play.'

'The devil,' said Cawdray. 'No honour among thespians, eh? I expect you'd like to run into Master Alleyn again?'

'It would be an . . . experience,' Marlowe admitted. 'They tell me Martin is just as good, so I'm sure Alleyn's lack won't spoil your enjoyment when you finally get to see us in action. Shaxsper is coming along too, now he has stopped being such a hot-headed idiot. But, tell me, Master Cawdray, do you think that Reginald Scot is guilty?'

Cawdray shrugged. 'I would have thought the bodkin speaks for itself,' he said.

'Yes.' Marlowe smiled. 'Yes, probably. So, you'll stay with us to Oxford?'

'I wouldn't miss it. What are you going to perform? I suppose with Master Sledd gone it will be difficult.'

'We'll send young Thomas on ahead tomorrow to look out the ground for us. We probably won't perform in a college; they'd expect erudition, scholarship, rhetoric.'

'Whereas . . .?'

'Whereas Nat Sawyer does a particularly good sketch with a balloon and a stuffed parrot, I understand.'

'Ah, comedy.' Cawdray smiled, sipping his wine. 'My wife's favourite.'

'Given what has happened,' Marlowe said, 'it's perhaps a blessing she's not with you.'

He saw the man's face darken. 'No,' he said, 'not so much a blessing as a curse.'

'I'm sorry,' Marlowe said, suspecting that he had committed a rather major faux pas. 'I don't understand.'

'My wife was taken from me, Master Marlowe,' Cawdray said quietly, looking thoughtfully into his goblet of wine, 'by her own hand, I fear.'

Marlowe looked at the man. 'I'm sorry,' he said. There was nothing else he could say in these circumstances.

Cawdray crossed to the flame-lit window and looked down at the huddled figure of Reginald Scot curled up in the hay of the yard below and still tied to his cart. 'She was to have had a child,' he said, looking now at his reflection in the glass. 'Something . . . and I don't know what . . . turned her mind.' He turned to Marlowe. 'So she killed herself and her baby.'

'You blame her for that?' Marlowe asked.

'No.' Cawdray shook his head. 'I blame God, the Devil, myself . . . anyone but her. People were very kind. She drowned herself in the lake in the grounds of our house. They said she had slipped in, swooned . . . but they didn't see the letter she left. No one did, save me.' He laid a hand over his heart. 'I carry it here, always.'

Marlowe could think of nothing to say to comfort this man, whose grief was so raw it seemed to fill the room.

'She had said we must fill in the lake before the baby came. So that the grounds would be safe.' He smiled. 'I still filled it in, you know, and sometimes, when I first wake in the morning, I am glad I did. To make it safe for the children.' He looked up at Marlowe. 'Most people smile at this point,

Master Marlowe. They think this story has a happy ending, that I married again and filled my house with children, sons and daughters. But you say nothing.'

'I am a poet,' Marlowe said. 'A playwright. A scholar. I know that life has more sad endings than happy ones. The tragedies get bigger audiences than the comedies. I am so very sorry for your loss.'

'I wish I could find someone who I could blame, you know,' Cawdray said, almost to himself. 'Revenge is sweet, or so they say.'

'Oh, yes,' Marlowe said. 'Perhaps I should have said: the revenge tragedies get the biggest audiences of all. And now, if you'll excuse me, I must check the prisoner before I go to bed. Goodnight, Master Cawdray.'

'And to you, Master Marlowe.'

'Hasn't this gone far enough?' Reginald Scot wanted to know. He ached in every limb and his wrists were rubbed raw by the ropes that had tied him to Martin's wagon. His left sole had parted company with its uppers and the straw he was now sitting on was sharp and scratchy.

'You are a murderer, Master Scot,' Marlowe said loudly, keeping up the pretence as he sat down next to him. Then he added, in a whisper, 'Sorry, Reginald, but it's paying dividends already, our little subterfuge.'

'Is it?'

'Well, no.' Marlowe had to confess. 'But it will. Joseph knows who killed Ned.'

'He does? He doesn't strike me as a man who knows his arse from a hole in the ground.' Reginald Scot was not an unkind man or one who usually resorted to obscene language but he had been sorely tried and he was not in the mood to be pleasant when there was a chance to be otherwise.

'A fair assessment, Reginald, I'll give you that. I put it down to a lifetime of drink and speaking other people's words. But it is locked in there, in whatever passes for his poor, befuddled old brain. God save us from turning into old actors, eh?'

'God, Kit?' Scot raised an eyebrow. 'That's an odd notion, coming from you.'

'Is it?'

Scot rested his aching back against the wagon's wheel. It was hard but it gave him support. 'I've been with you a few days now,' he said, 'all told. When men are afraid – as we all were at the stones – their old instincts show. Half these people are of the old religion – Shaxsper, Joyce Clopton, Boscastle and his people. They all, to a man and woman, crossed themselves in fear. But you,' he said, 'a scholar of Corpus Christi and a man destined for the church, as I understand it, you did not. You've left your God behind somewhere, haven't you?'

Marlowe smiled. 'Along with your friends the witches.'

'Ah, no,' Scot said, stony-faced. 'They are no friends of mine. Tell me, Kit, what's the date?'

'The date? I don't know. The twenty-ninth, I think. Why do you ask?'

'Lammas,' Scot said. 'Lammastide.'

'August the first,' Marlowe said.

'Shaxsper and company are of the old religion,' Scot said, 'but . . . my friends the witches, as you put it . . . are of an older faith still. They worship the horned god.'

'The Devil,' Marlowe said.

'The Devil, Satan, the Great Beast, Prince of Darkness. He has many names. And below him there are sixty-six infernal princes, each of whom command six thousand, six hundred and sixty-six legions of Hell. Each legion has six thousand, six hundred and sixty-six demons. Add that lot together and you have half the population of the world. Saint Athenius once wrote "The air is filled with demons". They are all around us, Kit.'

'I thought you didn't believe any of this claptrap.'

'Hocus pocus,' Scot said, 'the rubbish the witches chant. But what is that but *hoc est corpus*, this is the body of Christ, which all Christians chant every Sunday at communion? Just because we don't believe it doesn't mean it isn't real.'

Marlowe was impressed by this man who, bloody and sore, could still ride his hobby horse. 'So, what are you saying?' he asked.

'I'm saying that, come what may, I must be back at the Rollrights by Lammastide. To the witches, it is Lugnasadh, one of their great ceremonies. They dance widdershins, sky clad under the moon and prostrate themselves before their horned god.'

'And you want to see it?' Marlowe nodded. The scholar in him appreciated how important it was to get things *right*. Sometimes, only personal research would do and this was not a thing to find in a library. Even though he had known some very strange librarians in his time.

'If you remember,' Scot said, 'I went to Meon Hill for a new chapter to add to my book. That's why I was there. Although I admit the arrival of your troupe rather –' he shook his bound wrists – 'altered the direction of my life.'

'Why were you at Clopton?' Marlowe asked him. 'What has Clopton to do with your horned god?'

Scot looked at the man sitting cross-legged opposite him. 'I thought I might find him there,' he said.

'And did you?'

'No. But I found his handiwork. Lord Strange.'

Marlowe nodded. 'The poppet.'

'The poison poured into the man's goblet by someone working in the Clopton kitchens. The Maiden.'

'Who?'

'The Maiden is the creature of the horned god. She is at once his skivvy and lover. At the Sabbat at Lugnasadh she will be the first to feel him inside her and to receive his seed which, so they say, is as cold as ice.'

'Do you know who she is?'

Scot shook his head. 'No,' he said, 'but we'll find out if we go back to the Rollrights. That is their holy place and the coven will have been gathering for weeks now, preparing for their diabolical ceremony, for the sacrifice. They will have ridden there on toads and black horses and broomsticks.'

'An arresting sight on the road, I would imagine.'

'Indeed it would be. They also imagine that they stand ten feet tall and can fly over hedges and ditches, steeples if the fancy takes them. It's the hemlock talking, of course. They rub it into the skin and it causes hallucinations. It's very real to them.'

'Sometimes your hops can have the same result,' Marlowe

said with a smile. 'I've seen scholars in Cambridge who thought they could jump the river from a standing start.'

'Any successes?'

'Not as yet.'

'And so it is with witches. Even when witnesses swear to them that they have not moved, they have an answer for it, that their god has closed their eyes, that kind of thing.' He sighed. 'It makes them very difficult to research properly. That's why I want to see their Sabbat. And it's up to you, Kit, whether I can be there or not. Given that I'm here on a charge of murder concocted by you.'

'There are ways around that,' Marlowe said.

'Oh? What?' And Scot flinched as Marlowe's dagger scythed through the air and its razor edge sliced through the hemp around his wrists.

Scot knelt up, willing his numb feet to obey his brain and chafing his painful wrists with fingers that scarcely worked. 'Thanks for that. What now? Do I just vanish?'

'This Sabbat of yours,' Marlowe said. 'How many will be there?'

'Thirteen, of course,' Scot told him. 'It is a black parody of Our Lord and his disciples. Twelve and one.'

'The Dark One.' Marlowe nodded. 'Any idea who that might be?'

Scot looked puzzled. 'I told you. The Great Beast. Beelzebub. Lord of—'

'Yes,' Marlowe broke in. 'You told me *that*. But who *is* it, do you think? Who is . . . I can't think of any other way of putting this, Reginald. You don't really think it is the Devil, do you?' He looked at him closely. 'Or do you?' He was beginning to regret cutting him loose. The man was clearly barking mad. All that research into arcana had clearly clouded his senses.

'Oh, I see. Who *is* it? Well, I have absolutely no idea.'

'That will be fun then, to expose him.'

Scot looked puzzled all over again. 'Why would I want to do that?' he asked.

'Well, to stop him having sabbats all over the place, I would have thought. Depraving local crones, that kind of thing. It

can't be good for the morale of these villages, Reginald, to
have this kind of behaviour going on. And it is, as I understand
it, against the law.'

'Of 1562, yes, but I hadn't taken you for a prude, Kit,' Scot
said, still rubbing his wrists.

'And you would be right,' Marlowe said. 'But I have seen
some strange things in my life, and the fewer of them there
are around, the better I like it.'

'It is an ancient religion,' Scot pointed out.

'I seem to remember you mentioned sacrifice,' Marlowe
riposted.

'Of a goat, a kid. Perhaps a lamb or calf. Not a person,'
Scot said. 'They may talk of such things, but they wouldn't
kill a *person*.'

'What, like no one would have killed Ned Sledd? Lord
Strange? William Clopton?'

Scot looked thoughtful. 'I see you intend to come with me.
But I really don't want to interfere, Kit.'

'I have a compromise, Reginald,' Marlowe offered. 'If there
is no sacrifice, no one is in danger, everyone seems to just be
enjoying a roll in the hay under the moon, I agree to leave
well enough alone. But, if anyone is clearly coerced, in danger
. . .'

'Then you'll step out with your dagger?' Scot asked. 'Don't
forget there will be thirteen of them and only two of us. Unless
you have others in mind to have tag along. I can see my covert
watching is getting less likely to succeed.'

'No, no, Reginald. I won't spoil your spying. I do have a
plan.'

'What do you propose?' Scot asked.

'Help yourself to a horse,' Marlowe suggested. 'After mine,
Simon Hayward's is the best we have.'

'Why . . .?'

'I can't ask any of Lord Strange's Men to get involved in
this,' Marlowe said. 'They've been through enough. But
Masters Hayward and Cawdray have already proved they can
handle themselves – and in somebody else's fight. To be doubly
sure, however, if you just happen to have ridden off on Master
Hayward's horse, it's odds on he'll come looking for you.'

'Brilliant, Kit!' Scot snapped his thumb and forefinger, quite pleased that he could still do it. 'Wait a minute, though.' He stopped in his tracks as realization dawned. 'I can be hanged for horse stealing.'

Marlowe smiled at him. 'You can be hanged for murder too, Reginald. Life can be a bitch, can't it? Choice, choices, always choices.'

With a sigh, Scot walked off, limping only slightly, to where Hayward's horse waited for him in its stall.

Reginald Scot was sitting on an elder stump that afternoon, his ink and paper beside him, making notes for the new chapter for his book. The hot sun had made him mellow and perhaps a little light-headed and he found himself listening to the crickets in the long grass and watching the butterflies chase each other in their spiralling flights over the fields. His senses were heightened by the heat of the day and the breathless air so that he almost thought he could see the rainbow dust flick from their wings with every beat. The words of an old folk song came into his mind with its strange, haunting tune: 'Fly over moor and fly over mead, Fly over living and fly over dead, Fly you east or fly you west, Fly to her that loves me best.'

'That had better be Mistress Scot, hop grower, or there'll be Hell to pay.'

Scot shrieked and fell off his stump, ink and parchment going everywhere. He squinted up at the figure standing above him, half blotting out the sun. 'Marlowe,' he growled. 'Damn you, Kit, my heart is beating fit to burst out of my chest. You could have killed me.'

'That's what Master Hayward planned to do until I explained the circumstances,' Marlowe said and waved an arm to the two horsemen sitting on their animals on the slope of the hill.

'I didn't hear a thing,' Scot said. 'How did three men on horses creep up on me so quietly?'

Marlowe looked north into the hazy distance. 'Isn't that Meon Hill over there?' he said. 'I think you'll find that explains it all.'

And Scot threw his book at him. Rather pointedly, Simon

Hayward dismounted and strode towards the trees, patting the rump and shoulder of his stolen horse before untethering it and hauling it away. 'Just for the record,' he grunted to Scot, '*my* horse. You can have this bloody bag of bones I've been jolted around on all morning. *And* you can pick up the cost of the hire.'

Richard Cawdray led his horse forward by the bridle and helped Scot up. 'I hope this isn't some wild-goose chase, Master Scot,' he said. 'Marlowe here says you may need our help.'

Scot looked at the poet. 'I may, gentlemen,' he said, 'but I should warn you first that come midnight you may see sights you'd wish you never had. If you are of nervous dispositions . . .'

Marlowe clapped Scot on the back. 'There's no chance of that,' he said. 'The deal I promised Hayward is that if the witches didn't ride I'd let him hang you as a horse thief. Either way, his day is made.'

'I don't mind telling you, Martin,' Will Shaxsper said, 'I don't like this. What exactly did Marlowe say?'

The actor looked out from the tower of the church of Mary Magdalene, his eyes fixed on the camp of Greville's men that still clustered on the far side of the river. 'I told you,' Martin said. 'He and the gentlemen had urgent business, viz and to wit, to catch Reginald Scot, the murderer.'

'Yes.' Shaxsper gnawed his lip. 'Murder's out of tune and sweet revenge grows harsh.'

'Marlowe?' Martin thought it sounded familiar.

'Do you mind?' Shaxsper rounded on him. 'That's a small thing, but it *is* mine own!'

'Sorry,' Martin said, shrugging. He clicked his tongue with impatience. 'What are they waiting for?' he hissed, watching Greville's men, the distance making them look like ants, but ants who had lost their work ethic as they sat dicing and playing cards on the river bank. Every now and then a little lawyer with his arm in a sling waddled back and forth, looking at Woodstock through the summer's haze.

A new gloom had descended on Shaxsper. 'They're waiting to realize that we've lost our best people,' he said. 'Oh, no offence to you, Martin, and I fancy I can wield a reasonable sword myself, but Marlowe, Scot, Cawdray, Hayward, Lady Joyce and Boscastle have gone. Even Thomas has nipped on ahead to Oxford. Where *is* everybody?'

'Don't worry,' Martin said with a smile. 'You get used to this taking a show on the road. I've played to smaller houses scores of times. If you're going to be an actor, Will, it's just something you have to live with.'

'I don't care about the size of the *house!*' Shaxsper yelled. 'I care about escaping with my skin.'

'You have that worry when you take a show on the road as well,' Martin said, fingering his head reminiscently. 'Feel there.' He lowered his head to Shaxsper. 'Go on.'

The poet reached out a tentative finger. 'A bump.'

'Fire irons. Flung from the crowd in Highgate, summer of . . . oh, when was it? 1581, I think it was. I was out cold for nearly three days. Now, that *was* a tough crowd.'

A silence fell between them with only the distant sounds from the Greville camp to break it. Shaxsper dropped his chin on to his hands, folded on to the warm stones of Mary Magdalene. He missed his children, he even missed his wife. His nice little cottage, even if it was currently full of his father and various cousins and aunts. An actor's life was not for him, he decided. At this point he didn't really mind what life he had, as long as there was quite a lot more of it still to come.

FIFTEEN

Kit Marlowe had always had enough thoughts in his head to kill the slowest time and he had a facility for closing his ears to the babble around him without taking on a vacant look which would give the game away. Hayward had never had such an appreciative audience for his hunting sagas and even if the poet didn't wince quite enough at the disembowelling episode, then Hayward was still content. Cawdray and Scot hatched a complex plan to watch the coming Sabbat, involving all kinds of arcane lighting devices. It wasn't really important that Marlowe wasn't listening, because they didn't stand a hope in Hell of working. Scot realized this as soon as Cawdray started talking about walrus blubber, which apparently burnt with a particularly clear light. Witches had very sensitive noses, or so they claimed; they would be sure to smell it and besides, where would they get a walrus at this time of night? Marlowe was repeating the lines over and over in his head; he knew this poem was a keeper and had no means of writing it down in that he had a pencil but no paper. And anyway, what was the point of writing things down if actors could just walk off with it when they chose? As the evening wore on, the conversation grew more desultory until it ceased altogether.

Scot suddenly spoke in a harsh whisper. 'Kit!'

'Come, live with me and be my love,' Marlowe said, startled out of his internal poem.

If Scot was surprised he didn't show it. 'I'd have to check with Mistress Scot, of course, but I'm sure we would get on famously,' he said. 'But there are more important things afoot, Kit.'

Marlowe shook his head and smiled sleepily. 'Sorry,' he said. 'Miles away. Has something begun?'

'By no means,' Scot said. 'The Sabbat itself won't start until just before midnight. They like to come to the climax of the ceremony then. No, I thought we should perhaps think of getting into position. We won't be able to if it gets any darker. If we start blundering about in the dark we'll give the game away, I'm afraid. We don't want to be seen.'

'Why not?' Hayward asked sharply. 'I thought the idea was that we should unmask these fiends of Hell? As they take to the air of their evil steeds, we will leap out and drag them down to the earth that had . . .'

A strange light had come into Simon Hayward's eye and he was releasing rather too much spit. Scot stopped him by placing his hand gently on his arm. He had seen this kind of zealot before and it usually resulted in some poor old soul being trotted around a room until she dropped dead.

'Master Hayward,' he said. 'We are not here to unmask anyone. Don't forget that these are deluded women – and men, often – who think that the Devil is their God. They don't fly, except in their imaginations. They can't conjure storms or kill people. What I want is to see a Sabbat so I can write it up in my next edition. You do understand that, don't you? All of you?' He looked around their small circle. The men nodded, but Hayward looked unsure. Scot decided that he would keep him by him, so that he could make sure he didn't ruin everything.

Marlowe reached across and slapped Scot on the back. 'We understand, Reginald,' he said. 'And just to show you how much I want to help, I would like to give you this.' He held out his loaned pencil.

'How kind,' said Scot, dubiously. 'A small piece of wood, wound with string. Some kind of personal talisman, is it, Kit? You should know that I don't really believe in such things.'

Hayward eyed it superstitiously and Cawdray leaned forward and took it. 'Is this a pencil?' he asked Marlowe, who nodded. 'I have heard of them.' He turned to the others. 'It is graphite, from the north, Northumberland, I think. It is very soft and leaves a mark on paper, a little like charcoal but less messy. An expensive trinket for a wandering playwright.' He looked at Marlowe appraisingly.

'A gift,' Marlowe said. 'No, I should be more accurate, a loan, from Lord Ferdinando Strange. I am just a little tired of being splattered with ink when I am near Master Scot. Just look at my boots.' He thrust out one leg for them to see the fine spatter of black on the soft tan leather, but it had become too dark to see much more than shapes. 'It is dark, suddenly,' he said. 'Reginald is right, we should be in position. Where would you like us?' he asked the witch expert.

'I think we should stay in pairs,' Scot said, looking meaningfully at Hayward. 'Because you and I have discussed this at length over the last few days, Kit, I suggest that we split up and each one takes either Master Cawdray or Master Hayward. Which do you prefer?' But before Marlowe could express any kind of preference, he said, 'I'll take Master Hayward. As for position, anywhere out of sight but from where you can see the stones. If I were to advise you, I would say make sure there is something at your back.'

'Why?' Cawdray said. 'In case a witch creeps up on us unawares?'

'No,' Scot said, 'unless you have some kind of trouble with old ladies coming up behind you. No, I merely suggest that so your cover is more complete. Don't forget –' and again he glared at Hayward, who seemed immune to hints and suggestion – 'our aim is to watch and learn and remain undetected.'

'We understand,' Hayward said, testily. 'I'll go with Scot, then. We'll see you at the foot of the hill, when we have seen what there is to see.'

'That's the spirit,' Cawdray said. 'If you go first and conceal yourselves, we'll follow and choose our place.'

Scot and Hayward crept around the side of the hill and soon they could be seen as silhouettes against the darkening sky.

'How will we see where they have gone?' Marlowe said, suddenly seeing a flaw in the plan.

'If it doesn't get too dark before they are in position, this will help us,' Cawdray said, and took a tube from within his jerkin and handed it to Marlowe. 'Have you seen one of these? It is an array of lenses which can make distant things seem nearer.'

'I have heard of such things,' Marlowe said, 'but not seen one.' It seemed to him the kind of invention that Nicholas

Faunt would be keeping more than a weather eye on. It seemed
made for people like him and his dark doings. 'How does it
work?'

Hayward took it from him and held it up to his eye. 'It isn't
always easy to use,' he said. 'You need to focus your eye
through the tube on the distant object. This suits my eyes very
well, but some with shorter or longer sight than mine can see
less well. I think that there will be improvements, but for now
it serves.' He was quiet for a moment then said, 'I see them.
They are at the far end of the stone circle from here and have
concealed themselves in a bush, a tangle more than a bush.
We should try and find our hiding place on the other side.'

'May I try it?' Marlowe asked, holding out his hand.

'By all means,' Cawdray said. 'Look over there at the
horizon. It will be easier for you to see than the dark side of
the hill.'

Marlowe screwed up one eye and put the tube to the other.
He scanned the horizon from east to west and then swung
back a little, peering intently.

'What can you see?' Cawdray asked, looking in the same
direction.

'I thought I saw . . . but no, it was nothing.' He handed the
tube back and Cawdray stowed it away again inside his doublet.
'That thing is a great invention to trick the eye. I thought I
saw a horseman on the road, but when I looked again he was
gone.'

'It can mislead, you're right,' Cawdray admitted, 'especially
when you first use it. But –' and he patted his chest – 'I find
it useful every now and then. The hunt. That kind of thing.
But, Kit, I think we should be on the move. The moon is up
and if we wait longer we will stand out like a white hart in a
dark wood.'

'Very poetic image, Master Cawdray,' Marlowe said. 'Do
you dabble?'

'I wouldn't presume,' Cawdray said. 'I have no skill at any
of the creative arts. I merely observe. Shall I go first?'

Marlowe extended a hand and fell into step behind Cawdray,
who, if he wasn't creative, was certainly very good at keeping
to the shadows and at picking his way over rough ground.

They were soon at the top of the hill and at once discovered that Scot and Hayward had already collared the only comfortable cover. Marlowe and Cawdray would have to lie under the lee of a hedge, one arm around the bole of a tree and their legs braced against the bank.

'Do you suffer from cramp, Master Marlowe?' Cawdray asked. 'But perhaps not – your bones are younger than mine.'

'I have not found cramp to be a problem, no,' Marlowe said, squeezing himself closer to the ground and tucking his collar into his doublet so that the moon would not pick out the white. 'I hope tonight does not prove to be my first experience of it.'

'Unfortunately,' Cawdray said, 'I suffer sometimes with a nervous twitch in my legs. My late wife often complained of it. She said other men did not kick in the night.' There was a silence, then he said, 'I would tease her, saying that she ought not to know such things. How we would laugh.' He sighed. 'I miss her so much, Kit. She has been gone nearly a year and I miss her so much.'

'She is not gone if you think of her,' Marlowe said. 'The dead don't leave us if their names are still spoken.' He felt the man's hand on his shoulder for a brief second.

'A lovely thought, Master Poet,' Cawdray muttered. 'Thank you.'

There was no movement from the clump of stunted trees opposite and the moon was temporarily behind a cloud. There was nothing to do but wait. Marlowe let himself doze lightly but with one eye metaphorically open. Having to hang on with one hand made it impossible to sleep properly without jumping awake with every slight relaxation. The feeling of falling off a log that comes so often on the point of sleep was quite literally a fact in his precarious position. Then Cawdray tapped him on the shoulder with the fingers of his gripping hand.

'What in the name of all Heaven is that stench?' he asked. The words were scarcely out of his mouth before a shrill voice took over the silence of the night. 'Buy venny dollies mere piss kays,' it sang, over and over. The tune was a parody of a chant from the psaltery; the choirboy still buried deep in Marlowe recognized it as the setting of the Twenty-Third Psalm.

But the words eluded him, though they sounded vaguely
familiar. But that smell! He could hardly breathe for it and he
opened his mouth to try and minimize the horror. 'Breathe
through your mouth,' he whispered to Cawdray. 'You can't
risk being sick.'

The moon came out as though on a cue and into the circle
danced a young girl, naked as the day she was born. It was
her voice they had heard and in her upraised hands she carried
a wooden platter. As she whirled round in a mad galliard the
platter spun in the moon's beams. It was heaped with fish and
Marlowe realized that it was the source of the smell. He could
see them, piled up and slithering across one another. He
wondered why they didn't fall off as she spun and sang her
way around the circle. Then he saw that what he had taken
for movement was in fact the seethe of maggots over their
rotting scales. These fish had not swum for many a long day
and were stinking with putrefaction. The words suddenly made
sense too. 'Buy *veni dulcis me pisces*,' the girl was singing.
'Come buy my fresh fish.'

Marlowe and Cawdray looked like fish themselves, lying
caught in the toils of the hedge, mouths gaping. They rolled
their eyes at one another, unable to do more. The girl's song
and dance came to an end and she took up a place nearest the
biggest stone, with her back to Hayward and Scot. Marlowe
could almost imagine he could hear Scot's pencil skittering
like a mouse across his parchment. Either they were getting
used to the smell or the wind had shifted, because it seemed
less overpowering. The girl was standing unabashed in her
nakedness, her face turned up to the moon, her hands caressing
her breasts and thighs but almost absent-mindedly, as though
the body she stroked belonged to someone else. Marlowe heard
Cawdray catch his breath and when he looked he had turned
his face away and had let go of the sapling for long enough
to cross himself.

The silence after the piercing notes of her song sang with
echoes. Then, shuffling into the circle came the fat keeper of
the stones. She was carrying a plate of cooked chicken, also
teeming with maggots and smeared with something it was best
not to think of; Marlowe thought he heard a sound from the

bushes concealing Scot and Hayward which may have been a stifled retch, but if it was, the women didn't hear it. The fat woman was also naked, with folds of flesh hanging down, one over the other, like a frozen fountain in winter. Her thighs rubbed together and her knees turned in with the weight and her breasts almost covered her stomach, so pendulous were they. As she passed close to their hiding place, they smelt the vinegary tang of unwashed flesh long hidden in filthy clothes and basted in the sweat of years. The chicken was almost appetizing by comparison. Marlowe felt that the widower would not need to cross himself as she went past and a glance told him he was right. Her song was a mumbled groan, with no words discernible, but the tune, such as it was, was a parody of a psalm. She took up her place opposite the fish carrier and her buttocks filled Marlowe's field of vision so that when the next woman came into the circle he had to turn his head as best he could to see past her.

The next woman was not alone, nor was she carrying anything, although her companion carried a jug, brimming with something glutinous which ran down her leg as she stumbled occasionally on the rough grass. Here was the blind woman, the one with no eyes who had so frightened Lord Strange on the road. She was led by a statuesque blonde who even in her stumbles had a natural grace. She held her head high and keened in a voice which Marlowe admired for its range and velvety tone. She could charm the birds from the trees even in this strange and eerie setting and, as if to prove it, an owl fluttered like a white ghost ahead of her. The two took up position along the perimeter of the circle, at a point halfway between the others. The blonde woman put down her pitcher and ran a lazy finger through the liquid on her thigh. She offered it to the blind woman, who licked at it avidly. Marlowe didn't have to look to know that Cawdray was crossing himself again.

The songs were mingling now, no words to speak of but some kind of strange, atonal harmony was developing and Marlowe felt an almost irresistible urge to join in. Although the women were all looking at the sky, he could tell that they were very much aware of each other. Each one was beginning to sway, each in her own style. The first dancer who had entered the circle was shifting from one leg to the other, thrusting her hips to an invisible lover. The keeper of the stones was swaying her shoulders only, one hand in the small of her back, the classic stance of the old lady with a painful spine. Marlowe felt a twinge of pity for the grotesque thing, driven to this unnatural way of life when she should have been at home in a cottage dandling her grandchildren on her knee. For all it was summer the wind was beginning to blow a little chill and he could see the gooseflesh start to ripple in waves across her thighs and back. The blind woman had taken one step to the side away from her guide and was swaying like a willow in a gale. The blonde goddess was scarcely moving, squeezing her thighs together and smiling a secret smile as she reached out with her fingers daubed with the unspeakable liquid to feed her companion, who seemed to sense the fingers as they approached and sucked them greedily.

Then, the circle seemed full of processing women, some carrying plates of rotting or desecrated food and every one of them naked. They walked round the circle of stones, picking up the waiting witches as they went, until there was an unbroken ring of them, chanting, singing, shuffling, leaping or dancing according to their abilities. They were easy to count, unlike the stones, because no two were even a little alike. There were old and young, beautiful and almost unspeakably ugly, fat, thin, lissom and stiff and creaking.

Round and round they went, until Marlowe thought his head would never stop spinning. He and Cawdray gripped each other's shoulders for comfort and squeezed every now and again, to keep reality where it should be, inside their heads and looking out of their eyes. Marlowe believed in nothing but himself; he had no God and therefore no Devil, but even he could sense a presence in the circle, riding on the shoulders of every one of the deluded women as they circled and sang. There was a dark shape above each one, flying through the air and spiralling up to the bright face of the moon, shrieking its defiance to the sky. If he closed his eyes the image faded and the sounds from the circle became just the mumbles of old women, overlaid by the bell-like song of the bird charmer.

He shook his head and bit down hard on the inside of his lip. The salt taste of blood and the pain brought him back to himself again and he watched the developing scene with human eyes, with no deluding curtain in front of them.

Twisting his head, he could see that Cawdray's eyes were a little glazed, but every now and then he would squeeze them shut and duck his head. Then, for a while, he would focus. Marlowe knew that he was thinking of his wife, his fixed point in all he did. He just hoped that Cawdray's adoration of the dead woman would give him strength to resist the powers of the live ones who were now racing round and round in a tightening circle before their eyes. Something was happening, a climax was coming and they must keep their heads clear. The ground in the circle was a mess of trampled, rotting food, spilled wine, and what he thought must be urine from the smell. Some of the women had seemed to be peeing as they ran. Others had squatted briefly out of the dance and had smeared themselves with the results of their labours. He wondered what mind had imagined that the Devil would want his disciples to behave this way. In his experience, the most evil men he had ever met had been very fond of their comfort and the thought of a fat old woman smeared with piss and shit would not have been their idea of a companion for any purpose. He wondered as the women came together in a disordered rabble in the middle of the circle how Scot and Hayward were managing, over across the circle in their clump of trees.

SIXTEEN

Scot and Hayward had started off the evening's events in a much more comfortable hiding place than Marlowe and Cawdray. Hayward the hunter had a talent for constructing hides and, with a few deft movements, he had woven branches together to give them better cover and two clear areas to look through. Scot was pleased with his companion; although a little surly he clearly knew how to move through the dark and apart from the slightly acrid smell of the bushes, which Scot could not quite place, they were very comfortable. They didn't speak much and Scot had made a few notes, holding up his folded parchment to the filtered light of the moon.

'Do you know what these trees are?' he asked Hayward. 'You seem to be a bit of a countryman, from what I have seen so far.'

'I've always lived in the country,' Hayward replied. 'I don't like the town. These are elders. Don't you recognize that smell?'

Scot stiffened. Elder, the witches' tree. This was so exciting. He made a note. 'This is wonderful, Master Hayward. We are in the middle of a clump of witches' trees. This clump may even become part of the ritual. That is so exciting.'

Hayward didn't answer and Scot turned to him, a repeat of his remark on his lips. To his horror, he saw that Hayward was looking out of the hide with eyes wide with panic. Scot realized in that moment, as the first naked dancer appeared, that he had immured himself in a clump of elder waiting to watch a Lammas Sabbat in the company not only of witches, but a man who believed in them as he believed in his immortal soul. He muttered a curse and prepared for a rather difficult night.

By the time the women were circling in their lurching dance, Scot knew that Hayward was in another place. His mouth hung slack and his head nodded in time to their chant. He was even chanting it with them, in an undertone and Scot abandoned his notebook, alert for any move from Hayward which might look like an attempt to break cover and join them. Deluded women or not, unarmed as they clearly were, he would give Hayward no chance of survival if he burst in on them while they were in this heightened state. He had heard of men ripped limb from limb in these circumstances and whilst the researcher in him would appreciate some empirical knowledge of how that would work in practice, he was not an unkind man and would stop it happening if he could.

Hayward seemed to be in a fairly safe trance state, muttering, '*Magister, adjuva nos, magister, adjuva nos*,' over and over. The pronunciation was not quite classic, but Scot had been expecting the phrase so could understand it. This was another thing which he had been uncertain about. Would the witches say 'Master, help us,' in English or Latin? Now, he had his answer.

The chant was speeding up, and the drumming of the women's bare feet in the fetid mud churned up from the dust of the Rollright circle almost drowned out their voices. Like Marlowe, Scot sometimes saw ghostly forms riding on the witches' backs, but a quick pinch of flesh inside his arm brought him back to reality. He could quite understand how Hayward had been sucked in, although the speed had been a surprise. He only hoped that he and at least Marlowe would be able to resist, if things turned ugly later on.

Then, as suddenly as if he had gone totally deaf, the muttered chant and the drumming feet stopped. Hayward's mad paternoster stopped with the women's as though they shared but one throat. The silence was thick with menace and Scot could feel the goose flesh rise on his back and down the sides of his head as the hairs stood up in trepidation. The whole valley and hills seemed to have drawn in their breath. Not a creature moved, not a leaf so much as fluttered for what seemed to be a lifetime. Then, so near and so loud as to make bowels turn to water, there was a roar. It was pure sound, not from any human throat and was on such a note that every nerve stood on end and the desire for flight was almost unstoppable. Across the circle from

Scot, Marlowe and Cawdray almost rolled from their precarious perches. Hayward lurched forward to be stopped by his woven branches. Scot half rose but managed to force himself back into his crouch behind his witches' trees.

The roar went on and on, with no breathing or humanity in it, until the watchers felt their ears begin to dull with it, as the nerves to the brain gave up the unequal struggle. When it suddenly stopped, everything felt muffled and distant, as though they were drowning in thick, evil-smelling water. They found themselves holding their breath, then struggling to breathe as a drowning man might as he breaks the surface for the third and last time. Hayward lowered his head and looked through his spy hole from below furrowed brows. His breathing came hard and slow and Scot wound a hand in the man's belt, ready to hold him back.

The witches fell back and all went down on their hands and knees, heads down, hair hanging matted over their faces. The moon seemed to put in an extra effort and the light in the circle was almost as clear as day. Into the spotlight strode a hideous creature, seven feet tall, clothed in dazzling white with a black cope over his shoulders. His head rose massive to the stars, a long face with golden cat's eyes gleaming in the moonlight, with long hair running down like a dull river of jet down his back. The horns which sprang from just behind the ears were outswept like supplicating arms and banded with spirals of gold and gems. Although each part of him, the spotless robe, the golden eyes, the splendid horns, were all separately beautiful, somehow their proximity to the whole creature made them vile. He stepped into the filth in the middle of the circle and began to chant in a low, deep voice. Marlowe, a child of the church by accident though not design and a lover of words for their own sake, recognized the paternoster backwards.

'Amen. *Malo a nos libera sed, tentationem in inducas nos ne et.*' As he came to the end of each phrase, he placed a naked foot on the head of a witch and sent her sprawling on her back in the mud. Soon, all of the women were lying spreadeagled in a parody of crucifixion on the ground and the gross animal stood in the middle of the circle. Again, the silence enveloped the stones and Hayward pulled at Scot's restraining hand.

'Maiden!' The voice rang and echoed round the stones. Marlowe thought of Ned Sledd and how he would have loved the theatre of all this. He tightened his grip on Cawdray's shoulder and was rewarded by an answering squeeze. 'Maiden! Arise!'

The first dancer rose to her feet as though on strings and walked towards the creature, their Master, with her head down. When she reached him, he put out a hand, encased in a clawed glove, and raised her face to look at him, the wicked talon drawing blood under her chin.

'Maiden! Your time has come!' he boomed. 'Release me from these earthly trappings.' She reached up to his shoulders and unlaced the gown and cope which rippled to the ground like snow. He was revealed as a large man, muscular and well made, with strong legs and back. His manhood sprang out and seemed larger than any on a mortal man. The girl addressed as the Maiden was rooted to the spot. He lifted her around the waist and seemed to impale her where he stood. With his first thrust, he turned his evil face to the sky and she seemed to shudder with the pain. Then, he pushed her off on to the dirt and pressed his foot into her stomach, pinning her down. 'Liar!' he boomed. 'Liar! You do not come to me as a Maiden. You have known men. Many, I'll warrant.'

She wriggled under his foot, trying to get away from the deadly weight on her. Marlowe and Cawdray leaned forward, hands reaching for their daggers. She might think she was a witch, but they saw her for what she was: a young girl scarcely more than a child. Her mouth was moving, but no sound came.

The creature raised his head and bellowed to the moon. He kicked the girl away and she crawled from the circle, whimpering. None of the others dared to turn their heads as she left them, although a few closed their eyes and muttered what may have been a silent prayer, although none could say which way the words left their mouths.

The Master leaned forward now and hissed at his minions. 'Bring me a Maiden. Nothing is complete without I spill my seed into a Maiden's womb.' The women all looked at the ground. 'Is none of you a Maiden?' he screamed. 'I will increase my flock! One of you will bear the Devil's child inside her before tonight is out or all will die.' Suddenly, the blonde witch approached him, her glorious hair now matted with filth. He reached towards her, eyes glittering. 'You?' he purred. 'You, a Maiden? I had hardly thought . . .'

She took a deep and shuddering breath. 'No, Master,' she said. 'I am no Maiden and have not been since I was scarcely more than a child, but there is one on this hill tonight who is.'

'Who?' the voice sounded like the deepest bell and rang around the hills.

'Listen, Master,' the woman said. 'In the silence you will hear her voice. She is calling to you. She wants you, though she would deny it.'

Everyone strained their ears and there was, at the very edge of hearing, the sound of a woman sobbing. The beast raised its head and the eyes flashed with new fire. He nodded at the woman and dismissed her with a wave of a taloned glove. 'Fetch her,' he hissed. 'Fetch the Maiden to me.'

Four witches scrambled to their feet and hurried off out of the circle towards the Whispering Knights. They came out of the three-sided hut made by the leaning stones with a struggling figure between them. As they got inside the circle, they tore the cloak from her and she stood there naked, with her head raised defiantly. Shaking off the women, she stepped into the circle and walked towards the beast.

Marlowe drew in a sharp breath. Alone of the watchers he had seen the woman's proud nakedness before. 'Joyce,' he breathed. 'Joyce Clopton. I think now is the time to act, Master Cawdray, don't you?'

Cawdray nodded, but whispered. 'My legs are in a cramp, Master Marlowe. I shall fall if I try to run now. Can we wait just a minute, while I massage some life into them?'

'A minute?' Marlowe was aghast. 'You have seen what he can do! Joyce doesn't have a minute. With or without you, Master Cawdray, I am going to kill that evil thing.'

Marlowe was in the centre of the clearing by the time Joyce Clopton was forced, struggling, to her knees. The hags who held her forced her head back by the hair and pulled her hard to make her lie spreadeagled on the churned ground.

The witches saw only their Master, the blade of the athame flaring in both hands as he knelt astride the wriggling girl. Would it be his manhood or the blade tip that entered Joyce Clopton first? The cold of the Master's seed or the searing heat of his steel? Marlowe saw only a man in a mask and he leapt at him, catching the horned god off balance and they rolled in the dirt. The shriek from the witches was unearthly and they swarmed together like writhing rats with their tails in a knot, naked under the moon, screaming and clawing.

Hayward was still in his frozen position, his eyes glazed, his mouth open as in a silent scream. From the other side of the circle, Cawdray hobbled into the open, but his numb leg gave way and he fell beside a stone. It was Scot who found his voice first and he burst into the clearing where the bodies writhed over the struggling men. He had a dagger in one hand and the pencil in the other and he made the sign of the cross in the night sky. 'In the name of God,' he thundered, and the screaming stopped.

The naked women shrank back and Joyce Clopton rolled free of them, as mud-spattered as they were and gasping for breath. Two men stood upright in what had been their circle, one naked with a goat's head; the other, Kit Marlowe.

'Ever fought the Devil before?' the goat's head rasped, his right arm extended with the athame in his fist as he circled the poet.

'Every day,' Marlowe said. 'Reginald –' he didn't take his eyes off his opponent – 'get Lady Joyce out of here. I have business with this gentleman which won't keep.'

The witches swayed now, their heads jerking from side to side, their teeth bared and their nostrils flaring. Guttural grunts and sibilant hisses burst from their throats and their eyes seemed to flash as the daggers met under the moon. At each pass, Joyce and Scot winced. The horned one was more vulnerable but he was bigger than Marlowe and seemed to possess superhuman strength. Hayward was swaying like the witches against the stones and Cawdray was still nursing his useless leg.

The pair circled, parrying with their short, deadly blades,

now closing, now separating. The women behind Marlowe reached up, clawing at his legs, gripping his breeches as he turned, trying to unbalance him. He lashed out with his boot and kicked his way free, but the horned one saw his chance and lunged. There was a rip of velvet and linen as the blade sliced through Marlowe's sleeve, cutting his forearm almost to the bone. He dropped back, the pain shooting through his body like cold fire as he parried for his life.

'It looks as though there will be two sacrifices tonight,' the voice boomed in the goat's head. '*Bagali laca Bachabé*,' he said and lunged at Marlowe again.

This time, the poet was ready. He caught the athame on his own blade, sliding along it to the quillons and the blade snapped like a crash of thunder. He swung sideways, ramming his dagger to the hilt in the naked body, feeling it thud under the ribcage and burst a lung as the goat's head roared and crashed to the left, bringing both of them down into the fetid mud.

Now the only sound was of Kit Marlowe fighting for breath. The women were kneeling in their circle, the show over, the Devil dead. Now, long before the cock crowed or God's light frightened away the shadows, they were ordinary women again, sad, deluded and very afraid.

Marlowe wrenched out his dagger to leave a gaping gash, pouring blood bubbling with the last air escaping from the beast's lungs. He gripped the black hair and with an effort that made his gashed arm flare with pain, tore off the goat's head.

SEVENTEEN

After the events of the night, the little party rode in silence, padding along the old road south to Woodstock. When conversation began, it was in snatches and an attempt to make sense of the senseless and to ward off the dark shadows that still seemed to cling like wraiths to their backs and in dark places on the road.

Joyce rode with Marlowe, wrapped in an old cloak to cover her modesty. 'I don't know how it happened,' she said. 'One minute Boscastle and I were saying a prayer for Ned Sledd, the service for the dead, and the next . . . he burst into the chapel, this . . . creature in a cloak and cowl. Like some mad monk he smashed a crucifix over Boscastle's head and grabbed me. I don't remember any more . . .'

'You were in a faint, as like as not,' Marlowe said. 'After all you've been through, even before last night, it's not surprising.'

'No.' Joyce was adamant in her dignity. 'I am a Clopton. We don't faint.'

Marlowe smiled and shifted his bridle arm which was stiffening like the blood over his sleeve and doublet. He went to a good school; he would never call a lady a liar.

'It was the damnedest thing,' Richard Cawdray was telling Simon Hayward. 'I was rooted to the spot. Even when I tried to help Marlowe, my legs just wouldn't work. The damnedest thing.'

'All I remember,' Hayward said, still shaking his head every now and then to clear it, 'is those appalling women. The smell. And the black shapes they flew on. All kinds of beasts, some I can't describe, with wings and jaws and . . . well, you know all about the theatre, Cawdray. How did they do that, do you think?'

It was Cawdray's turn to shake his head. 'I have no idea,' he said. 'But I'd wager a fat purse that Lord Strange's Men would kill to know the answer.'

Scot had reached his horse tethered at the foot of the hill to find a filthy Merriweather waiting for him, clothed just about in whatever she had been able to grab for herself as the witches had run for their lives, out of the circle of stones, away to Meon Hill. She had looked out for Dorothy, out of habit, but she had disappeared before the rest, disgraced by the Master in front of her sisters. Merriweather was surprised he had not seen through the girl from the start. She was notorious the length of the county for her wanton ways, always behind some hedge or wall, whoever asked her, and sometimes even when they hadn't asked. Merriweather's legs were old and her head was screwed on the right way and she had seen Scot at Clopton and been struck by his aura of common sense. She had come to the Sabbat because she had been summoned and it wasn't as if she didn't like a bit of witchery now and then. But this had soon got out of hand and she hadn't got the guts for all the filth and stink these days. Old bones were more comfortable in front of a nice warm fire and with a little luck she could find a nice corner back at Clopton, or anywhere Lady Joyce found to lay her head.

'Hello,' he said, looking her in the eye. 'Are you waiting for me, mother?'

'Don't you mother me,' she said. 'I am waiting for you, if you will give me a ride to where My Lady is going.'

'And in exchange?'

She looked at him and suddenly tipped a wink. 'In exchange, you can ask me all you want to know. Although I can't promise I know all the answers. Tonight took a turn I wasn't ready for, so I think my style might be out of joint. But I will tell you the truth as I know it.'

Scot climbed on to his horse and reached down to put his arm around her. 'Come up here, then, on my saddle bow, and we can talk as we ride,' he said. 'But before I lift you up, don't try any clever tricks, because I know them all.'

Merriweather chuckled quietly to herself. She doubted that he knew them *all*, but it would be nice to ride on his saddle. He wasn't young, but nor was she and it was a while since she had had a man's arm round her. So she sprang up, light as thistledown and settled her back against his chest.

'Now, Master Scholar,' she said. 'What would you like to know?'

The warden of Woodstock had already raised the hue and cry and the town constable had marshalled the people at his disposal and sent them over the River Ray to the crooked little houses of Islip; south to the thatched village of Bladon; north-west to the tree ridge at Charlbury. Nothing. No sign of the Lady of Clopton or whoever had abducted her.

And so Marlowe had some rapid explaining to do when the warden's men came upon the horsemen on the road, with the kidnapped woman riding behind Marlowe on his bay. All was well, all had ended and Joyce, shaken and pale after the night's events, fell into Boscastle's arms, sobbing quietly. The stew-ard's head was bandaged and he could barely see out of one eye, but he held Joyce close to him for all he was merely a retainer and a tear trickled down from beneath his unbruised lid.

'Kit,' she said softly, as the time came for her departure with the warden's men. 'I can't find the words.'

'Don't try,' he said, 'your father can rest in his grave now. Will you go home, to Clopton?'

'Yes,' she said, breathing fiercely to stop herself crying all over again. 'There is work to be done. Bridges to be built. I can bring myself to attend their nasty little church in Stratford, at least for one day of the year.'

He smiled, while Boscastle arranged a horse for her and sent riders to stand down the hue and cry. They all turned to the thudding of hoofs on the road to the south and shouts from a rider, tousle-haired and standing in the stirrups.

'Kit! Kit!'

It was Thomas, as lathered and sweating as his horse. He reined in hard and the animal blew and snorted, glad the mad race with the wind was over.

'Devil on your tail, boy?' Scot asked.

'Martin said I'd find you here,' the boy said breathlessly, sliding gratefully out of the saddle. 'He didn't know what to do and said I should ask you. Master Shaxsper had some ideas, but Martin said we should still ask you. So here I am.'

'One damned riddle after another,' Hayward grunted, adjusting his girth by the roadside.

'Ask me what?' Marlowe asked when he could get a word in edgewise.

'Wait . . . got to get my breath back,' Thomas said, bending over with his hands on his knees and breathing in deeply through his nose. He paused and stood upright, sniffing more delicately then his nose wrinkled. 'What is that terrible smell?'

'Better for you that you don't know,' Marlowe told him.

'No, but, honestly . . . I don't believe I have ever smelt anything worse.'

'Breathe through your mouth,' Cawdray advised. 'But you do get used to it after a while, I promise you.'

Thomas looked dubious and stepped a few paces back from the men. 'I've just come from Oxford,' Thomas said, wincing at the stitch which still gripped him in the side. He felt he had galloped the whole journey, not the horse. 'We can perform on Christ Church Meadow. Nice place. Views of the Isis, Merton College, Corpus Christi.'

'Yes.' Marlowe nodded. 'I'd heard they'd pinched that one from us. Rumour has it there's an Eagle and Child Inn, too.' He shook his head, tutting. 'Is nothing sacred?'

'Usual deal,' Thomas said. 'Quarter of the gate to the Town Guilds. No fornication. No blasphemy. If God's in it, we can't be allowed to see His face.'

'Forgive me, Thomas,' Marlowe said. 'I have had rather an unusual night, to tell you the absolute truth for once in my life. So if I sound a little stupid, you really mustn't judge. But it seems to me that news of a possible performance in a meadow, even an Oxford meadow, is not so important that you would ride Hell for leather and almost kill a horse under you to tell me. And why doesn't Martin know what to do? He's been in this business for much longer than I; surely he can decide whether to go ahead or not. He must have done this scores of times, with Ned and others.'

'No, no, Kit.' Thomas was shaking his head and accepting a welcome swig of water from Cawdray's bottle. 'You don't understand. The Earl of Worcester's Men are in town.'

'Is that a problem?' Scot asked.

'Oxford is big enough for both of you, surely?' Hayward said.

'Oh, yes,' Thomas agreed. 'Worcester's boys are performing in Brasenose College – on account of it's got its own brewery.' There were chuckles all round, but Thomas was deadly serious. He had not yet told his news. 'No, gentlemen, don't scoff. There is more to this.'

'Well, out with it,' Marlowe said. For a lad who had spent his whole career so far playing girls by the time-honoured method of swinging his skirts and giggling behind straw hair, he certainly knew how to milk an audience.

'Alleyn's with them.'

'Who?' Scot asked.

'Ned Alleyn,' Marlowe repeated, grimly. Then he turned. 'Your favourite, Master Cawdray. Don't worry. We won't find it disloyal if you go to watch him rather than our little offering.'

'I can't wait,' Cawdray said with a smile. 'To have two plays to see is far more than I could ever have hoped for.'

'What's the play they're doing, Thomas?' Marlowe asked. 'I don't think I could stand another round of *Rafe Roister Doister.*'

A strange light flitted across the boy's face. 'Well,' he said, 'apparently, according to the playbills, it's something Alleyn wrote himself. It's called *The Tragedy of Dido, Queen of Carthage.*' Thomas stepped back. He had never seen a messenger actually shot, but he had often seen one dealt a nasty one in the mouth and he was anxious to avoid that if he could.

'*Dido,*' Marlowe said, calmly, '*Queen of Carthage*, no less. Well, gentlemen,' he turned to Scot, Hayward and Cawdray. 'Please don't get too worked up about the exciting prospect of the great Ned Alleyn as Aeneas, although I am sure his performance would have been one to tell your grandchildren about. He won't be appearing after all.'

Thomas looked doubtful. 'It's on all the playbills, Kit,' he said.

'Very possibly,' Marlowe said. 'But he won't be appearing, nevertheless.'

'Why not?' Cawdray asked. Thomas was smiling now, having worked out the likely reason.

'Because I will have killed him,' Marlowe said, simply. 'Well . . .' He rubbed his hands together as well as his wound would allow and turned towards his horse. 'Shall we, gentlemen? I am stopping off at Woodstock. And your good selves?'

'Straight back to Oxford,' Thomas said.

'I may go home for a day or so,' Hayward said. 'And a bath.' He turned to Cawdray. 'You're most welcome, if you would like to stay. Or I could meet you in Oxford. You could get the rooms.'

'I could do with a hot bath,' Cawdray said. 'If not several. I'll consider my plans as we ride.' And the two men mounted up and walked their mounts off down the road.

'Master Scot?' Marlowe asked.

'I think I have all Merriweather has to tell me,' Scot said. 'I will accompany Thomas, I think, straight to Oxford. Hart Hall will doubtless be happy to provide me with a bath and a change of clothing for old time's sake.'

'Well, until Oxford, then,' Marlowe said and he turned his horse's head to Woodstock and whatever he might find there.

Marlowe took the winding road through Over Norton and cantered through the growing dawn light down the Glyme valley, the horse's hoofs thudding on the hard, dry ground. The cocks were crowing and the harvesters were on their way to their fields by the time he crossed the old Roman road called Akeman Street and saw the lazily smoking chimneys of Woodstock and the pale, mellow bulk of its church.

'Halt!' he heard a shout and the clash of weapons as he reached the camp by the river. 'Who goes?'

'Edward Greville,' he called back.

The guards looked at each other. Even in the silver grey of dawn it was clear that the man was the wrong size, the wrong age and he was riding the wrong horse. Halberds came to the level, men tumbled out of canvas, bleary eyed and regretting their flagons of the previous night. Captain Paget was among them, his right hand heavily bandaged and his arm hanging oddly, numb to the shoulder, the nerves exhausted with the constant pain.

'What's the meaning of this?' he snarled at Marlowe who sat his horse calmly, staring him down.

'Paget?' a dishevelled Henry Blake was at his elbow, struggling into his robes and trying to look important. 'What's going on here?'

'You may remember me, Master Lawyer,' Marlowe said. 'I have a little present for you. Call it an offering.' He suddenly turned in the saddle and hauled a bundle over in front of him, using his left hand. He unknotted the white cloth from round something big and threw it down, letting it hit the ground with a thud at Blake's feet. It was the head of a hideous goat, its glass eyes staring dumbly up at Greville's men who stood back, nonplussed. One of its gilded horns was bent at a rakish angle and the hair was matted and wet.

'What *is* that?' Blake felt obliged to ask.

Marlowe shook his head, tutting. 'The rubbish the Inns of Court are turning out these days is a disgrace,' he said. 'See if you do any better with this.' Marlowe threw something bright and shiny to the lawyer, who stepped back, confused. Paget was faster and caught it deftly in his left hand, something he would have to do for quite a while. His eyes widened as he realized what it was.

'Sir Edward's signet ring,' he said.

Blake snatched it from his open palm and scowled at the Greville arms in enamel on the ring's surface. 'How did you come by this?' he asked Marlowe.

'I took it from the dead finger of Edward Greville as he lay naked at the Rollright Stones. That –' and he pointed to the ghastly head – 'was on his shoulders at the time and he was the . . . guest of honour, shall we say . . . at what the witches call a Sabbat.'

Paget gaped and most of his men crossed themselves.

Blake was flustered. 'No,' he said. 'No, you're lying.'

'You have been serving Satan, Master Lawyer,' Marlowe said, 'but now the time has come to give up your soul.'

'My soul?' Blake blinked and was suddenly aware that Paget and the others were moving away from him, their halberds and pikes pointing in his direction.

'You will be dragged to Hell any time now,' Marlowe told

him. 'Isn't that how it works?' He smiled as Blake dropped to his knees, mumbling what sounded like the Lord's Prayer, only in English and very definitely the right way round. 'Or –' Marlowe leaned forward in the saddle – 'to be a little more prosaic for a moment, you are out of a job, lickspittle. When news of Greville's little debauchery reaches the authorities – as it more or less has by now – his estates will be forfeit to the crown. You and Paget here will be lucky to escape with a year or two in the Clink. Unless of course it can be proved that you were actually part of the infernal happenings at the stones.'

Blake still knelt there. 'As God is my judge and witness,' he gabbled, 'I know nothing of that. I knew there were some cunning women, but surely every village has those. His friends, Sir Edward called them. He would . . . consult them, now and then. There was one, he called her the Maiden. Dorothy, her name is, she works in the Clopton kitchens. Everyone around knows Dorothy.' He threw a glance behind him. 'I would wager half these men know Dorothy. So when Sir Edward called her the Maiden, well, I thought he was having a joke.'

Marlowe knew for certain that Sir Edward didn't joke about things like that. He gestured Blake to carry on.

'He wasn't doing anything wrong. The Queen herself has her own magus.'

'Dr Dee.' Marlowe nodded. 'He's a friend of mine. A more honourable man never drew breath. Edward Greville was a devil-worshipper. Last night he even played the part himself.' He half smiled. 'As a playwright, I have to say he wasn't half bad.'

'That's enough!' Paget shouted. His men were already dashing to saddle their horses, leaving the makeshift camp as it stood. He turned back to Blake. 'You're on your own now, lawyer,' he grunted and, sneering at Marlowe, made for the horse lines.

Blake knelt there, terrified and lost, trembling for what was and what might have been. Marlowe urged his horse past him, then reined in and looked down into the man's abject face. He held his gaze for a heartbeat or two and then came to a decision. He drove his boot into Blake's injured shoulder, without malice or temper, but in pure retribution. Blake screamed and clutched his arm as he fell sideways in the dust.

'That,' Marlowe said, 'is for Sir William Clopton.'

He had done this before. It wasn't his college or even his town, but there was a monotony about university buildings, a predictability about the proctors who patrolled them after curfew. He recognized the tap of their pattens, saw the darting beams of their lanterns and did what he had always done at Corpus Christi, melted into the background, merged with the dark. Blackness now, as then, was his friend.

He'd learned all he needed on the streets that evening and while Lord Strange's Men were setting up camp on Christ Church Meadow and Cawdray and Hayward were unpacking their few overnight traps in bedrooms in a cosy inn, Kit Marlowe was creeping up the back stairs of Brasenose College on a mission to right a wrong. He tapped on the studded door at the stair's top, where the landing twisted to the left and he waited.

'Who is it?' a voice called from inside the room.

'Butler's pantry,' Marlowe said, affecting what he hoped was an authentic Oxford burr.

'I didn't order . . . wait a minute . . .'

He heard the scrape of furniture and the padding of feet. The door squeaked open to reveal a ferret of a man with wild grey hair and an elaborately smocked and embroidered night-shirt. Lights from candles danced on his spectacles. He looked his visitor up and down. The man appeared to be carrying no tray, no flagon, no platter. And were Brasenose doing so well they could dress their servants like roisterers?

'Who are you?' the little man asked. He peered through his spectacles and then over them, pushing them back up his nose with the knuckle of a forefinger. 'You are not from the Pantry.'

'That is very true,' Marlowe said. 'I am Christopher Marlowe.'

'Never heard of you.' The little man started to close the door. 'I don't buy at the door. Go away.'

Marlowe was quick and had a booted foot between the door and the jamb before the other man could give the wood any momentum. 'I want to speak to you,' he said, leaving his foot there despite the increasing pressure.

'What do you want?'

'Just some answers,' Marlowe said. He took advantage of a slight reduction in the man's efforts with the door and pushed him back into the room. He closed the door behind him.

'You *do* know who I am?' the man in the nightshirt checked with his unwelcome visitor.

'You are William Somerset,' Marlowe told him.

'That's the third Earl of Worcester to you, sonny. This may be Oxford, but Jack is not, I'm afraid, as good as his master. I'd like a bit of respect, if you please.'

Marlowe liked the cut of this man. For all he knew, Christopher Marlowe was a hired assassin bent on slitting the throat of all nobility, but, unarmed and alone as he was, he defiantly looked his would-be killer straight in the eye.

'When you have earned it, My Lord,' Marlowe said, smiling to put the man even more at ease. 'And that will be when you explain this.' And he threw a handbill on to Worcester's desk. The Earl adjusted his spectacles and held the paper out at arm's length. 'Not a misprint, surely?' he growled. 'I really can't be held responsible. The University printers . . . not really up to rush jobs, I'm afraid. Their usual print time is measured in decades, I believe. Now, hush and let me read.' He ran a finger along the lines, muttering under his breath, pausing now and again with a querulous little mew and then continuing. Finally, he said, 'A few mistakes, I grant you. An unusual way of spelling Carthage, with a "j" like that, but far from the worst I have seen. As I say, the University printers . . .'

'. . . have got the name of the playwright wrong,' Marlowe said flatly.

'What?' Worcester blinked and took off his spectacles, polished them carefully on a small unembroidered piece of his nightshirt and replaced them on his nose. 'Alleyn? No, I'm sure there is always a "y" in it.'

'The only why, My Lord,' Marlowe said, 'is why you believed such a callow youth could write a masterpiece like *Dido*.'

Worcester nodded. 'It is rather good.' His face changed immediately. 'Now, I won't have that. Ned Alleyn may be rather young . . .'

'And he may be rather light-fingered,' Marlowe said, adding to the man's credentials.

'What do you mean, sir?' Worcester asked.

'I mean, sir,' Marlowe said through gritted teeth, 'that Ned Alleyn stole the play from me. What should be written there –' and he stabbed at the playbill with an angry finger – 'under that emotive little word "by" is the name Christopher Marlowe.'

Worcester peered at him closely and then turned away and picked up a candle, holding it so close to Marlowe's face that there was a faint smell of burning beard. Marlowe backed away, pushing the man's arm down to a less dangerous level.

Worcester gave a spluttering laugh. 'You say that Alleyn could not have written this work because he is too young,' he said, checking his facts.

'I do, sir.'

'So, my next question, Master . . .'

'Marlowe.'

'Yes, Marlowe, is this. How old are you?'

'I am twenty-one, sir.'

'So, in the thirty-six long months that you have lived longer than Master Alleyn, you have learned to put these golden words each in line, one after the other, have you? Three years ago, you would have been unable to do this?'

'No.' Marlowe realized that this little man in his over-decorated nightshirt was no fool. 'No. I could write like this . . . or almost like this . . . when I was eighteen. But –' as he spoke he knew that he could only sound petulant, but he carried on anyway – 'I don't think that you believe Master Alleyn can.'

'Why not?' Worcester asked, simply.

'Because . . . because he is a foolish popinjay who looks well on stage and can seduce any woman alive. Because he is a thief and a braggart and walked off with my play when my back was turned.' He felt his anger all but boil over. 'I wrote it, dammit, plain and simple. The play is mine!'

'The Devil you say,' Worcester thundered.

'I do,' Marlowe said, standing his ground.

The little man put down his candle and folded his arms across his chest. 'There must be a way out of this impasse,' he mused, ostentatiously putting a finger to his brow as though in deep thought. 'I know.' He narrowed his eyes at Marlowe and said, 'Prove it. Tell me the story, quote me some lines.'

Marlowe sighed. 'The play concerns the Queen of Carthage . . .'

Worcester held up a hand. 'I must stop you there, Master Marlowe. I don't want to waste your precious time, nor mine. I think most people out there on the street could tell me that much.'

'My Lord,' Marlowe said, clenching his fists behind his back and speaking with more control than he thought he had in his entire body. 'Please let me speak for at least a sentence or two before you interrupt me, or we will never get this matter brought to any kind of conclusion.'

Worcester waved a hand and smiled. 'My apologies. I am sometimes a little precipitate. I will try to keep quiet. Proceed.'

'Where was I?' Marlowe had had the worst night of his life and a long, hard ride to get to this point and had suddenly completely lost his way.

'Queen of Carthage,' Worcester told him helpfully.

'Thank you. The Queen of Carthage and her lover, Prince Aeneas, lately come from the sack of Troy. It is written in iambic pentameter, five beats to the bar which, I believe has never been heard on any stage in the country.'

'The world,' Worcester corrected him, then, catching the bead in Marlowe's eye, smiled and closed his mouth firmly. Marlowe still fixed him with a glare. He had worked out this man's method and an interruption was not considered complete until he had said at least two phrases. Worcester looked at the handbill again, then back at Marlowe. 'Who's on first?' he asked and Marlowe bowed a tiny bow and continued.

'Unless Master Alleyn has tinkered with my genius,' he said, 'it is Jupiter. Ganymede is sitting on his knee and Mercury is asleep stage right.'

'Yes.' Worcester narrowed his eyes. 'Act One, Scene One,' he said, rummaging on his desk for the relevant pages. 'Venus says – and I'm quoting here – "Ay, this is it; you can sit toying there, And playing with that female wanton boy . . ." I meant to mention that to Alleyn as a matter of fact.'

'What?' Marlowe asked.

'Well . . .' Worcester felt a little awkward. 'Jupiter, Ganymede. I mean to say, the lad is sitting on the man's lap and the boy is asking for jewels in exchange for hugs. Alleyn does *know* this is all illegal, doesn't he?'

'I really don't know what Alleyn knows,' Marlowe told him. 'But I know the Greeks not only tolerated such relationships but positively lauded them.'

'Good Lord.' Worcester was amazed. 'Did they?' He looked at Marlowe. 'All right, you've talked me into it. *Dido* is your play. What happens now?'

'Now you print another batch of handbills with my name on them. I've already saved you the trouble of removing the old ones by tearing them down myself.'

Worcester looked like a dog chewing a wasp. The costs were already soaring and even a belted earl wasn't made of money. 'Very well,' he said. 'Anything else?'

'I take it Alleyn is playing Aeneas.'

'Handsome lead,' Worcester said. 'Of course.'

'He's too young. Give it to somebody else. Give Alleyn Ganymede.'

'I can't do that. He'll go mad. He's my main draw. All the ladies come to see him. I can't lose Alleyn.'

'Why not, My Lord? You are the third Earl of Worcester and you own Alleyn and all the rest of the troupe. You can buy yourself another handsome lead who will have the ladies flocking, just like Alleyn. And one who isn't a liar, to boot.'

Worcester stepped back a little and looked at Marlowe with his head on one side.

'Before you ask, My Lord, the answer is no. My interests lie elsewhere and I am no actor. Tell Alleyn he is Ganymede and brook no argument.'

'He's not going to like it,' Worcester warned, wagging a finger at him.

'Ah, but I am,' Marlowe said with a smile. 'And there's one thing more.'

'Name it.' Worcester sighed. He had resigned himself now. There was no doubt in his mind; Marlowe *was* the author. And one word from him to the Master of Brasenose and the whole show would close. It was ironic, really; unlike Strange, Worcester never travelled with his Men. This was his first time and the way things were going, it would be his last. He knew what was coming. This was the clincher: money.

'Where can I find Ned Alleyn at this hour of night? He and I have a little unfinished business.'

'Before I tell you,' Worcester said, relieved that it didn't mean more personal expense, 'may I ask one thing more of you?'

'One good turn deserves another,' Marlowe said.

'When you hit him, don't mark the face.'

Marlowe had entered Worcester's room with the white heat of indignation coursing through his veins and this had helped to keep him awake and upright. It was getting hard to remember when he had last slept in a soft, clean bed made up with cool linen sheets. He had longed to lie down in Worcester's bed and just close his eyes. Yes, confirming the authorship of *Dido* was important, but sleep was becoming an all-encompassing obsession. His legs felt like lead and he seemed to see the world through a long, dark tunnel, with a bright point of detail at the very end which never came any nearer. There was a buzzing in his ears which came and went, like a high wind on a hilltop will sound to a man down in the valley.

He looked down the stairs as he took them one by slow and careful one. The shadow at the bottom looked like a pool of ink. There was nothing to see and he didn't really care. You could probably float in ink. It was lovely, warm and welcoming ink. If he just floated in the ink and shut his eyes for a little while, he could go and . . . do whatever it was he had set out to do. Not so important, that thing, that thing he was going to do.

Christopher Marlowe sat down on the bottom step of the stair and closed his eyes. Sleep spread her blanket and he dreamed of absolutely nothing for an hour at least. Then, suddenly, in the blackness of his head, a screaming face was inches from his, bared fangs dripping with something indescribable. He was on his feet, trembling and wide awake in a second, his hand at his back for his dagger. The pain from the instinctive movement finished the job the nightmare had begun and he was back to reality, standing at the bottom of the silent stair, looking out through the arch of the porch into a silent court.

Black holes denoting the start of other stairs broke the gold of the stone at intervals around the walls. He looked up at the sky and was rewarded by a moon in its first quarter giving a clear light, but not enough to see well by. He remembered the Sabbat being under a full moon; was this the only way in which the hypnotic chant of the witches had affected him? Or was he still sleeping?

He shook his head and shook himself down, squaring his shoulders in his borrowed clothes. The warden of Woodstock had been a gentleman throughout the entire episode. Marlowe smiled at the thought of the man's face when he had clattered into his courtyard that morning. He had called immediately for a bath, had clothed Marlowe from his own son's linen press and had lent him a horse. He had asked no questions, he had asked for no security. He had just given what was needed and graciously waved Marlowe off without seeming to worry that he was possibly waving goodbye to a very substantial amount of money. A good man who shone like a good deed in the naughty world Marlowe was inhabiting.

Thoughts of the warden of Woodstock brought another thought into Marlowe's head which hit him like a blow in the chest. He had forgotten Ned Sledd in all of the excitement and although he knew that his friend would not be brought back by finding his murderer, that he would lie as cold in his Woodstock grave whatever the outcome of any investigation Marlowe could make, even so, it was a sobering thought to the playwright that he had not progressed one more inch along the path to seeking retribution on behalf of the Player King. The cricket-calling night drew Marlowe out of the darkness of the stair and he stood, irresolute in what light the moon could throw. He lifted his face to the sky and let some tears spill from his eyes for Ned Sledd. Somehow, until now there had been no time for tears.

Then, he wiped his face and made up his mind. Find Alleyn

and give him a piece of his mind and, while remembering the Earl of Worcester's request, give him a few resounding slaps. From what he remembered of him, the man was a bit of a fop, handsome in the pretty style, not much meat on him; definitely a lover not a fighter. He could deal with him in a wink of an eye and then give the rest of the night over to puzzling out who murdered Ned.

Making the decision, forming a plan, made Marlowe feel much better. It might be the middle of the night to other people, but to Marlowe it could have been noon. He had had an hour's sleep and he could go for days more on that, no trouble at all. He took a step towards Alleyn's stair and stumbled on a tussock of grass growing between the slabs of the path. His tired brain could either think or control his legs and balance and he fell heavily, rolling to avoid more damage to his arm. He lay there for a second or two, gathering his wits and his breath. Perhaps a better plan would be: deal with Alleyn, using the element of surprise, then go and have a long sleep, *then* work out who killed Ned Sledd. He rolled up into a sitting position and then from kneeling to standing. His arm was beginning to hurt him a lot now, almost more than when the blade had bitten first, but this wasn't the first injury he had sustained and he doubted it would be his last. It always got worse before it got better, something he had learned in the nursery and still held true.

EIGHTEEN

As he crept up the stairs, he shook his head again to get rid of the strange and random noises in his ears. He knew it was just the tiredness. He had experienced it many times before, lurching home in the wee small hours after a night out with his fellows scholars in Cambridge. It was as if the night sounds got stuck in his head and bounced around, creating a tinny music of their own. He knew it wasn't real, but it was very distracting and he needed all his concentration now.

He reached Alleyn's door. The Earl of Worcester certainly knew how to look after his Men. Ferdinando Strange was an excellent patron in many ways, but he was a man who didn't mind personal discomfort, so if he was prepared to camp in a wet field, he saw no reason why his Men shouldn't do the same. The Earl of Worcester used the same principle; he needed a soft bed and all the comforts of home when on the road, so his Men got those too. Clearly, Brasenose College had come up trumps too, with the best linen and the downiest feather. It was all about funding these days and Worcester's funds, men said, were limitless. Marlowe fought down a desire to join the Earl of Worcester's Men on the spot and tapped lightly on the door. He cleared his throat delicately and waited for Alleyn to answer. His plan hinged on Alleyn having not scooped up some willing wench for the night already. From what he heard, the chances were that he already had company, but hope sprang eternal.

Straining his ears he heard footsteps cross the bare floorboards of the room on the other side of the door. A voice sounded, muffled by the oak, but clear. Alleyn clearly took his enunciation seriously, even at dead of night.

'Who is it?'

'Is that Master Alleyn?' Marlowe fluted, in a falsetto voice high up in his head.

Marlowe sensed rather than heard that Alleyn was running fingers through his hair and unlacing his nightshirt a notch or two. 'It is,' he said, dropping his voice a tone and injecting it with honey. 'And may I ask who you are, dear?'

Marlowe cast his eyes up. Did the man never give up? When *he* was eighteen, he was intent on his studies, lost in the world of Ramus and Aristotle and Plato. His brains were in his head, not tucked into his breeches. But, Alleyn was Alleyn and if the stories were true, he never missed a chance of a roll in the hay or any other soft surface. 'Ooh, Master Alleyn!' he said, with a knowing chuckle. 'You must remember me, surely. After what you said to me this evening at the tavern. Ooh, my friends did bait me about it, so here I am. Like you asked.' For a moment, Marlowe thought he might have gone too far, but no. The bolts were drawn back and Alleyn stood there, one hand on the door jamb, the other holding the edge of the door in a nonchalant pose.

'Come in, my . . .' His eyes started in his head as he recognized Marlowe. 'You!' he breathed and went to slam the door, but Marlowe was quicker and slipped inside like a cat.

'Good evening, Master Alleyn,' he said, smoothly. 'Or is it good morning, by now? It's hard to tell, isn't it, when it is that hour of night when good things of day begin to droop and drowse and night's black agents to their preys do rouse.'

Alleyn drew himself up and pulled his nightshirt together. 'I'm an actor, Marlowe,' he said. It amused Marlowe that he put emphasis on the second syllable. What an insufferable poser; he might go for the face after all. 'Don't you come in here quoting at me.'

Marlowe blinked. 'I'm not quoting. It just seemed like a good way to say it was dark, late and no one's about. If you are an ac*tor*, Master Alleyn, then I am a po*et*. And a playwright. Unlike your good self, perhaps I should add.'

As they spoke, Marlowe was walking steadily towards Alleyn, pushing him further into the room until the backs of his legs made contact with the bed and he sat down with a bump. Marlowe kept walking until he was knee to knee with the man and he had to lean back on his hands to look up into his adversary's face.

'What is it you want, Marlowe?' he asked and Marlowe was impressed that, even in extremis, he could keep up his bluster.

'*Dido.*'

'She isn't here . . . oh, you mean the play.'

'No. I mean *my* play. Where is it?'

'I don't have it.' Speaking the truth, even with lies by omission buried within it, gave Alleyn more confidence still and he pushed with his knees and managed to stand up. 'Write it again. I understand you have a very ready pen. And those lines just now; you don't seem short of ideas.'

Marlowe drew his dagger, using his bad arm gingerly. He hefted it and then put it down on the table. 'I'm not going to fight you, Alleyn,' he said. 'I've been to see the Earl of Worcester. He knows now what a conniving, lying, thieving little shit you are and your career as an actor is well and truly over.' He was gratified by the light of panic that flared in the actor's eyes and saw him suddenly for what he was; just a boy who had had too much, too soon. 'It's all over, Alleyn. Perhaps you should make a career out of women. You seem to be good at that. An innkeeper's wife here, a farmer's wife there. Perhaps a short stint as a groom in some big house, pleasuring the master's wife for the extra food and clothes she might give you. Even a gold coin now and again, if you are really as good as they say.'

'Look, Marlowe, can't we talk this over? Have you really been to Worcester?'

'Yes. He was very interested to hear of your . . . I can only call it theft and deception, Ned. I can call you Ned, can I? I feel I know you well enough to call you Ned.'

'Call me what you like!' the boy spat. 'You've ruined my life so what's in a name?'

'Ned, Ned, Ned.' Marlowe took a step back. He wasn't a fists man as a rule, but he would make an exception in Alleyn's case. He looked at him and made a decision. The face it was. He raised his arm and saw the actor's eyes widen in terror. 'It's only a thump, Alleyn,' he told him in disgust. 'You'll only get a black eye.' Then, he leaned closer. There was something other than terror in the other's eyes. There was the glint of metal in candlelight.

Marlowe turned and pushed Alleyn to one side, all in one movement. He realized as he did so that he had not had noises in his head; he had been followed.

'You,' Alleyn said, from his position on the floor by the bed.

'Yes, me. I've been searching for you for nearly a year, you worthless excuse for a man. I've nearly had you once or twice, but you have always been one step ahead. If I thought you had done it with skill, I would applaud you. You'd like that, wouldn't you? Applause.' The intruder lifted his voice an octave and mocked. '"Ooh, Ned. That was lovely. Can we do it some more, Ned? Can we, Ned? My husband can't do it like you, Ned. Not as hard. Not for as long. Have some money, Ned. Have some nice clothes. He'll never miss them, he has so many."' He took a step nearer to the actor, scrabbling now to get further from the murderous knife.

Marlowe moved towards his own dagger on the table, but the intruder caught the movement and turned to him.

'Don't do it, Kit. I don't want to hurt you. I just want to kill this worthless turd. I'll be quick. He won't suffer, more's the pity.' He turned back to Alleyn and, using the high voice again, he spoke to him, but the words were wrenched from his heart. '"Oh, Ned,"' he said, the voice full of pain and fear, '"Oh, Ned. I'm going to have a baby. I haven't let my husband near me, Ned, not since you came along. He'll know it isn't his. Let's run away, Ned. Let's be together, us and our baby."' Dropping the high voice, he took a step nearer. 'And you did run away, Ned, didn't you? You ran as fast as your legs could carry you. Leaving my beautiful wife, with child and desperate.'

'I was sixteen,' Alleyn said. 'She was a woman and I was a boy. She could have said no.'

Cawdray stepped back, as if in shock. 'Well, that's perfectly in order then. She could have said no.' He sheathed his dagger and held out a hand to Alleyn as if to help him up and by reflex the actor took it. Marlowe started forward but Cawdray grabbed his injured arm and squeezed it viciously. 'Stay out of this, Kit, I said. This is not your battle.'

The pain was so intense that for a moment everything went black for Kit Marlowe. When he came to his senses, Cawdray had pulled Alleyn from his place on the floor and had him pinned against the wall by his throat. The actor was shorter than his attacker and his toes barely touched the floor. He was clawing at the fingers around his neck, but Cawdray was wearing gloves, some rather ornate ones, a gift from Shaxsper a lifetime ago. Alleyn's lips were turning blue when Marlowe spoke.

'Richard,' he said quietly. 'Don't do this. What Alleyn says does not excuse him, but there is some sense in it. He didn't force your wife to do anything.'

In reply, Cawdray just squeezed a little harder.

'Let him go, Richard. You don't want to become a murderer. What would your wife say if she knew?'

Cawdray froze as the shot went home then let go of Alleyn's throat and let him crash to the ground, making horrible cawing sounds as he tried to drag air into his lungs past his tortured throat. It flew through Marlowe's mind that it would be a week or so before he could deliver much of a line on stage.

Richard Cawdray turned to face Marlowe as though mounted on a spindle. His face was lifeless and he unsheathed his dagger and took a step towards him. 'I have always liked you, Kit, from the moment we met. Hayward didn't like you. He doesn't really understand anything except perhaps making money. And what he doesn't understand, he doesn't like, on principle. But me, I'm not like him. I take in waifs and strays.' He paused and looked over his shoulder at Alleyn. 'I taught my wife to do the same. She was always around the estate, doling out comfort and charity. She was a good woman. Everyone said so.'

Marlowe smiled at him and took a step backwards to match the man's progress. 'From what you said, she certainly sounded . . . pleasant.'

'Don't patronize me, Kit,' Cawdray growled. 'She was indeed a very pleasant woman. Then, she changed. She wouldn't let me share her bed. She became distant and was out from the house at all hours. When she came back she would be happy and laughing for an hour or two, then she would become tearful and quiet. This went on for weeks.'

The coughing huddle on the floor that was Edward Alleyn

seemed to be trying to speak. Cawdray went over to him and
kicked him viciously in the head and he slumped back.

'Then, one day, she came back to the house crying and
screaming. The servants called me and I went to her. Her
maid had put her to bed, but she threshed and struggled and
called *his* name constantly. She wouldn't speak, so I asked
her maid what was going on. She didn't want to tell me,
but . . . well, I persuaded her.'

Marlowe could almost feel the slaps and punches which he
had dealt to make the woman tell. How could he have missed
this side to Cawdray?

'When I had what information I needed, I went back to my
wife. I told her I knew everything and she started to speak to
me. As it turned out, I knew only a little. She had met this
animal –' and he turned and spat on Alleyn's recumbent body
– 'while out for a walk. He was staying with an aunt in the
village. They talked. And more, of course. It is the only
language he knows. She fell in love with him. She thought he
loved her too. But when she told him she was with child . . .
well, the craven creature ran away. She thought they were
going together, but when she got to their meeting place, the
only person there was his little cousin, with a note. And that
was the last she saw of him.'

'And so she killed herself.' Marlowe could feel the man's
pain.

'Kit. Sometimes, you really let your lack of years show.
Of course she didn't kill herself. She was carrying his child
and wanted to keep it as a lasting reminder of him. When she
got over her hysteria, she closed in on herself. She walked
around the house cradling her growing belly, crooning to it.
She was sure it was a boy. She intended to call it Edward. I
was to be shown to the world as a cuckold. A stupid cuckold,
with another man's bastard in my wife's belly, in my house.
So –' his eyes became colder and he seemed far away – 'I
went to her, when her bastard was almost ready to be born.
I went to her and said she needed fresh air. For the baby's
sake. She had prepared a room for it, with a crib and all any
gentleman's son would want. She had ignored me, but she
didn't see what I was planning. She said her pains were

coming, not often, but she had been told by her old nurse what it meant. She was an innocent in many ways, my wife.'

'Richard,' Marlowe said. 'Why don't we sit for a while? Look at Alleyn. He's unconscious. Maybe even dead. Why don't we sit? If you are as tired as I am . . .' He held his hand out to the man. 'Come, over here. Put the dagger down and we'll sit.' His words seemed to calm the man and he sat on one of the hard chairs at the table, but the dagger he kept in his hand. He moved Marlowe's dagger absent-mindedly away from his elbow, without really seeing what it was.

'She was an innocent. We went for a walk near the lake. She was talking of filling it in, when the baby came, so he would be safe.' He supported his head in one hand and took a deep and shuddering breath. 'I walked her round the lake at a pace she couldn't keep up, even before she was with child. I walked her and walked her, with her crying out that her pains were on her, that the baby was coming.'

Whenever he paused in his narrative, the room seemed to hum with what more horrors he still had to reveal. Marlowe edged his hand across the rough table top, inch by careful inch, until he was touching the dagger's hilt. He waited for the tale to begin again before he curled his hand around it and slowly drew it towards him.

'She fell to the ground and hauled up her skirts like the slut she was. The baby came in a rush of blood and water. It was a boy, as she had said it was all along. I held it up to her.' He turned his face to Marlowe and it was wet with tears. 'In all her fear and pain, her eyes lit up. She smiled and held out her arms to it. "Edward," she said. "Edward. Please give me my son." So, I did. I gave her her son into her arms, and then I picked them both up, took them to the lake and held them under.' He took a deep and shuddering sigh. 'I feel better for that, you know, Kit. They are right who say that confession is good for the soul.' He smiled brightly and pulled himself together in an instant.

Marlowe had known some terrible people in his life, and had heard some terrible things. It wasn't just the content of the man's tale that chilled him to the bone. It was his lifeless voice, the soulless description of snuffing out the life of two human beings. While he hesitated, Cawdray struck, stabbing with his dagger and pinning Marlowe's arm to the table.

'I am merciful sometimes, though, Kit. I could have stabbed your arm, but, see, I have only pinned your sleeve. Now, I will just finish off Alleyn and be away.'

Marlowe thought quickly. 'Tell me about your hunt for Alleyn. Where did he go when he left your village?'

Cawdray looked at him, head cocked on one side. In his funereal black he looked like a crow, a raven, some scavenging carrion eater eyeing up something found rotting in a hedge. Then he glanced at Alleyn, still and silent in the corner of the wall. He sat down again, holding his dagger so that Marlowe was no longer a threat. 'It was a long hunt, Kit, and one I didn't start until my wife was . . . let's just say dead. I don't have to pretend any longer, to you, at least. I left my estate in the care of my steward. Everyone was sad for me because I had lost my wife and child. Ned Alleyn was forgotten. Even his aunt played the part; she didn't want to lose her cottage. I didn't blame her for the behaviour of her wanton nephew, but she wasn't to know that. I am a kind man.'

To Marlowe's astonishment, the man meant it.

'I listened to talk around the village. My wife was not the only woman to fall for his big brown eyes and handsome face. Before I kill him I will be able to tell him of at least two more bastards he left behind. I was on his trail quite quickly, but always it seemed one step behind. Then I heard he had joined Lord Strange's Men. Because of the plague, if there is indeed a plague, in London, the Men had gone into the country and, I now realize, they were not the most organized of troupes. When Ferdinando Strange joined them they were easier to find. I have friends in fairly high places and I discovered that the Queen had insisted on having someone to guard him, someone clandestine, secret.' He looked up at Marlowe, suddenly alert. 'Was that someone you?'

'No,' Marlowe said. 'But I think I know who it was.'

Cawdray slapped his hand on the table. 'York! I knew I knew him from somewhere.'

Marlowe inclined his head.

'Well, I found out where they were going and . . . joined

in, as it were. Hayward was a bit of a nuisance, to be honest, but his was a roof over my head and he is quite the organizer, getting rooms and so on. He has found an excellent inn for us here in Oxford. I would have invited you to dine with us, but . . . well, you see how I am placed. When I kill Alleyn, as I will as soon as he wakes, then I am afraid you will have to be next, my dear Kit.'

'But tell me about the chase.' Marlowe encouraged him to keep talking. Michael Johns, his tutor and mentor in Corpus Christi, had once told him of an ancient manuscript which told of a woman who told tales every night to keep herself from execution. This was that story, but told in a mirror; Marlowe must keep his executioner telling the tales, to save his life. Or at least buy time. It must be nearly dawn.

'Hither,' Cawdray said. 'Thither. The attempt on Strange – that wasn't anything to do with me, I must assure you – rather skewed my plans. You all ran about as though someone had poked your little ants' nest. But finally, I caught up with you.'

'And you asked for Ned,' Marlowe said, quietly.

Cawdray gave a little grimace which may have been remorse, but somehow Marlowe doubted it. 'I got the wrong one. Yes, that was a nuisance.'

Marlowe had never claimed to be a patient man. He was not bad tempered as such, but he had his limits on what he would accept as reasonable behaviour. And dismissing the death of any man, let alone a man he liked and who he had called a friend, was very much beyond that invisible line so that he scarcely had to consider his next move. Heedless of the warden of Woodstock's sleeve, he wrenched sideways and tore free of Cawdray's dagger pinning him down. Such had been the man's arrogance that he had left Marlowe's dagger in his fist and it was the work of seconds to bring the hilt round and smack the man in the side of the head with it, buying time until he could adjust his grip.

Cawdray was only momentarily stunned and was on his feet and lunging at Marlowe in one fluid movement. He was at the advantage in that he knew of Marlowe's injury and played on it, chopping at it with the side of his hand and banging that arm down on the table. Alleyn was still dead to the world and would be no help and Marlowe was faint with the pain. He managed to strike a few useful blows; if he survived this, the bruises would be a good piece of information to give to the Constable. Without them, Cawdray could blend into the crowd and might never be found again. And as a killer of at least three people, he had to be found, or Marlowe and Alleyn would have to watch their backs for ever.

Marlowe fell back against the chair, which gave way under him, throwing him on to the ground, trapped between the table and the fireplace and the door, ajar since Cawdray had crept in what seemed like hours before. Cawdray loomed over him, his dagger gripped so tightly that Marlowe could see his knuckles white in the growing daylight in the window.

'I really *do* like you, Kit,' Cawdray said, regretfully. 'And I would have let you live, if you hadn't fought me like this. If you had just listened, I might have spared you, but I know now I can't leave you alive. For some reason, you seem to think what I have done, what I still plan to do, is wrong in some fashion. I had decided from our chats that you were a man of the world.'

'It isn't the world which interests me,' Marlowe said, 'so much as the people in it. And when one of them goes around killing indiscriminately . . .'

'Not indiscriminate,' Cawdray protested.

'Ned Sledd?' Marlowe asked. He knew there was no point in discussing Cawdray's wife. Her husband had dismissed her as a human being long ago.

Cawdray shrugged and raised the knife. 'A tragedy of errors,' he said. Then, he half turned towards the door, eyebrows raised in surprise. A thin trickle of blood oozed out of his mouth and he fell first to his knees and then on to his side, knocking over the chair as he went. Marlowe struggled to his feet and looked round the door, not knowing quite what he would find. He didn't believe in witches, not as such, but he was tired, the light was bad. If a demon in full fig had stood there, he would have not been in the least surprised.

'Thomas?'

'Hello, Kit,' the boy said. 'Someone seems to have killed Master Cawdray.'

'Indeed they do, Thomas. Fortunately, I don't see anyone with any blood on them.'

'Except you, Kit. You're bleeding.' Thomas pointed to Marlowe's arm, where blood was seeping through the sleeve.

'That's my blood, Thomas, as you well know.' Marlowe was speaking gently. The boy was trembling from head to foot and his teeth would soon be chattering. Killing someone will do that to a person.

'I . . . I . . .' With an effort he pulled himself together a little. 'Before I took the girls' parts, Kit, I used to be a tumbler. Did you know that?'

'No, Thomas. I don't think you ever told me that.'

'I used to be the one they throw, you know, the little boy. I used to be dressed in all sorts of things, sometimes they put me in a ball and I would come out at the end. Other times, I was dressed like a cat, or a dog. It was fun, then.' His voice caught and he coughed before he carried on. 'Then, when I got a bit bigger, Ned – he ran a tumbling troupe before he took to plays – Ned asked me if I wanted an act of my own. So he taught me how to juggle. I'm a bit rusty now, but at one time I could keep eight things in the air. I used to juggle all sorts. Eggs. Clubs. Knives.'

Marlowe looked at him shrewdly, but let him carry on at his own speed.

'Then, I started practising in private, something of my own. Till I was good, you know. Then, I showed Ned my act and he let me do it for the audience. They liked it.'

'What was the act, Thomas?' Marlowe asked, although he already knew.

'I was a knife thrower.'

The poet put an arm around the boy's shoulders and held him tight. 'Why don't we walk and talk? It isn't very tidy in here, is it? What with the bodies and suchlike?'

'No.' Thomas let himself be guided to the head of the stairs. He turned to Marlowe. 'I followed you, Kit. I didn't want you getting yourself into trouble. Not over a play. It's never worth it.'

'We'll agree to differ on that one, Thomas. But it was a kind thought.'

'Then, I followed you here. I saw you fall over on the path and I could tell you were tired. I thought you might need a bit of help with Ned Alleyn. He's a coward, but a tricky bastard.'

'Well, no differing there.' Marlowe smiled at the boy.

'You seemed to be coping on your own, so I slipped into a dark corner on the landing and waited to see what would happen. I loved that girl's voice you did, by the way. Can you teach me how to do it?'

'Of course.' Thomas was wittering to keep from the moment of truth, Marlowe knew that, and so let him witter on.

'Then, Master Cawdray came up the stairs. He didn't close the door quite to, so I pushed it a little, every now and then when you weren't looking, until soon I was in the room almost, in the shadow. I . . . heard what he said about Ned.' He turned his face to Marlowe, and it was wet with tears. 'He shouldn't have killed Ned Sledd, Kit. Ned was the nearest I ever had to a father. My own one . . . well, I only know I have one because I couldn't have been born otherwise. Ned . . . Ned was . . .' And his voice broke down altogether. He buried his head in Marlowe's chest and cried as though his heart was breaking.

Which it was.

NINETEEN

He hated to admit it. But he had to admit it. The ale they served in the Eagle and Child wasn't up to Cambridge standards, but it wasn't bad. He sat with his back to the oak panels watching the scholars who in turn watched the door for the proctors who prowled the town. For a while, Cambridge came back to him, like a ghost; the wind that whistled around Petty Cury; the grinning gargoyle outside the Devil; the Gothic splendour of King's and the soaring notes in the chapel there – notes that had come from his own throat and his own heart. Should he, even now, go back?

'Can I buy you a drink, Kit Marlowe?' A voice with a Warwickshire accent brought him back to the here and now.

'You can, William Shakespeare,' he said, and waved to the serving girl with the blonde hair and the bouncing breasts. The serving girls of Oxford had more time for their customers with Ned Alleyn laid up in bed with severe injuries to almost everywhere.

'No, just Will Shaxsper,' Shaxsper said. 'The glover from Stratford.' He scraped back a stool and sat down. 'I thought you'd be at Brasenose, watching your play.'

Marlowe looked at him. 'I thought *you'd* be at Brasenose watching my play.'

'To be honest, Kit –' Shaxsper waited as the foaming jugs were placed in front of them – 'I've learned a lot over the last couple of weeks. Most of it from you.'

'Oh?'

'I've learned that the playwright's life is not for me. When I was at home, surrounded by gloves and wool and bailiffs' writs and the ghastly Hathaways—'

'Hathaways?'

'My in-laws.'

'Ah.'

'When all that was going on, the theatre was all I thought of. The wooden O, the strutting players. It was all so magic.'

'And now?'

'Now, I'm not so sure. Now, Anne and the children seem . . . well . . .'

'Family?' Marlowe suggested.

'Exactly. Let's face it, Kit, I'm never going to be Christopher Marlowe, am I? Who'd pay to see a play written by somebody who had to change his name to be recognized? The nearest I'd get to a theatre is holding the horses of the gentlemen in the audience. No thank you.' He shook his head and raised his tankard. 'The gloving trade,' was the toast he proposed.

'The gloving trade.' Marlowe raised his cup too, but with his left hand because of the pain still in his right.

Shaxsper stood up and extended a hand. Marlowe stood up too and gripped it, less heartily perhaps than he might have done a day or two ago. 'Will we meet again, do you think?' Shaxsper asked.

'I'd put money on it.' Marlowe smiled. 'You're not a bad writer, William Shakespeare.' He looked into the eyes, diverging slightly as always. He looked at the receding hair, the heavy chin. 'Perhaps one day you'll be as good as me.'

And they laughed together before Shaxsper strode to the door. 'If you're ever in Stratford on the Avon,' he said, 'and you're in need of a new pair of gloves, you know where to find me.' He winked solemnly. 'I'm sure we can sort out some kind of discount.' And he was gone, into the Oxford night.

Marlowe sat down heavily and wished he hadn't. Something sharp was sticking through the wooden partition at his back and he didn't have to turn round to know what it was.

'Lord Strange sends his regards,' a familiar voice said. 'So does Sir Francis Walsingham.'

'Is that your dagger in the small of my back, Nicholas?' Marlowe asked. 'Or are you simply pleased to see me?'

A smiling Nicholas Faunt coiled around the partition and took up Shaxsper's stool, the dagger already sheathed and a goblet of wine on the table between them. 'You'll be pleased to know,' he said, sipping slowly, 'that Ferdinando is in the best of health. The Yorkshire air, he says. That and vomiting whatever poison he took out of his system. Even so, he says it will be a while before he ventures out with his troupe again. But what news of you? Anything eventful happen while I've been gone?'

Marlowe looked into the cold, grey eyes of the projectioner, the man of a thousand secrets. He opened his mouth to say something, then changed his mind. 'No,' he said, sampling his ale. 'Absolutely nothing.'

'I hear Ned Sledd is dead.'

'Tragic accident.'

'And Alleyn. I met him once, you know. A bit of a poseur, or so he struck me at any rate. Badly beaten, or so I'm told.'

'Yes, by almost everybody. Edward Alleyn always was an accident waiting to happen,' Marlowe told him shortly.

Faunt smiled his thin-lipped smile. 'So. What now, Kit Marlowe? Cambridge? Canterbury? London? In the end –' and he closed to his man – 'all roads lead to Rome, don't they? Do you intend to travel one of them?'